THE MAMO MURDERS

by Juanita Sheridan

The Rue Morgue Press
Boulder, Colorado

For that guy with luau feet,
my favorite son, Ross

The Mamo Murders
Copyright © 1952, 1978
New Material Copyright 2002
by The Rue Morgue Press

ISBN: 0-915230-51-8

Reprinted with the permission of Ross Hart,
the author's son and literary executor

The Rue Morgue Press
P.O. Box 4119
Boulder, Colorado 80306
Tel: 800-699-6214
Fax: 303-443-4010

Printed by
Johnson Printing

PRINTED IN THE UNITED STATES OF AMERICA

Those individuals fortunate enough to know Maui will recognize that certain topographical liberties have been taken with the island for the purposes of this story. No one will find Alohilani, for the ranch was created in the author's nostalgic imagination. If it seems to resemble any existent property, or if any of the fictitious characters in this book appears to resemble an actual person, living or dead, such resemblance is purely coincidental.

About Juanita Sheridan

Juanita Sheridan's life was as colorful as her mysteries. Born Juanita Lorraine Light in Oklahoma on November 15, 1906, Sheridan claimed in a lengthy letter to her editor at the Doubleday, Doran Crime Club that she came by her knack for murder naturally, since her maternal grandfather was killed by Pancho Villa in a holdup while her own father may possibly have been poisoned by a political rival.

After her father's death, Sheridan and her mother hit the road, touring the American West. When she was on vacation from boarding school, Sheridan was often put by her mother on a train "with a tag around my neck which told my name and destination. I was never afraid, and never lost."

That self-reliance came in handy years later when at the height of the Depression (ca. 1930) Sheridan, with an infant son in arms, found herself dropped off at the corner of 7th and Broadway in Los Angeles with only two suitcases and five cents to her name. She used the nickel to telephone a friend, who loaned her five dollars, and went out and got a job as a script girl for $20 a week. Her son Ross went to live with a rich Beverly Hills foster family and at about the age of six was legally adopted by his maternal grandmother. After the adoption, Sheridan, who had by then sold a couple of original screenplays, headed for Hawaii to begin her writing career. Life wasn't all that easy in Hawaii and once again she hit the pawnshops, although, as usual, "the typewriter was the last to go."

To those people, editors included, who thought her plots contained more than a touch of melodrama, Sheridan said she was only writing from life, having been clubbed by a gun, choked into unconsciousness by a man she never saw, and on two occasions "awakened from a sound sleep to find a pair of strange hands reaching for me through the dark. . ."

Sheridan, who married as many as eight times, never used much of the material she gleaned from real life, figuring that no one would believe it: "One of my most interesting friends in Hawaii was the madame of a 'house.' She looked like a schoolteacher, wore glasses and spoke New England. She had a record collection and a library. She was 26 and her annual net was higher than that of many high-voltage executives. I visited her place occasionally, and after the girls learned to trust me I heard some biographies which can't be printed—no one would believe them."

While in Hawaii, Sheridan began selling short stories. She also married architect Fritz Elliott, at which time she asked that Ross be allowed to join her in Honolulu. When the boy's grandmother—and legal guardian—refused, Sheridan came to the mainland, snatched the boy while the older woman was out for a walk and sneaked the two of them on board the *President Hoover* with the steerage passengers, "down where they eat with chopsticks at one big table, the toilets are without doors, and there is no promenade deck." Ross remembers that they embarked on the ship the very day his mother "kidnapped" him, but Sheridan claimed that she and the boy hid out in San Francisco for a week while the FBI hunted for them.

Sheridan sold several stories, including two mysteries with Asian characters, which won $500 prizes. Ross left Hawaii in May 1941 and went back to live with his grandmother. Sheridan, with the manuscript to *What Dark Secret* in her hands, left Hawaii in November of the same year, just a couple of weeks before the Japanese attack on Pearl Harbor.

At some point during this period she settled down (for the time being) in a housing cooperative on a 130-acre farm in Rockland County, New York where she and her current husband bathed in a stream and slept in a tent while helping to construct their house.

Sheridan returned to Hollywood briefly when one of her Lily Wu books was sold to television as the basis for the pilot of a mystery series set in Hawaii. She "left after a couple of sessions with the Hollywood movie types," son Ross reported, because "she couldn't stand the hypocrisy."

Eventually Sheridan settled in Guadalajara, Mexico, with her last husband, Hugh Graham, and found work as a Spanish-English translator. A fall from a horse (she learned to ride while working as a polo horse exerciser in Hollywood in the 1930s) left her with a broken hip. The last time Ross saw her she was in extreme pain and would "lock herself in her room and mix painkillers and alcohol to try to ease the pain." She died in 1974.

Her mystery writing career was brief but memorable for its depiction of mid-20th century Hawaii and for creating one of the earliest female Chinese-American sleuths. If Sheridan called Lily "Oriental," rather than today's accepted term, Asian, she was only using the civilized parlance of the day. Her books are a fierce defense of the many cultures that make up Hawaii. Unlike Sayers or Christie or countless other writers from the first half of the century, she was able to rise above the petty prejudices of her time.

For more information on Sheridan see Tom and Enid Schantz' introduction to Rue Morgue Press edition of *The Chinese Chop*.

CHAPTER ONE

HONOLULU had been sweltering all that week. It was Kona season and the trades weren't blowing; the island lay suspended in heat. Trees stood as if carved; flowers blazed through stillness. We were having the kind of weather which makes tourists wonder why they've come to the Paradise of the Pacific, which makes islanders restless and irritable, which means there will be storm or earthquake. Old-time Hawaiians believe it is a warning of disaster.

Trouble of any sort seemed far from us; our principal concern was keeping cool. Lily Wu and I were living in the house of Mary Tong, who was in Europe on a photographic assignment. Mary's house is on a shaded hillside of Tantalus, and on this day we were grateful for the exquisite austerity of its furnishings. Lying on the polished floor, I gazed through the window wall at pale sky which seemed to flatten over a metallic sea. It was probably scorching at Waikiki.

Except in the ocean, of course. I thought of green waves topped with froth, the crash of salty water against my skin, and half rose to a sitting position. Then I considered the effort of dressing, the drive through traffic, beach noises and crowds. . . I lay back and muttered, "No. Not worth the effort."

"How about a drink instead?" Lily Wu asked.

I turned. There are times when Lily's 10,000-watt intellect and tempered-steel will make her seem years my senior, but this was not one of them. Today she might have been fourteen instead of twenty-five. She was lying on the teakwood *k'ang*, her head pillowed on a square of blue silk, black hair touching the floor. She wore nothing but a white crepe slip, and while I perspired in that oppressive air, she looked cool as alabaster. As I looked at her I found it difficult to believe that I had once seen this languid little creature club a man unconscious.

"What kind of drink?" I asked.

She counted on her fingers. "Iced tea, gin, pineapple juice, bourbon, coffee, lemonade."

"A collins," I decided. "In one of those tall crystal glasses with plenty of ice cubes. What will you have?"

"Iced tea. Alcohol makes too much heat. And we're drinking tonight; there's a gallon of rum punch in the refrigerator."

I grimaced. "I'd forgotten the party. How many are coming?"

"Only about twelve. It won't be hectic. Hilda's going to play some of Dai Keong Lee's things, and Boyd's bringing a recording he just acquired—*The Family Reunion.*"

"T. S. Eliot? Where somebody says, 'In a world of fugitives the person taking the opposite direction will appear to run away'?"

Lily nodded. " 'We do not like to walk out of a door and find ourselves back in the same room.' That's the one. It plays for about an hour. Which of us is going to get those drinks?"

"You're closer to the kitchen."

The dimple in her cheek deepened. "But I was the one who made the suggestion."

"Don't turn that phony charm on me, you little hypocrite. Men may fall in droves, but you know very well that as far as I'm concerned it won't do any—" I broke off as brakes squealed and a car stopped in front of the house. The car door slammed, someone brushed past the willow which trails its leaves on the path, and feet clomped to the octagonal moon door.

"Damn! I hope it isn't that goon of a Henry Leung. If I have to watch him sit and drool at you on an afternoon like this . . . !" I started to go for kimonos.

A familiar voice bellowed, "Janice! Are you home?"

I slumped to the floor again. "Come on in, Steve."

The door opened and Stephanie Dugan strode into the room, her horsy face wearing a broad, beautiful smile. She works for a Honolulu paper and knows more about the citizens of Hawaii than the FBI; she could become rich overnight if she decided to put the squeeze on some of our Better Families. But Steve's heart is as big as the crater of Haleakala; she takes the smug hypocrisies, the scandal—and our local hypersensitivity about mentioning same—as one vast joke over which she never stops chortling. She drives a 1941 model sedan, admits that she's never had more than five hundred in the bank, and adds cheerfully that she probably never will have, either.

She stood by the ebony Steinway blinking at the change in light, while she automatically kicked off her number nines and wiggled her toes on the bare floor.

"You lucky, lazy *wahines,*" she said, "loafing here half-naked while an honest woman beats her bunions on the hot streets. And me in my newest creation, too."

"That's some creation," I said. "Are you sure you dumped all the potatoes out before you put it on?"

Steve drew herself up and made a chest. "I'll have you know, dearie, these are *not* potatoes!"

She turned to Lily. "How did you happen to choose this disagreeable wench for a roommate, anyway?"

Lily smiled. "I must put up with her, Steve. She's my foster sister."

"And Lily has only herself to blame for that," I added. "She saved my life once, and according to Chinese belief, she's responsible for that life forever after."

I became silent, considering what this friendship has brought to me. There is a room in the Wu home in New York's Chinatown, and its teakwood furniture is polished, the silky rose carpet is spotless, my bed is ready for me at any hour. I have been familiar with loneliness, frustration, and insecurity. Knowledge of such permanent sanctuary gives me priceless comfort and peace of mind.

Steve was saying with a grin, "Damned funny people, these Chinese."

"Yes, aren't they?" Lily agreed amiably. "You look hot, Steve. How about a drink?"

Steve beamed. "That's Hawaiian hospitality, Lily. Got any rum?"

"In the kitchen," Lily told her. As Steve started in that direction I added, "Bring us a couple of glasses of iced tea, will you? There's a pitcher of tea on the sink, and some lemons."

"Thoughtful of her to arrive just now, wasn't it?" Lily commented. We both knew that otherwise I would have prepared drinks for us. Lily is useless in a kitchen. But at times when we don't have domestic help she irons my blouses, and she keeps my dresser drawers beautifully neat. We consider it a fair exchange.

Steve brought a tray and distributed glasses, then sat on the floor with her back against the chow bench. She took a long, grateful gulp of rum collins and sighed gustily as she fished in her bag for cigarettes.

"A reporter has a dog's life! Sometimes I'm sorry I didn't buy that house on Water Street when Charlene offered it to me."

My tea went down the wrong throat. "House?" I choked. "Does that mean what I think it means?"

"The kind of house that's never a home? Un-huh." Steve was grinning. "It was just after Pearl Harbor, when so many people were leaving the islands. I could have got a fifty-thousand-dollar investment for five.

Oh well. Might have developed calluses somewhere else besides my feet." She chuckled. "Don't look so shocked, Janice. The only guy who'll ever call me madam is the Fuller Brush salesman."

She took another gulp of collins. "Mmmm. Heavenly. Look at the frost on that glass!" She lit a cigarette, leaned back, and said, "It was brutal out there at the airport."

"Been meeting somebody?"

"Yep. With *leis*, photographers, and all the trimmings."

"Celebrity?"

"Worse than that. Sixty eager *malihinis*—overflow from the American Livestock Convention in San Francisco." She stuck her tongue in her cheek. "Some of them are wearing ten-gallon hats and high heels."

"I've seen them in New York during rodeo season at Madison Square Garden," Lily said. "They look uncomfortable."

Steve nodded, but her mind was not on the odd habits of cattlemen. She was looking at me as she raised her glass again. She finished her drink, rattled ice cubes absently, and set it down without removing that intent gaze.

I said, "What is it, Steve?"

She stretched for the ashtray behind her, and as she tapped ash from her cigarette she said, "Ran into something odd today. Thought you might be interested."

"Something odd? Where?"

Instead of answering directly she asked, "What's on your little blond head just now, Janice? Are you working?"

"If you mean am I writing another pulse-stirring romance of the tropics—the answer is no. I have some galleys to correct. They weigh a ton."

I waved toward the chair by the door where the package lay. It had arrived that morning and I had unwrapped it to see what kind of type the publisher was using, had flipped long sheets containing thousands of words to be read, and dropped it with a groan.

"Anything else planned?" Steve pursued.

"Not at the moment. Those lovely Hollywood checks continue to arrive. Somebody from the studio will show up pretty soon and I'll have to start earning my pay as technical adviser. In the meantime we're having a vacation. Or we would be, if it weren't for this heat. What's on your mind?"

As Steve started to answer, a palm leaf crashed to the roof, scratched slowly down the tiles, and dropped to the lawn. A hot breath whooshed toward us as if exhaled from the big tree in the garden, and the smell of overripe mangoes filled the room. The atmosphere seemed to grow almost palpably thicker in the silence which followed. The islands were brewing something for us: a volcanic eruption, possibly—or a Kona storm.

Steve seemed to register atmospheric tension too—or perhaps she felt uneasiness from some more tangible cause. For a moment she lapsed into withdrawal, scowling with concentration.

Seeing this, Lily became alert. She turned sideways on the *k'ang,* her head on one arm, and reached for a cigarette. "So you ran into something odd today?" she prompted.

I added, "Tell us about it, Steve. We're interested."

Steve turned to me. "Do you remember Don Farnham?"

"From Maui?"

"That's the one. He owns a ranch there."

"I know the ranch, it's called Alohilani. Dad and I visited there once, years ago, when Don's father was alive."

"How about Don? Know him personally?"

"We weren't close friends. Don finished college while I was still in Punahou, but I remember him. Dark curly hair, brown eyes, sort of fierce black brows. A lot of girls liked him but he wasn't having any; he played polo, did a lot of swimming. He was in Dad's Hawaiian language class at the university; he used to come to our house for advanced tutoring. Rather a serious type, intense, I'd say."

"You seem to remember Don very well indeed. Were you one of the gals who had a crush on him?"

"Hardly. He was seven years older than I—that would make him thirty-four now—and when you're high school age, seven years might as well be a century. But what about him?"

"Well, I had to meet this delegation of ranchers today, here on two weeks' vacation. When I was interviewing one of the big shots from Arizona, a guy by the name of Hopper, he mentioned that Don was to meet him, he and his wife had been invited to visit the ranch. He was surprised when Don didn't show, and when I asked about the appointment he said it had been arranged a month ago, and showed me Don's letter. Hopper had been looking forward to seeing a Hawaiian cattle ranch; he was very disappointed. I drove him to the Royal and we asked the desk clerk if there had been any message. There was none."

"That's not alarming. Don might have been delayed. Perhaps he telephoned later from Maui."

"I thought of that. But I know Don Farnham—if he couldn't meet the Hoppers as he promised, he would have sent *leis* to the airport. So I called the ranch myself, after I left the hotel. They told me Don was out of town. And the woman I talked to, the housekeeper, rang off before I could ask any questions."

"That *is* odd," I admitted. Steve had seen plenty of real drama; she had no need to conjure it out of nothing.

"There's something odder," she said. "And this I definitely don't like. While I was waiting for the ranchers' special, another clipper arrived. And a girl got off. Mrs. Don Farnham. He wasn't there to meet her, either."

"Mrs. Farnham? I didn't know he was married. When did all this happen?"

"This summer, just before you came back from New York. I happened to be present at their first meeting, when I was covering the Hulihee swimming meet. This girl, Leslie, was entered in the amateur class and did some sensational diving. Don was there; he asked me to introduce him to her, and the minute they looked at each other . . . !

"I ran into them next day at Waikiki; Don was teaching her to surf and she was crazy about it. Crazy about him, too. Leslie was on vacation; she taught physical education in some girls' college in California. But she never went back to her job. They were married here, and he took her to the Volcano House for their honeymoon. That was two months ago."

"And now she's *arriving* on a clipper from San Francisco? That's confusing."

"It is. I didn't know she had gone back to the mainland. But she arrived today—and Don didn't meet her. I saw her look around for him—and I saw the expression on her face when she realized he wasn't there. I went over and spoke to her, asked if I could do anything. The girl simply froze, said a polite little no, thanks, and walked away. My ranchers arrived just then and I was busy, I didn't see her again. But I checked with Inter-Island, and she's got a late reservation on the plane to Maui."

"So she's going home to a bridegroom who isn't there," I said. "That does seem strange."

"It seems more than that," Lily said. "It is rather frightening."

"Why do you think she wouldn't talk to you, Steve?"

Steve shrugged. She hoisted herself and bent to pick up her glass. "I'll have a refill, if you don't mind, then I've got to get back on the treadmill. About twenty more important tourists want their pictures in the paper, and there's a big *luau* tonight for the boys from the wild West."

She waggled her hips and did a couple of bumps so violent that her knot of ginger hair came loose. "You know the kind, Janice. Mass *hulas*, a 'pageant of Old Hawaii,' *poi* pounding, *tapa* making—"

"Please, Steve," I said. "Those rotten mangoes are enough, in this heat. Get your drink and hurry back."

While Steve was out I looked at Lily. She was smoking, brows drawn together slightly, a faraway look in her oblique eyes. I decided that Lily was thinking, as I was, of the emotions of a girl arriving in Honolulu—where meeting friends is a tradition, and welcoming home the ones we love is practically a religion—to discover that her bridegroom had not met her.

I said, "I wonder how she'll feel when she reaches Maui. I wonder if anybody will be there to tell her Don is out of town—or to offer any kind of explanation . . . ."

"You know Don Farnham," Lily said. "Is he the kind of man who would let his wife wait alone at an airport? Would he give an invitation to another rancher and then fail to appear or to send an excuse?"

"No-o-o. Don wouldn't do that." As I concentrated, his memory became more vivid. "I remember Father saying that Don had an unusually strong sense of responsibility. For instance: most of the employees at Alohilani are Hawaiians, and he learned the language from them as a child, but Don wanted to read it perfectly as well as speak it. He had some sort of project he used to discuss with Father, about collecting old Polynesian myths to preserve them for the people. It was a sort of trust to him. No, he would never—" I stopped as Steve returned.

She nodded vigorously. "I agree all the way. There isn't a man in the islands who'd be more scrupulous about hospitality to an invited quest. And I know damned well he feels the same sense of responsibility about marriage, now that he's got a wife. Don married that girl with his mother's wedding ring, designed three generations ago for Farnham women. It's a circle of *mamo* feathers carved in gold, to represent the feather capes of the old chiefs."

"That's right," I said, sitting up straight. "The Farnhams are chiefs from way back—the *alii* of Alohilani."

Steve said, looking out the window, "I remember the look on Don's face when he put that ring on her finger. Doug Rowe and I were their witnesses, you know. That's why it rocked me when Don wasn't at the airport, and when Leslie Farnham acted the way she did. Pilikia there. I'm sure of it."

She was right. There must be trouble. I glanced at Lily and saw that she agreed.

Steve picked up her shoes and began to pull them on. "Well, Janice?" she said. "Would you like to make a trip to Maui?"

I squirmed. "But I can't just go barging in on a strange girl like that. I wouldn't know what to do or say. And I don't see—"

At that moment the telephone rang.

Steve went to it, saying over her shoulder that she had left word with the paper that she would be at our house until four. "Hello," she said. "Yes, this is she. All right."

She clutched the phone against her and hissed, "It's Maui calling!"

I rose and moved to her side to listen, while Lily sat erect on the *k'ang.*

"Hello," a man's voice said. "Is this Miss Dugan? From the paper? The lady who wants to talk wit' Don Farnham?"

"Yes. Go ahead. Is he there now?"

"No. Don's not here. But I got somet'ing to tell you. Somet'ing important." He began to speak very fast in Hawaiian which Steve didn't understand and I couldn't hear.

"Wait a minute." She handed me the phone. "You talk to him."

I took the instrument and spoke in his language. The voice sounded relieved, words poured forth. I listened, and presently a shiver went over me. I asked a question, reassured him, made a promise, and hung up the phone. Steve and Lily were waiting, and I told them briefly:

"His name is Eole and he sounds quite young. He's Don's calabash brother and he loves Don Farnham more than anything on earth. He lives at Alohilani, and he says evil has been done there, and a dreadful thing is going to happen soon if somebody doesn't stop it—at least that's the best I could make out; the boy was hysterical. He said he didn't dare talk over the telephone but if I will come to the ranch he will tell me."

"Well?" Steve said.

"Can I get plane space at this late hour?"

She waved a hand. "I've got a pal at Inter-Island who'll get you aboard if he has to off-load the governor. How will you find this Hawaiian after you arrive?"

"He'll be at the stables. I told him I'd identify myself by my Hawaiian name, Kulolo. He said he'd wait there all night if necessary."

I turned to Lily. "Wouldn't you like to fly to Maui? It's cool at the ranch." I didn't add that I would rather have her with me than blunder into such a situation alone.

"I can't go," she said. "There are guests coming. And David Kimu's taking me to see *Lady Precious Stream* tomorrow."

Steve was at the door. "Why don't you get the lay of the land and then call Lily from Maui? I'll check with her for news. This may be all hysteria on somebody's part. You'll probably be back right away."

Lily went to my room to help me pack, and as we folded things into my overnight case we didn't need to exchange comments to know that neither of us agreed with Steve's last optimistic words. Lily moved quietly, efficiently, while I found it difficult to follow her example. Some of the panic in that unseen caller had been transferred to me.

I grabbed cosmetics, gown, brush and comb, and had to restrain my-self from tossing them in and slamming the bag shut. The feeling I had, which I couldn't escape any more than I could escape the still, ominous heat of the islands, was that I ought to hurry, hurry. I ought to reach that terrified Hawaiian boy before it was too late.

CHAPTER TWO

THE STORM broke when we were still twenty minutes from the island. Our plane lurched, dropped, righted itself, and shuddered on through howling darkness. Rain crashed against the window and I drew back with a start. Then I glanced past my seat mate toward the passenger across the aisle.

Too late I had remembered that I forgot to ask Steve what Leslie Farnham looked like. After studying other women passengers I decided it must be the girl in navy blue who had boarded the plane with such a set face, and who now sat opposite me staring at the seat before her. She wore a brimmed hat which concealed her eyes, and all I could appraise was a small straight nose and an unsmiling mouth over a neat but deter-mined chin. She was shorter than I, which made her five feet two or three, and the manner with which she planted her blue calf pumps, the firmness of the brown hands which held her bag on her lap, seemed to indicate self-confidence which was at the same time belied by the rigidity of her pose. I had been wondering how to approach her when we arrived; I felt more diffident each time I glanced toward her and saw that she hadn't shown the nervousness manifested by other passengers; she hadn't even shifted her position when the plane dropped under the first onslaught of the storm.

Studying her, I decided that either the girl had nerves like steel cables or she was deep in a personal problem of such gravity that cataclysms of nature seemed comparatively insignificant.

I was brought out of absorption by the voice of the plump, white-haired woman in the seat beside me. "We're heading right into it, aren't we?"

"I'm afraid so."

"I'm not used to flying and must admit I'm terrified," the woman went on. "When I climbed into this metal monster and heard that door lock, I started to get cold chills."

"You could have gone by boat," I suggested.

"I know. But it takes more time. And my vacation's not very long."

I wondered what sort of work she did. Most women of her type and age were comfortably enmeshed in family life, visiting grown sons and daughters, fussing over grandchildren.

"I've been dreaming of a trip to Hawaii for years," she confided. "I've read everything about the islands that I could find. And I have a notebook filled with things to do and places to see—"

I glanced at my watch; ten minutes more. The girl across the aisle had opened her purse and was looking into a mirror as she touched lipstick to her mouth. Perhaps she expected to meet someone soon and wanted to make her best impression—as she raised the mirror in her hand I saw the circle of tiny gold feathers. I hoped she would be met by Don Farnham.

If Don were there, I decided, I'd greet him with surprised pleasure, explain that I had fled Honolulu's heat in order to correct galleys in comfort, and accept his invitation to stay at Alohilani. He would invite me; Farnham hospitality was legendary. Once at the ranch, I'd go to the stables and meet the Hawaiian boy, find out what was worrying him, and then be guided by what I learned. I felt strongly that if Don appeared to meet his wife, whatever threatened them would be on the way to solution.

"—have read about Maui," my seat companion was chattering. I gave her my attention; she needed to relieve tension and it wouldn't hurt me to listen. "King Kamehameha fought some famous battles here. This might even be the island where he's buried; they say his body has never been found. A strange custom, isn't it, to bury the dead secretly! Most people perform such elaborate public ceremonies at a funeral. Just imagine Kamehameha lying hidden somewhere, wrapped in his feather cloak—I saw one at the Bishop Museum yesterday which they say is worth a million dollars. Have you been to the Museum?"

"Yes," I said. "Many times."

"Then there is Haleakala—House of the Sun—isn't that a wonderful name? Ten thousand feet high, with a crater of twenty-five square miles. Who could imagine such a mountain on an island in the Pacific?"

"It's magnificent," I told her. "You mentioned a job. How long is your vacation?"

"Three weeks. It's sick leave really, at this time of year. I had a rather bothersome operation recently, and the manager insisted—I'm housekeeper for a hotel in Bakersfield—that I take an extra week to rest up."

"Fasten your seat belts, please. We're about to land now." The stewardess passed, grasping seats for balance as the plane began to lose altitude and tossed; momentarily, in a ferocious gust of wind.

I looked at the white-haired woman beside me. She was pale, but managed a smile as she tightened her belt.

"We're here!" she said. "The worst is over. It's such fun arriving somewhere, isn't it? I love to watch people meeting each other, giving *leis*, everybody happy and smiling. Have you ever noticed how much more attractive people are when they're eager for something?"

I had noticed it often, at shipside in Honolulu. I had not previously met someone who found it worthy of comment. No one was going to meet this friendly woman with flowers. The girl across the aisle had pulled her knees up, feet flat as if ready to rise the instant we landed. I hoped that someone would welcome her.

The plane bounced to a landing and wheeled, motors roaring, toward lights of the airport. As we made our way along the aisle the older woman said, "I'm Mrs. Bessie Watson," and waited. I murmured my name, my eyes fixed on the girl in blue. She was ahead of us, she started toward the lighted building the moment her feet touched earth.

I stopped just long enough to buy a red carnation *lei* and fling it around the neck of Mrs. Watson with a hurried, "*Aloha!* I hope you enjoy your visit to Maui." Then I evaded her astonished thanks and went in pursuit of Leslie Farnham.

Just inside the building I almost bumped into her. She was standing by the door, searching the faces of people milling around the terminal. No one approached. As the crowd thinned, her shoulders began to droop; she picked up a small dressing case and started indecisively toward the exit.

Someone behind us called, "Mrs. Farnham?" and we both turned. The speaker was an Oriental in chauffeur's uniform.

"I'm Mrs. Farnham," she said. When her face lighted up like that, she was a different girl. "Were you sent for me?"

He tipped his cap. "I'm from the hotel. A reservation has been made for you. May I have your luggage check?"

"The hotel?" The smile left her face. Then she said, "But I'm not going to the hotel. I'm going to Alohilani Ranch. Or"—and her voice rose—"has something happened there? Is someone sick?"

The chauffeur's face grew blank. "I work for the hotel. They said to pick you up." He reached for her dressing case.

She jerked it from his grasp, and her chin lifted. "You can tell the hotel there has been a mistake. The reservation is canceled." She turned away and I followed her toward the taxi stand in front of the terminal.

Most of those drivers were Hawaiians, the friendliest people in the world. But toward Leslie Farnham they were not friendly. Instead of jumping forward, arguing good-naturedly with each other over priority, they stared, unsmiling. They knew who she was, but not one moved toward her. Their attitude, with what it implied, shocked me more than anything else could have done. I stood at the side of the building, watching. She walked toward them, then slowly past the group to the last driver on the rank; an old man whose cotton pants and shirt hung loose on his skinny body. She stopped in front of him.

"Can you drive me up to the Farnham ranch?" she asked.

The old man looked searchingly at her, and curiosity in his eyes changed to something very like pity. *Pity?* He muttered, "Too much storm. Big rain come down from mountain tonight."

"But it's a good hard road," she pleaded. "I'm very anxious to get home, and nobody—nobody was able to meet me." By then I had started forward, and was close enough to see how her chin trembled on the last words. She bit her lip and raised that chin again. "Can't you take me, please?"

The old man looked uncomfortable, but continued to shake his head. I said, "I am also going to Alohilani. How about taking the two of us? It's a bad storm, and the trip's worth double fare."

I smiled at him, then glanced significantly toward the other drivers. *"Like Pu, makule, maikai no ia."*

He gaped at hearing a *haole* girl speak Hawaiian. He hesitated another moment, then nodded abruptly and opened the door of his ancient sedan. "All right. I take."

I said to Leslie Farnham, "Go ahead."

She gave me a brief glance in which gratitude, relief, and resentment were all mixed, then climbed into the car.

As we drove away from the airport I glanced out the rear window. The other Hawaiians had turned, they were still watching.

"I'm Janice Cameron," I said to the girl. "And an old friend of Don's. It's fortunate we happened to need a taxi at the same time."

She flashed a look at me and then said in a low voice, "Yes, it is."

The girl was under such strain that she didn't trust herself to talk. I couldn't tell her then about my reasons for being there, for practically forcing myself on her. I explained awkwardly that I had known her husband since childhood, that I had recently sold a novel which was to be filmed in the islands, and wanted to consult Don about a mountain sequence to be shot on Maui. All this was true except the latter, which was improvisation. She listened without comment, except to ask abruptly, "What did you say to our driver?"

"I said that if he didn't want to drive us it didn't make any difference. He knew I'd find somebody else. He was taking advantage of your being new here to get double fare."

She started to say something, possibly to deny this and offer the true explanation, but closed her lips tight instead. Between us lay uneasy aware-ness that some other reason had provoked the stares, curious and hostile, with which the Hawaiians had greeted her. She didn't want to talk about it—or, for that matter, to talk to me—and I subsided into worried silence.

Rain pounded savagely on the roof as the car skidded onto the hard-surfaced road which led up to the ranch. The old man drove as if demons pursued us, and we clung to the seat while the sedan rocked and bounced across gullies and around curves. Wind whistling through the windows brought the smell of drenched earth, and presently I knew we were near the sea by the sullen boom of breakers against the rocky coast. The night was charged with fury, an elemental force which threatened to sweep us from earthbound security with each renewed assault of wind and water. The driver never spoke; he stared at the road, which seemed in the weird glare of headlights to be completely screened by the deluge.

Finally I called to him, "Isn't this an unusual storm, even for the Kona season?"

The old man did not answer. Maybe he had not heard me, I thought, and repeated the question.

His head didn't move, his bony hands gripped the twisting wheel. "This no Kona rain," he announced. "This *alii* rain, fall only when chief is dead." He added something under his breath, Hawaiian words which sounded like an incantation.

I wished that he had not spoken. I remembered uneasily that ancient beliefs of the Hawaiians still survive in older generations on whom the veneer of white civilization has not been successfully applied. I glanced at the girl beside me, hoping she had not grasped the implication of the old man's words: certain torrential rains of Hawaii are supposed to fall only when one of the nobility dies and the gods welcome a new member to their ranks. Don Farnham was *alii*. I shivered and pulled my coat around me, then sat hunched in my corner, mute for the remainder of the journey.

The big ranch house was lighted. That warm yellow glow seemed the most cheerful sight I had ever seen. As the car rolled along the driveway and stopped before the house I heard Leslie Farnham release a deep sigh. The old man opened the door, swung our bags to the lanai, and extended a hand. We stepped from the car—to stand suddenly rigid.

From somewhere in surrounding darkness came an inhuman scream, unbearably high and prolonged, its tortured ululation rising above the wind.

Involuntarily I clung to the old man. *"What is that?"*

He began to tremble. He tore my hands from his shoulders and shoved me toward the lanai steps. He jumped into his car and was gone, careening toward the road by which we had come. As I regained my balance the scream rose again, quavered horribly, and stopped.

"That's coming from the stables," Leslie Farnham cried. "It's a horse!"

She started running and I stumbled after her. Wind whipped my coat around me, rain hard as pebbles struck my face; I crashed into a fence, turned and followed her through the door of a darkened building. She pressed a light switch inside and we stood panting on the rough wooden floor. Something moved near by shuffled and snorted. We turned.

An enormous black horse stood in the first box stall, eyes rolling, red nostrils flared. Immediately Leslie spoke to him. "Pilikia!" Her voice was warm, affectionate. "What's the matter, boy?" He tossed his head and snorted, gathering his muscles. He reared with a scream and came down, front hoofs pounding something which lay beneath him.

"He's a stallion," the girl said. "Nobody can touch him except Don and the ranch foreman." She murmured soothing words and laid a hand on the wooden half wall which kept the black beast imprisoned.

And someone groaned.

Leslie peered over the wall and gasped, "Eole!" as I reached her side.

He lay there, Eole—the Hawaiian boy who loved Don Farnham—huddled in the straw. His eyes stared at us, glazed with agony, his face—I swallowed scalding nausea. Leslie never hesitated. Keeping her gaze fixed on the trembling stallion, she swung the door open and commanded, "You take one ankle and I'll take the other."

When we had got him out, she turned to close the door of the stall, while I knelt on the floor by the injured boy.

"Are you badly hurt, Eole?"

He raised his head slowly. His lips drew back from white teeth in a bloody, gallant smile. "Kulolo?"

"Yes."

"*Aloha.* I waited, Kulolo." He groaned. His eyes closed.

Leslie knelt, she touched his shoulder. "We'll get help. Don't try to move."

He opened his eyes. He said in Hawaiian, with terrible effort, *"The coffin is almost ready."* His head thumped on the floor.

"Don't talk," Leslie said. She turned to me. "Go and get help. I'll stay with him."

I ran through rain to the house, struggled with the door, and burst inside.

It was like entering another world.

Three strangers were in the living room, two men and a woman, grouped around a blaze which crackled in the lava rock fireplace. The woman held a cigarette in jeweled fingers; its smoke feathered through hennaed curls. The man nearest her rose hastily, pulling a maroon crepe kimono around his tall body.

"Hello!" he said. Light reflected from his scalp under fine brown hair as he bent to set down a highball. "Who the devil are you?"

I ignored the question. "There's an injured boy in the stable!" I cried. "The stallion trampled him."

Something flickered in his pale eyes; he recoiled, then sat down heavily. I turned to the younger man, who was blond, good-looking, and equally disconcerted.

"Don't just stare like that!" I burst out. "Can't you understand? Somebody's hurt. We need help!"

They stared and didn't move.

At that moment Leslie came to the door and called, "Hurry, please!"

Her appearance seemed to startle both men out of their paralysis. They got themselves together and started out of the room. I glanced at the woman by the fire. She hadn't spoken; now she flicked her cigarette into the flames and picked up a glass. I turned after the others and followed them as far as the lanai.

Sheltered there from the storm, I watched through the open stable door as the two men lifted Eole and carried him into the tack room opposite the stallion's stall. Through the window, then, I saw them lay him on a cot under a row of saddles, after which the blond man bent over, straightened again, and shook his head. Leslie protested and stepped toward the figure on the cot; the older man caught her arm and said something. From the shocked, incredulous expression on her face, I knew what they were saying.

They were telling her that Eole was dead.

I went back to the living room and flopped into the nearest chair. I was still wearing my coat, my feet were soaked, I could feel wisps of hair lank on my neck. I sat looking at my muddy feet and absorbing realization that what Eole had wanted to tell me I would never learn from him now. The henna-haired woman was looking at me; she started to say something but what she saw in my face stopped her. She turned her eyes away and we sat in silence unbroken except for shrieking wind and rain which assaulted the house.

When the others returned, the woman looked up at the tall man and he said, "The boy is dead. There's nothing we can do. The *paniolos* will take care of him when they come back."

I wondered where the cowboys were at this hour but didn't ask; I was watching Don's wife. She crossed the room to a chair and sank into it; she took a handkerchief from her pocket and wiped blood from her wrist and did not look at anyone.

Finally she raised her head. "I'm Leslie Farnham," she announced. "Where is my husband?"

The thin man produced a smile. "Well, Leslie. We didn't expect you to turn up in this storm. I reserved a room for you at the—"

"Where is Don?" she said. "Is he with the *paniolos*? They don't go out at night unless—" Her voice sharpened and she said, "There's something wrong here! *What is it?*"

No one answered.

She turned to the younger man. She looked at the flannels and T-shirt he wore, which were too large for him. "Where did you get those clothes?" she demanded. "Who are you?"

"I'm Denis Desmond, a new neighbor of yours," he told her. His smile was self-conscious. "Got soaked in my boat coming over here, and borrowed some gear from Howard. Let me take your coat—it's sopping."

"Better give her a drink, Denis," the woman said. Her voice was startlingly low and hoarse, as if she had a cold. She added, "The horse was afraid of the storm. The Kanaka must have tried to quiet him."

"But Eole would never have—" Leslie stopped, she made an impatient gesture. "Who are you?" she asked again. "And when will Don be back?"

The thin man leaned forward. "I'm Howard Farnham. Don's cousin. This is Edith, my wife. Now, my dear, if you'll just relax for a moment—give her a drink, Denis."

I looked at Leslie. These people were trying to make her feel like an intruder. I wondered whether—then I saw that she was aware of it.

She sat straighter in the big chair and said clearly, "I don't want a drink. I want to know—"

"Better take one," Edith Farnham said. "You'll need it."

Leslie gave her a resentful look. "I don't want a drink. Now, will you please tell me—"

She stopped as Howard Farnham moved to stand with his back to the fire, looking down at her. Whatever he had to say, he was going to enjoy it; his pale eyes glinted and he couldn't quite keep satisfaction from his voice.

"Don has disappeared," he said. He added, watching her, "We have every reason to believe that he is dead."

Leslie gasped, "No!" Her eyes widened, she said in a queer drowned voice, "Then that's why—" She shook her head, looked up at Howard Farnham, and said, "Don? *Dead?*"

Life seemed to drain from her with the words; her eyes dulled, she swayed and then pitched forward to the floor.

CHAPTER THREE

I SAT BY THE BED and waited for Leslie Farnham to return to consciousness. Her lids fluttered and lifted and she looked at me without recognition from eyes of a deeper blue than the blanket which covered her. She had short, coppery hair; against the pillow it seemed very bright, perhaps because every other trace of color had gone from her. She sighed and closed her eyes again as if she could not bear awakening. I turned toward the other two who waited.

Denis Desmond had helped Howard carry her to this bedroom and had then disappeared. The Farnhams stood together at the window, he with his back to the room, his wife turned so that she could watch all of us. While Leslie's eyes remained closed, I studied Edith Farnham.

She was middle-fortyish, possibly a few years older than her husband, although her age was hard to judge, since she had the sort of face which matures early, deriving its expression from singleness of purpose unhampered by any kind of scruples. She had greenish eyes, her nose was fleshy and prominent, her wide mouth glistened. She wore makeup with no attempt at subtlety; her eyelids were oiled, her lashes mascaraed, her cheeks rouged. The effect was vulgar, ugly, and strangely fascinating. Equally so was her long velvet housecoat—which was the color of newly printed currency.

Some men might find her face repellent, but none could be unaware of what was under that green velvet. Her full breasts might well have carried a neon sign announcing that here was a superb instrument of pleasure, animated with a vitality which would attract a man tormented by certain inhibitions. It was as if she set rich food before a hungry child and said that he was to forget the silly things he'd been taught about manners, he was to eat his fill—his face in the trough if he felt like it.

She herself had apparently two appetites. The first was evidenced by the jeweled platinum watch on her wrist and about thirty carats of assorted diamonds flashing from her strong, manicured hands. The second was apparent in every movement of that body under the green velvet. One might search several continents, I decided, and never find a woman less likely to fit into the background of a Hawaiian cattle ranch.

Yet she had chosen this and was staking her claim. She directed her husband's activities; it showed in the way she watched him and the habit he had of looking to her for cues. He muttered now, as he faced the window, "I hope the girl doesn't have hysterics. I've got enough on my hands here already."

She answered in that hoarse voice, "Why don't you go downstairs? I'll talk to her."

Leslie's eyes had opened again as they spoke, although she still lay like stone. Finally she drew in a deep breath and clenched her hands into fists, shaking her head as if telling herself this couldn't be true, it must be a horrible dream. As nightmare assumed the dimensions of reality she accepted it; her face settled into profound sadness and she made a small involuntary moan.

Howard Farnham turned. Seeing the look on her face, he frowned and started toward the door.

She said, "Don't go."

He asked perfunctorily, "Feeling better?"

"I'm all right," she said. "Don't leave."

He brushed thin hair back over his scalp and moved to the side of her bed. "I'm very sorry, my dear, that I had to break this tragic news so suddenly. To tell the truth, I've been under a terrific strain myself. Please forgive me."

Those were his words. The smile didn't reach his eyes; they watched her with wary appraisal.

As she made no response he added, "Let me assure you that whatever Edith and I can do to help"—spreading hands indicated the boundlessness of his sympathy—"you need only to call on us—"

"Thank you," she said. "Now, please tell me what happened to Don."

He glanced at his wife, who gave a slight nod toward me. He looked pointedly at me then, waiting for me to go. I felt relief that I'd taken advantage of her unconsciousness to introduce myself as a close personal friend of Leslie Farnham rather than Don, and hoped that her attitude toward me would not contradict that claim. She seemed hardly aware of my presence. Fine. I settled and looked at Howard Farnham with an air of taking for granted my right to be there. He waited, returning my regard with resentment.

I thought I could gauge what was in his mind: my arrival had been disconcerting. Leslie was new to the islands and not established as chatelaine of the Farnham kingdom; possibly she wasn't yet emotionally adjusted to her relationship with Don. A girl alone, confused by the strangeness of this place, stunned by the shock of widowhood before she had even learned to be wife, should be easy to intimidate, to dispossess; she should accept the ignominy of a hotel room.

But she hadn't submitted to dispossession. And she wasn't alone. So he glared at me and stalled for time.

"Wouldn't you rather wait until tomorrow, Leslie? You'll feel better then:"

"No:" She braced herself against the pillow. "Oh no. I want to—Talk now."

He glanced at his wife; she brought a chair to the side of the bed, and as he seated himself she pressed his shoulder briefly.

He began by shrugging to indicate helplessness. "It's a simple story, Leslie, a familiar one here in the islands. Don was drowned."

"Drowned?" Leslie said. "How? Don was a champion swimmer:"

Her mouth trembled and for a moment she seemed about to cry. She shook her head as if to clear her thoughts, and gave attention again to Howard.

"Don wasn't swimming," he told her. "He went on a fishing trip. His boat didn't come back. It was never seen again:"

She started to protest.

He said in a sharper tone, "There's no doubt that he was drowned. You must accept it. Don disappeared four days ago—vanished without a trace."

"Why wasn't I told?" she asked. "I was in California four days ago."

"Because Karl King"—Howard's voice hardened on that name— "wouldn't believe that he was dead."

"Who is Karl King?" I asked.

"The ranch foreman," Leslie said. "His wife, Mele, is our house-keeper."

Howard sent me an annoyed look before he resumed. "We happened to be in Wailuku last week, and the moment we heard of Don's accident we came up here to the ranch. I sent you a cable that day. I only found out later that Karl had canceled the message."

"Why?"

He answered with reluctance. "Because Karl insists that even if Don's boat sank he would make his way ashore and get word to us."

She said quickly, "Karl should know. He has worked here for six years. And Mele was born here. They're Don's good friends as well as employees. If Karl believes that Don is still alive—"

"Nonsense!" Howard burst out. "Karl doesn't want to face the truth, Leslie, for his own reasons. Why, he even took the *paniolos* out tonight in this storm, on a crazy search party. Some fishermen reported a light along the coast, and Karl claimed it was a signal."

"It could well be," I interjected. "There are coves here, small beaches where wreckage would wash ashore, places a strong swimmer could reach. Don might be unable to get out because some of them are walled in by sheer rock. But if he carried waterproof matches, or if he found a piece of glass, he could make a signal fire."

Leslie turned to me with an expression of relief and gratitude, while Howard Farnham looked as if he would like to knock the words back into my teeth. It was then that his wife spoke from the window.

"How do you know so much about Maui?" Her question was a challenge.

I sent her a level stare. "Because I was born in the islands. I've been on Maui as many times, possibly, as you have." My voice was sharp with antagonism.

"But you told us you were such a close friend of Leslie's." Her keen eyes probed for the lie. "She's only been here a few months."

I remembered then a talent possessed by Lily Wu which I have long been trying to develop—the ability to dissemble. It might be useful here. Lily's technique would be the ingenuous smile, the sweet obtuseness, which serve to mask hostility.

I said, trying to sound conciliatory: "Leslie and I have been friends for several years; we went to school together. When we finished, she took the teaching job, and I came home to work as secretary at the Ramsey Residence."

I didn't know Leslie's age but hoped she was not too much younger than I to have been a classmate. My book hadn't been published yet, so my name wasn't known; I *had* held such a job, and Leslie had been a teacher. That teamed us in a social and economic bracket which might influence this woman to consider us negligible. I watched her as I spoke, but Edith Farnham's expression told nothing.

"In fact," I improvised, "it was I who introduced Don to Leslie this summer, at the Hulihee swimming meet." I turned back to the girl with a casual, "Steve Dugan was with me that day. Remember, Leslie?"

That would explain, if she were quick enough, how I happened to be at the ranch. She must surely recall Steve's attempted approach at the Honolulu airport. She said slowly, "Of course—I remember."

She considered for a moment and then asked, trying to keep her voice even, "So you think Karl is right—Don could be still alive?"

Before I could answer, Howard spoke. "That's utterly impossible! Don disappeared four days ago. If he were still alive he would have made some sign before now; there are planes flying over this island constantly and one of them would have spotted him. Karl won't admit his death because that means he will lose his job. And I must say, Miss Cameron, that I consider it cruel to give this girl hopes which are so obviously unrealistic."

He rose and stood behind his chair, holding its back with both hands. His eyes fixed on Leslie as he announced, "I am the owner of Alohilani now. And—I have plans of my own."

"The owner?" She put a hand to her brow as if her head had begun to ache. "I don't understand."

"It is quite simple, Leslie." He spoke as if she were a foreigner for whom he had to enunciate English very clearly. "This property is held under what is called a life estate, and the heir cannot sell. Don's grandfather was fanatic about the place—he wanted it to remain in our family. On Don's death I inherited—as next of kin."

Leslie took this announcement with a gasp, then sank into silence. The Farnhams watched, and as we waited for her to recover, I thought, rapidly reviewing family history, that Howard's claim to inheritance might be valid.

Farnhams loved their land with a passion near obsession. I recalled what I'd heard when Don's father reminisced of how his forebears began to tame these wild acres into the magnificent property which became Alohilani. He had spoken of struggle and almost unimaginable labor, of vision carved into achievement as mesquite-covered wastes were developed into pastures, of pumping water miles over black lava for cattle which were nourished by those pastures and which in turn nourished the population of Hawaii. He told of family conferences when the homesite was chosen and gardens laid out, of planting thousands of trees as cattle shelter and windbreak for the house when Kona storms howled their way up from the equator to convulse the land.

I wondered how much of this Don had told Leslie. Most of it, probably. In those intimate hours when a man reveals his heart to the woman he loves, he must have talked to her of the roots from which he had sprung, the way of life they would follow. Don had shown little interest in girls when I knew him; this one he had chosen in his maturity must possess qualities which made him feel that she was the woman, at last, with whom his world could be completely shared.

I couldn't estimate Leslie as a person. There was something vital lacking in her at this moment, but then what woman might not be diminished, confronted with sudden announcement of her husband's death? Shock did strange things to people, and she was certainly in shock now, almost unable to assimilate what she had been told. Gradually, also, I had begun to perceive that part of her mind was not on the news that she was to be displaced from the home she had inhabited so briefly. Some deeper and more immediate problem seemed to preoccupy her; she had withdrawn to face it.

Howard Farnham interpreted her silence as acceptance. Relief showed on his face, his mouth curved in the faintest smile of triumph as he started to the door.

Leslie straightened against the pillow. She said in a speculative voice, "You say you have inherited Don's land. Is that why you are so sure he is dead?"

He whirled so fast that his kimono flew open and showed long hairy legs. "Why, you little—!"

"Howie," his wife's husky voice warned from the window.

He regained control. He pulled the kimono around himself. "All right, my dear." He went to the side of the bed. "You insist that Don could not drown, he was too good a swimmer. That is possibly true, but—you must accept facts. *There are sharks in these waters.*"

Leslie sat erect, both hands clutching the blue blanket as if it were the last solid thing left in a reeling universe. She tried to speak and could not; when she began to tremble Howard's wife said, "We'd better go. Miss Cameron can take care of her now."

I was glad to see the door close behind them.

Leslie's teeth had begun to chatter and she could not stop trembling; she shuddered and gulped air which came out in gasps, she put both hands to her throat to stifle the cry rising there. I went quickly to the bathroom and filled a glass with water; she couldn't hold it so I held the glass to her mouth and she swallowed and gradually recovered. I lit a cigarette and sat by the bed to wait until she regained control of herself.

"Would you like a cigarette?" I offered.

"No, thanks." She managed a faint smile. "I don't smoke."

She had been a teacher of physical education. If she had won a swimming meet she must be very good; maybe she took sports seriously. I smoked and waited until she should indicate a desire either for conversation or solitude.

Finally she said, "You told me you are an old friend of Don's. Is Hawaii really your home?"

"Yes, I'm a *kamaaina*—island-born. From Honolulu."

"Then you might know—" She hesitated, and braced herself. "I wouldn't believe what that man says—but you'll tell the truth. Are there really sharks here?"

"There are a few," I admitted. "I've heard of sharks attacking cattle when they were being loaded at Makena—you know how they're towed out to sea and hoisted aboard the cattle boats?" She nodded. "But I have never heard of any shark attacking a man."

Her eyes closed. Finally she looked at me again and made an effort. "I've been inconsiderate." She glanced around her and something made her wince as she said, "This is one of the smaller guest rooms at the rear of the house. You'll find a room on the other side of the bath, next to it—" She stopped and started to push back the blanket. "Really, I'm not so rude as a rule—I'm not thinking straight just now. I'll show you—"

"No you won't," I said. "I'll find it myself. You're exhausted. You probably didn't get much sleep on the clipper, did you?"

"No. And I couldn't eat either—I was so excited about meeting—" She caught her lip in her teeth. I wanted very much to know why she had left Don when they had been married only two months. I didn't ask.

"Then you made another flight through a Kona storm," I reminded her, "and landed in this nightmare. What you need now is rest. I can take care of myself. But first I want to give you something to help you sleep—"

She started to protest and I said, "Maybe you never take a sedative, but there are times when it helps and this is one of them. Remember, Leslie: you're going to have a long and difficult day tomorrow."

She said then: "You are right. And tonight would have been even worse if you hadn't—when I'm able to thank you properly—"

"Thank Steve Dugan. She's the one who sent me over here."

I told her briefly how I had happened to come to the ranch, leaving out all mention of Eole. She was already near enough to breaking, without reminder of the boy who lay in the stable with a stallion's hoofmarks on his body. As I talked, I opened my dressing case and found some luminal which I always carry and never use. Leslie swallowed it and seemed relieved to know that she'd have time to prepare for bed before the drug took effect.

Before I started out to find a room for myself I said, "Speaking of Steve; she's going to worry until she hears from me. I'd like to call Honolulu now and leave a message, if you don't mind."

"Of course not. There are two telephones downstairs; one in Don's office and one in the library."

"Can I help you with anything?"

"No, thank you."

"Then I'll clear out and let you sleep. Good night."

I took my bag and coat and went in search of a room. The hall was lit by a small bulb in the baseboard near the head of the stairs; a bright streak of light under a door at the front of the house indicated where the Farnhams might be settled. I found an empty guest room opposite it and dumped

my things, then started downstairs. I had taken off my wet shoes and
stockings; in Hawaii we're accustomed to going barefoot so it didn't seem
unnatural to go soundlessly to the lower part of the house.

The living room was dark except for the glow of the fire. A log flamed
briefly and highlighted book bindings on the wall of an adjoining room,
and I went toward the library. I stopped halfway across the floor and then
made a quick detour to the side of the room and stood there. Somebody
was already talking on the telephone, and his words brought me to full
attention.

"—and tell the police if you want to. Then see how much good it will
do." The speaker was the man named Denis Desmond. He spoke to someone he knew well, someone he disliked or feared—his voice was harsh
with animosity.

"God damn it!" he said, apparently interrupting the person at the other
end of the wire. "Haven't you got sense enough in your head to understand—no, I can't! In this storm? I certainly cannot. I'll get there as soon
as I can make it and no sooner." His voice roughened. "If that doesn't suit
you, go and talk to anybody you like, go to the police, or go to hell—it
doesn't make a damned bit of difference to me!"

He banged the receiver on the hook then, and I made a hasty exit and
started back up the stairs, wondering about him as I went. He had spoken
like a man on the ragged edge of nerves; whatever emotion shook him—
rage, fear, or hatred of his unseen communicant—it had reached a critical
stage. I'd have to give Mr. Desmond close attention tomorrow.

Lying in bed a while later, I began to try to think, to sort out impressions and arrange a coherent report for that telephone call which I must
make in the morning. It was difficult to think; there was much to consider, and I felt depressingly unable to cope with it.

The rain had slackened but a cold wind prowled the house and
whined at the windows. A colder thought whimpered for admission
and finally I recognized it. Eole was dead. Eole had tried to warn me
of something, and now he was dead. *The coffin is almost ready.* Ready
for whom?

For Don? But Howard claimed that Don had been dead for several
days. He insisted on that fact—any denial disturbed him. If he had indis-
putable right to the ranch, why couldn't he and his wife have been decent
enough to meet Leslie, to help her through this ordeal with some gesture
of sympathy, no matter how grudging? They didn't want her even to sleep
on the property—why? They wanted to get rid of the ranch foreman too.
Howard Farnham seemed unfitted to be a rancher, and on a property of
this kind someone had to be always in charge. Howard had mentioned

"plans" of his own. Whatever they were, I decided, I was opposed to them.

Then I reminded myself that his plans were not actually my affair. My concern was to see that Leslie Farnham didn't get pushed around any more, to stand by until we were certain what had happened to Don. I didn't know what to do to help her, and wished fervently that Lily were there. I should try to call her now, but didn't want to go downstairs again in a darkened house, at an hour when even the elements seemed malign.

So many questions. Eole again. What had Leslie started to say about him, when she said, "But he would never—" and failed to finish that comment? If the stallion was so wild that hardly anyone went near him, what was the boy doing in his stall? I thought of Eole lifting his head to tell me something, and that brought a picture of the dark, agonized eyes, the bloody face—I had to shut out further thought of Eole until daylight.

The wind whined and sobbed intermittently. Somewhere near the house I could hear tall trees twisting and groaning like tortured spirits struggling to free themselves from a place where evil has been done. It's going to be a bad day tomorrow, I thought, and dreading it, I finally slept

CHAPTER FOUR

IT DIDN'T start like a bad day. Before I opened my eyes I knew that the storm was over, that golden light flooded the island and wind flowed from the east, bringing the stir of a fresh new morning. I lay absorbing sounds of life outside the house: chickens cackling, the bawl of a calf in the corral, doves cooing on the roof of the stable. Presently the door opened and a round face with bright black eyes peered in. Seeing that I was awake, the Japanese maid opened the door wider and bobbed her head in greeting.

"Good morning," I said. "Is Mrs. Farnham up?"

"Missus Don bedroom stop, say you come her side. Okay?"

"Tell her I'll be right there." She nodded and withdrew while I reached for my kimono and headed for the shower.

I found Leslie fully dressed, standing at a window with her eyes fixed on the mountain slope behind the house. I joined her and for a moment we watched two *paniolos* jogging through a pasture; *leis* around their hats made bright spots of color against rippling green over which their horses moved.

Finally Leslie turned. "Such a beautiful morning! I can't—" She straightened her shoulders. "I've sent for Mele."

"She's the housekeeper, isn't she? Hawaiian?"

"Yes. She and Karl are devoted to Don. He says he couldn't get along without them."

She wasn't using past tense. I said, "You don't believe Don is dead."

"No. I can't. I won't! Unless Karl and Mele tell me—I've only known the Kings for a week, but I have more confidence in them than any— you'll see why."

Steve had said Don and Leslie were married two months ago. Yet Leslie had known the Kings for only a week. When I showed confusion she explained that she and Don had had two weeks of honeymoon at Volcano House, during which time Don kept in daily touch with the foreman by telephone. When he brought Leslie to Alohilani she spent a week learning details of household management from Mele, while Karl brought Don up to date on ranch affairs. At the end of that time Don sent the Kings— over Karl's protest, for he had not left Maui since he came to work there— to Honolulu on vacation. This, I gathered, was to give the newlyweds more time alone together.

Leslie's voice had been warm up to that point. Her tone changed as she added, "Then, just before Karl and Mele returned, something came up, and I went to California very suddenly. I *had* to go—" Before she could continue there was a knock on the door and the housekeeper entered.

Leslie went to her. "Mele! How glad I am to see you!"

"Good morning."

The Hawaiian woman stood at attention in a starched blue uniform. She didn't utter a word of welcome, and her face was stony.

Leslie's smile vanished and her hands dropped to her sides. I concealed my own amazement while I was introduced to the wife of the ranch foreman. She was much taller than I, she nodded a head wrapped with thick braids and turned immense dark eyes toward me, but she didn't speak. She stood and waited.

Leslie's candid face registered disappointment, incredulity, then fear in quick succession. She made a second attempt; she smiled again and said, "Thank you, Mele, for carrying on when—during Don's absence."

"That was our job," Mele said. Her beautiful mouth was far more grave than Hawaiian mouths are meant to be. She looked down at her common-sense oxfords and her voice quickened as she added, "Now that Howard Farnham has taken over, we will be leaving."

Leslie was staring at her, speechless with dismay. It was time for a friend to step in.

"Mele," I said crisply, "this girl has had a great shock, as you undoubtedly know. And she hasn't eaten for a long time. How about bringing some coffee up here for us before we talk any further?"

Mele leveled an appraising look on me. I met it with a smile which said that I was perfectly willing to be friends if she wished, but in the meantime I expected orders to be obeyed. She turned to Leslie. "Is there anything else you wish sent up? Fruit juice, toast, perhaps—"

Leslie's back was toward us. She shook her head.

I answered for her. "Nothing else, thank you. Just coffee." I added, for I was sure she meant to send one of the maids and thus avoid what had to be brought into the open, "And bring a cup for yourself, so we can sit down together and talk this over."

She nodded and left the room.

I went immediately to Leslie, drew her over to the bed, and sat beside her. "Now listen," I said. "You've got to pull yourself together and make up your mind who's going to be in control here. The way you handle your housekeeper may determine the morale of your entire domestic staff. For some reason, which we can't figure out yet, you seem to be getting a beating from all sides. Are you going to stand up to it—or do you intend to let everybody push you around?"

Leslie had caught the edge of the spread and was twisting it. I picked up her left hand and said, "You're wearing the Farnham wedding ring. Do you know what those little gold feathers mean?"

She didn't answer.

"Those are *mamo* feathers—they signify that Don is a chief here—and you are a chief's wife. A long time ago the great chiefs of Hawaii wore capes made of those golden feathers. The birds from which they came are extinct now, and the few capes left in the world are in museums, or buried with their owners where they'll never be found. You can see one in the Bishop Museum someday, if you're interested. But in the meantime, it's important to remember what that little gold circle on your hand means.

"Farnhams are considered chiefs because they love and protect the people who live on their land. According to Hawaiian belief, when you marry nobility you acquire the responsibilities as well as the rank. That's very important to the people on this ranch—and to you. During Don's absence—and that's the expression you yourself just used—you have to take his place."

Leslie dropped the spread. She began to trace with one finger the raised feather design of the golden circle she wore.

I caught my breath and went on. "I've known Don since he was a very young man, and I can tell you that he took a long, long time to fall in love and marry. When he put that ring on your finger—" I stopped as she raised a wet face to me.

"Thank you, Janice. I may never be able to tell you—well, that was just what I needed." She straightened and began to dry her cheeks like a child, with her two hands. "When Mele comes back, I'll—"

I gave her a little shove. "Better go wash your face. Put on some lipstick, powder, whatever you use. And get set for the first round." She went to follow my suggestion.

Mele returned presently with a tray which held cups, a pot of coffee, fruit juice, and buttered rolls—service for two. She did not intend to sit with us and discuss anything. As she set the tray down Leslie came in, coppery hair brushed behind her ears, her mouth touched with pink, and her chin high. Her eyes showed that she registered Mele's further rebuff, but she made no comment. We drew chairs up to a table and as Mele began to take things from the tray Leslie talked.

"You startled me a while ago, Mele, when you spoke of leaving Alohilana. I'm sorry if you and Karl have been made to feel you're not wanted here—but surely you realize I am not responsible for that. I'll correct this situation immediately."

Mele's hand halted in the act of serving coffee; she hesitated and then finished pouring as Leslie continued.

"Mr. and Mrs. Farnham may stay here for the present—*as my guests.*" She drew in a breath and finished decisively, "But Howard Farnham is not in charge of this ranch. While Don is away, that responsibility is mine. And in case you had forgotten, since we had so little time to get acquainted since I came here, I will remind you that I grew up on a cattle ranch. I am fully acquainted with the details of this business, and capable of supervising any aspect of it." She softened this by adding with a tentative smile, "Not so well as you and Karl, of course—and even if I were, I should never want you to leave. So let's not hear any more such talk from you." Mele straightened. Under starched cotton her breasts heaved with quickened breath. She started to speak—surely she wasn't going to protest?—then her mouth closed tight.

Something was wrong with this woman. Or had the searching party brought back news which we had not yet learned? I asked, "Has your husband returned yet?"

"Yes." Her voice was sullen. "But he is sleeping now. They did not come home until five this morning."

"Did they find—is there—" Leslie could not finish.

"I do not know."

Mele set down the coffeepot and went to the door. She said, "The *paniolos* took Eole's body to his house."

"I'll see his family this morning," Leslie told her. Then: "Wait a minute!" she called, as Mele opened the door. "Please have my bags moved into our room and send someone to unpack—what's the matter?"

"Mr. and Mrs. Farnham have taken that room. Your things were removed."

"They have taken *our* room?" Leslie's cheeks began to flame. "Then have them moved out of it—at once! Put them somewhere at the other end of the house. Get Suma and Haru to help you. Are the Farnhams up yet?"

"He and Denis have gone to the village. She—"

Leslie interrupted. "Is Mr. Desmond staying here too?"

"Yes. "

Leslie glanced at me. I made a gesture which said, one thing at a time, and she looked back at Mele. "And Mrs. Farnham?"

"She is having breakfast on the terrace."

"Then don't disturb her. I'll talk to her later."

"As you wish."

After Mele left I said, "You know, you don't have to put up with these people. Howard Farnham is trying to bluff you. He has no rights here. His title depends on a court decision and it takes a long time."

She said reluctantly, "You are probably right. But he is Don's relative—"

I set down my cup. "That's for you to decide, of course. I'll go now and get dressed."

When I came out again I almost bumped into a Japanese maid; I drew back to let her pass and waited while a second woman followed her. They carried garments over their arms; their feet in white *tabes* padded in and out under dark kimonos as they trotted toward the far end of the passage. Leslie appeared then and beckoned from the door opposite mine, from which I'd seen light the night before. I went across the hall into a large room furnished with modern mahogany twin beds and huge *koa* chests which looked like family heirlooms. Sunlight filled the room, a breeze billowed white curtains from the windows and brought the briny smell of the sea, mingled with eucalyptus. Through an inner door I glimpsed a smaller room containing a desk, bookcases, radio, and comfortable chairs.

I settled on a cushioned window seat out of the line of traffic. Leslie smiled briefly at me as she stripped a bed and tossed linens into the hall. She helped Mele stretch fresh sheets and unfold blankets, she plumped pillows and smoothed white candlewick over them with a firm hand. When

Don returned, her expression said, his bed would be ready for him. Leslie welcomed this activity; it showed in the purposeful gesture with which she removed dresser contents and dumped them, Edith's nylon lingerie tumbled with Howard's socks and shirts, in the empty bureau drawer which Mele held for her. Under the shirts was a manila envelope which I thought I should not, in her place, have hesitated to examine. As she tossed it I craned to read the return address. A satin lastex girdle fell over half the printing and I could decipher only:

DON & CO.
eers
ingham Bldg.
lulu, T.H.

I made a note of that.

The little maids beamed; they exchanged comments in Japanese as they pattered out of the room and returned to stand on tiptoe hanging Don's and Leslie's clothes in the two closets where they belonged.

In contrast to Leslie and the housemaids, Mele's demeanor was noticeable. Reluctance slowed her; she worked with eyes down, glancing up resentfully only when Leslie spoke. Once she stopped and looked at me; for a startled instant I fancied that she sent some message of wild appeal; then her face was averted and she moved again in stolid silence. I watched, wondering if I had imagined fear and desperation in her eyes—and decided that indeed I had. I looked out the window.

The crushed coral driveway where we had stood last night in pouring rain was dry now. Nasturtiums trailed between lava rocks which outlined it, scarlet geum and daisies bordered the walk which sloped, dropped a few steps, sloped again to a concrete terrace far below the house. A swimming pool there reflected light like a green mirror; beside it were benches, deck chairs, and an umbrella-shaded table where a woman was sitting.

Edith Farnham's figure was not visible but her legs and feet were extended beyond the shade of the umbrella to the seat of a chair; she sat in the position of one surveying her kingdom.

Kingdom is the right word, I thought, for this place. East Maui is wild bluffs, headlands plunging to the Pacific; the few ranches there are in high altitudes—except Alohilani. Don's is one of the rare properties; it lies in a wide valley—tree-studded through the plantings of generations of Farnhams—which begins westward on the sumptuous flanks of Haleakala, curves abruptly, then gently, and stops as if sliced straight down, only thirty feet from the sea. The water was still disturbed from the storm;

I watched breakers crash into white spume which thundered back onto wooden steps angling down toward a small pier where a few boats were moored. Beyond the little bay the Pacific rolled to Hawaii—the Big Island—across the channel.

Somewhere in that deep blue water—I blacked out the picture, refusing to think of Don at that moment. Apprehension might show on my face and I didn't want Leslie to see it. The maids had finished; she was thanking them as they bowed out of the room; I heard her unsnapping the locks of her luggage.

I'd like to talk to Lily, I told myself, looking at my watch. Nine o'clock. I'd give her another half hour of sleep—maybe she would break her date— she would relay a message to Steve and perhaps that hardy soul could get away from her job and join forces with us.

There were a lot of things I wanted to find out: who and what the Howard Farnhams were, why they were in such a hurry to get rid of Leslie; ditto for Denis Desmond, and explanation of why he had so suddenly become neighbor to an isolated place like Alohilani. Some of these questions, Steve, with her amazing fund of information about islanders, might be able to answer. Lily could tackle the rest of them, using her own methods, while I stuck close to Leslie Farnham.

A kimonoed figure went down the walk toward the big umbrella, carrying a covered tray. Edith Farnham's breakfast. I glanced at Leslie but she was at the clothes closet. Over her shoulder she asked, "Do you ride?" and looked relieved when I said yes. She laid whipcord jodhpurs on a bed, found boots, and we compared sizes and decided I could wear them. I had a cotton blouse which would do, and Leslie gave me her own jacket. It was of cocoa-colored suede, and when I demurred at taking something so obviously new and prized, she said with a smile that she had its twin.

"It belongs to Don but I'd rather wear it and let you take mine. He had them made for us."

She brought the larger jacket from the other closet and her fingers lingered over the soft leather as she laid it on the bed. Watching her, I recalled that I had once carried a big linen handkerchief, looking at it a dozen times a day. It bore the initial E, and its owner had long ago changed my life by marrying another girl. It was difficult now to remember how he looked, but I remembered the emotion—I smiled at Leslie and accepted her jacket so she could have excuse to wear the one which belonged to Don.

She took riding clothes from a traveling bag: slim-legged frontier pants which were faded and threadbare, high-heeled boots of reversed leather. "I got these from storage in California," she explained, and I perceived that they were the kind of clothes in which she felt most at ease. Don hadn't chosen blindly . . . .

A maid brought a breakfast tray to the sitting room next the bedroom and we settled to it. We were almost finished when we heard a bang on the bedroom door.

"Come in," Leslie called, and laid down her spoon.

The door swung wide and Karl King strode into the room.

CHAPTER FIVE

HE WAS A BIG MAN, a hearty man with tremendous vigor and power. When I first saw him his huge frame drooped with weariness, his cheeks were dark-stubbled, but the force of his personality was apparent nevertheless. Karl's eyes lighted when he saw Leslie, his smile was warm, and I could almost see her spirits lift as she drew strength from the welcome he gave her.

"Leslie!" he boomed. "*Aloha nui loa!*"

"Karl!" She went toward him, her mouth was tremulous as he dropped a *lei* of gardenias around her neck and kissed her.

"Welcome home, Leslie! Can't say how glad I am to see you."

"Karl, that goes both ways." She turned, holding his arm as she introduced us to each other. He gave me one of those big smiles and said, "Certainly glad to meet you, Miss Cameron."

She urged him toward the room where we had been having breakfast. "Have you eaten yet?"

"Had fish and *poi* with the Makele family, hours ago. I could use some hot food."

"I'll call Haru—"

"Don't bother." He strode to the hall and bellowed: "Mele! Bring me some *kaukau—wikiwiki!*"

Lines around his eyes deepened as he twinkled at Leslie. "You'll have to excuse me a minute. Haven't given my wife her good mornin' kiss yet.'"

Mele didn't appear; she sent Haru with food for him. Karl waited until the maid had put the tray down, then went to the hall and yelled: "Mele! Come up here!"

When his wife came to the door he stepped into the other room. I turned my eyes away but not before I glimpsed his arms going around that rigid figure, his mouth pressed down on hers. There was sound of a struggle, a smothered exclamation; then he came back to the room where we waited, and pulled his breakfast tray toward him.

I smoked and drank coffee, Leslie fiddled with the silver; Karl grunted satisfaction after he swallowed his first mouthful of food. His bronzed and weather-beaten countenance, the way he bore himself in worn riding clothes, indicated a life in the open, while his table manners were those of mess shack instead of dining room. I judged that here was a man of rugged character; he could evict the Farnhams for Leslie if she decided that they should go. He would probably enjoy it, too.

As Karl ate he corroborated the story we had heard from Howard Farnham, saying in answer to my question, "No, it wasn't anything special for Don to take off for a day's fishin'. Most often he went with Eole. This time he was alone."

"Did anyone see him?"

"The Makeles did. They were spearin' squid off the point that afternoon. Said Don waved as he went by. He was alone."

Leslie's eyes never left his face as he spoke. She leaned forward now and said, "Karl, what do you honestly think has happened? Please tell me the truth."

He gulped coffee, then pulled a battered pack of cigarettes from his shirt pocket and struck a match on his boot. "Eole said the damned kerosene stove on Don's boat needed fixin'. Don must've had trouble with it. A Kanaka came into the village yesterday talkin' about a flash of light he saw along the coast. When I heard about it I thought he meant on land, maybe a signal. Took some of the men and rode over there last night. The fella told us he saw the flash at sea, just off the point. So maybe there was an explosion—"

Leslie caught her breath.

Karl laid a big hand over hers. "Hold tight to the curb, girl. You know that man of yours is first cousin to a fish. He's made his way ashore somewhere. Why, there's dozens of hidden valleys here, deep places you can't get to by land. A few natives live in some, but there's more that've been deserted for years. Hell, Leslie, a guy could live in one of those places forever. Eat raw fish, seaweed, bananas. We've had plenty rain now, so even if the cove was dry he'd have drinkin' water. A man'd make out, specially a guy like Don, born on this island."

"That's what Janice says."

He turned to me with a smile, pleased at what he heard. "Island girl, eh?"

"Yes. Born in Honolulu."

"I thought so. Then you're the *aikane* Leslie needs right now."

With that I agreed. Aside from Karl, I was the only one here who seemed to be a real friend to her.

He turned back to Leslie and resumed: "One of those little coves—that's where we'll find Don. I've been ridin' all along the damned coast. Borrowed Don's glasses and carry 'em with me. Lucky the roundup's over. We've let some of our jobs slide, but we're joggin' along all right. If we have to, we'll get some boys over from another ranch. Everybody wants to help. Let's see, I've got two mares due to *haanau* in the lower pasture. And Lani's ready for breedin'. That's why I had Pilikia brought in."

Leslie spoke of Eole then. "You heard what happened last night?"

His rugged face became grave. "Yes. Can't understand it. Eole wouldn't get in ropin' distance of that stallion."

"The Farnhams thought he might have tried to quiet the horse," I offered.

The big man scowled. "Not that boy. Anybody else but Eole." He looked at Leslie. "What was he doin' at the stables, anyway? Did he tell you?"

"When we found him he couldn't talk much, Karl. All he said was—" Her brows drew together slightly as she tried to recall those words.

"I heard what he said, Leslie," I interrupted. She might remember that he had called me by name, and I didn't want anyone to know about my rendezvous with Eole. They looked at me and I smiled apology for my rudeness and explained, "Leslie was closing the door of the stall while I knelt by him. He told me he had been waiting for her."

"He said more than that," she insisted, and I stiffened. "He said something in Hawaiian—it sounded like '*lolo*.' "

"Oh yes!" I agreed quickly. "He said something about being '*lolo*' and then that he was waiting for you. He must have heard that you were coming home."

Karl scowled again. "Probably got the news from the kitchen, like I did. Don's cousin never bothered to tell us about your cable. Eole—Howard and Eole had a helluva row yesterday." His face lighted with an idea. "That's why he was waitin' for you, Leslie. Wanted to tell you about his sampan."

"Sampan?"

"You know how crazy the boy was about fishin'. Don promised him the down payment on a boat. I got to admit it was a relief to me, the kid was useless around here and I was glad to get rid of him. '*Lolo*'—that means stupid, Leslie. He was tryin' to tell you he'd done a dumb thing, goin' into that stall."

I must have shown my distaste for the way in which he spoke of the dead boy. Karl looked directly at me and said, "Leslie will tell you, Miss Cameron—"

"Janice."

"Janice. Leslie, here, will tell you, or my wife or anybody else who takes orders from me, that I'm a guy with very rough manners. I never learned to use the soft, polite words. And I'm afraid it's too late now."

Leslie touched the flowers which lay around her neck. "We all know how tough you are, Karl. Go on."

"Well, this sampan just arrived from Molokai. When Eole came to the house to get the money Howard told him the deal was off. I felt sorry for the kid—if you coulda seen the look on his face! That bas—" He bit off the word and substituted, "That guy Howard had a fight with Don too—just before Don disappeared."

"But he told me they only came here after they heard of Don's accident."

Karl leaned back and ran a hand over the stubble on his jaw. "Howard was here the day before. I heard 'em myself, goin' at it hot and heavy in Don's office."

He asked, and anxiety crept into his voice in spite of himself, "Did Don write you he was worried over anything? He started to say somethin' that day about *pilikia*, about wantin' to talk to me. Had a sick heifer in the corral and was in a rush. He said he'd see me later."

"No." Leslie's face grew troubled. "I had no—very little news from him."

What did that mean? That she had heard nothing at all? I was still wondering why she had left Don so soon after their marriage.

Karl sighed, and lines deepened around his mouth. Leslie said quickly, "Karl, you've been riding all night. Why don't you go back to bed?"

"Me? I'm not hamstrung yet, girl." He shoved back his chair and stood up, grinning at her. "I'm good for another twenty-four hours."

As he reached for his hat Leslie asked, "Who is that man I met last night? He's staying here. He told me he's a new neighbor of ours. And, Karl, he was wearing Don's clothes!"

Karl's face became as expressionless as if a shutter had been drawn. "He bought Auohe."

Auohe. Hidden place. I grew tense. This was a thread leading to some of the elements which disturbed me.

Leslie didn't know that. But she was disturbed, too, over another facet of this information. "But that's your wife's land! I thought Mele would never sell—she refused Don's offer. I couldn't understand why Don wanted it, except that it adjoins the ranch."

"The valley's worthless," Karl said. "Except for the stream there. Don wanted to pump water to storage in the upper pastures; the cattle walk off pounds if they go too far to drink." He hesitated, then said, "I thought Mele wouldn't sell her land, too. But"—his jaw shot out—"she sold it to Desmond."

"But it's inaccessible, isn't it, except by boat?"

"There's an old trail down the face of the cliff. Nobody uses it."

"What does he want inaccessible land for?"

Karl shrugged. He rammed his hat over his head and went to the door. He hadn't told her all he knew. He didn't want to talk about Denis Desmond.

I concluded that the man must be a friend of Howard's, since Howard had given him Don's clothes. As if he knew that Don would never need them again. And the blond man felt as secure as the Farnhams, apparently, in whatever he was doing here; he had told somebody over the phone to go to the police and be damned. I wondered whether to mention this to Leslie and decided against it. She had too much to worry about already.

I'd tell Lily Wu; she might sort impressions and facts and come up with something significant as she so often does. I knew now that Leslie had some courage with which to face her trouble, but I was not sure that it was enough. And this situation had ramifications of which she was not aware. From what Eole had said, from the way the Hawaiians had treated her at the airport, and from the uncharacteristic behavior of Karl's Hawaiian wife, I feared that this was *pilikia nui*—great trouble. And its source might be deep Hawaii. Apparently it was something that not even Karl, the *haole,* was permitted to know. I could help Leslie hold her own against the Farnhams and Denis Desmond, but in the meantime it was imperative to search for some purpose moving beneath the surface, inexorable as the lava which seethes in the vitals of Hawaii's mountains.

Leslie had walked into the other room with the foreman. "Karl, I don't know what to—it's hard to sit and wait, I feel so helpless. What are you doing about—"

"About Don? We'll never give up till we find him. I've got men out, coverin' every acre of this island, from daybreak to dark. But I have to spend some time here, Leslie, to keep things goin' right."

"I know that. I shouldn't even have asked. You're in charge; do what you think best."

"Think you can handle the Farnhams?"

"I'll handle the Farnhams," she said. "We'll proceed exactly as if Don were here, until—until he comes home."

As soon as he had gone she began unzipping her flannel skirt, looking at me to ask, "Do you mind changing now? I must ride over to see Eole's parents, and I hope you'll go with me."

"I'll be glad to. But first I want to call Honolulu. I wasn't able to get the call through last night."

"Certainly. And please give Steve my regards and thanks."

"I'm not calling Steve, but your message will be relayed. I'm calling my roommate, Lily Wu. I'd like to ask her to come over here, if you don't mind."

"Please do. She will be very welcome."

I went down to the library and put in my call. Lily answered immediately.

"This is Janice," I said, looking from the library toward the dining room. Haru was there, arranging hibiscus on the big table. "How was the party last night?"

"Delightful. We missed you, of course. It is very hot here. I am sleepy. And is someone listening while you make this call?"

"Very likely," I told her. "Lily, you mentioned that you intended to visit some cousins on Maui." That was safe, because Lily seems to have cousins everywhere we go.

"You mean you want me to come over there? What has happened?"

"You know I wanted to get out of the heat while I corrected those galleys. I'm visiting an old school friend, Leslie Farnham, at Alohilani Ranch. Incidentally, it's cool enough here to wear a coat. But we're having a bit of *pilikia*. Her husband recently disappeared while he was out on a fishing trip."

"I see," said her cool voice. "You remember that I have a date with David. Is it all right if I wait until that happy event is over or do you think this is urgent?"

"Yes, of course. Come whenever you feel like it. But please bring me some clothes." She knew what I would need.

"Anything else? What shall I tell Steve?"

"Oh yes. Tell Steve that her Hawaiian friend, the one she wanted me to look up at Hana—well, just say I'm staying on here for a while and won't be able to see him. Lily—do you remember Maude?"

She would understand that reference. Maude Benson was dead. And it was in exposing her murderer that we had encountered some of the superstitions of primitive Polynesia.

Lily's voice sharpened. "Yes, I remember her very well."

Haru had gone from dining room to kitchen, leaving the swinging door ajar. Mele was in the kitchen, standing before the open refrigerator. She didn't touch anything on its shelves; she stood very still.

"Tell Maude I'll write," I said casually. "Just as soon as I can." By which I hoped Lily would get the idea that I wanted her to break that date and come to Maui now. "Call me when you decide to come over, Lily, and I'll drive down to meet you and pick up my clothes."

"I understand, Janice." The line began to crackle and her voice sounded faint and far away. "I'll call you. I'll tell Steve. Good-by."

I replaced the instrument and went back to my room. As I slipped a belt through the loops of Leslie's jodhpurs, I tried to shake off a feeling of depression, or maybe it was apprehension, I don't know which. It wasn't only that I dreaded meeting the family of Eole, although that was part of it, knowing as I did how almost unbearably tragic is the Hawaiian expression of grief. Talking to Lily had made me realize that, although I possessed a few miscellaneous facts, I hadn't so far got the faintest clue to what was really happening in this place. As I dressed, I tried to straighten out what little I knew.

Eole was Hawaiian. He feared something which he called "dreadful," and which to him must have been even worse than Don's disappearance, because when Eole spoke to me Don had already been gone for four days. The "dreadful" thing he feared was yet to happen, and he was so terrified that he called for help from a total stranger. And a *haole,* at that. Why, I wondered, hadn't he confided in Karl?

Now that I had met Karl I understood why Leslie had such confidence in him. Possibly something had developed late that day which had sharpened Eole's fright, and he couldn't tell Karl be cause the foreman was out with the search party. Or was there an other reason?

Talking to Lily had reminded me, as her presence generally does, that in order to analyze something one must have concrete facts to consider. I hadn't enough. Well, I decided, if I can't do anything else, I can stick close to Leslie.

I went to her room and found her pulling on her boots. She stood up and tucked her cotton shirt in more neatly, then went to Don's closet for his suede jacket. Her faded frontier pants, with their reinforcing worn through inside the knees, fit her slim body perfectly. She looked very young, and vulnerable, and deeply troubled.

She said, "I'm glad you're here."

"So am I," I told her, and reached for the other jacket. "Is this for me?" She said yes and I picked it up and carried it over my arm as she carried Don's, then followed Leslie down the stairs toward our interview with the parents of Eole.

CHAPTER SIX

WE FOUND three *paniolos* at the blacksmith's shop behind the stables. One was currying a horse which stood at the hitching rail waiting to be shod by the Japanese smithy. A second man sat at one side of the wide door-way with knife and whetstone in his hands. The third was much younger, a slim youth wearing a bright shirt, a *lei* of red roses around the hat which was tipped to the back of his dark curly hair. He squatted easily on his heels with shoulders against the building, oiling a bridle. As we approached he looked up; he appraised each of us in turn with bold black eyes.

The older men waited. Leslie said, "Hello, Ikua. Hello, Mahoe." She added timidly, *"Aloha.* I am glad to see you again."

That was the greeting they should have given her. The young one spoke instead; he sent us a flashing smile and said, *"Aloha,* Leslie Farn-ham. Welcome home to Maui. I am Kolea." He stared at me.

"Thank you, Kolea. This is my friend, Janice Cameron."

I smiled and started to say something in Hawaiian, then thought bet-ter of it. Leslie asked the big man with the currycomb, "Mahoe, can you saddle horses for us? Has Panini been brought in from pasture?"

"Ae, he is here," the Hawaiian said. "He plenty devil, mebbe bettah you no ride Panini today."

"I can manage him," she insisted.

Mahoe's face became expressionless.

He turned to Kolea and spoke in Hawaiian. "Go and get the horses, worthless one. We are tired, we rode through the storm last night while you lay drunk in your bed."

Kolea rose with lazy grace, the bridle swinging from his arm. "Mind your own business, old man. How do you know I was in my bed?"

"Too bad for you if you were in somebody else's. You've got trouble enough now as it is," Mahoe said angrily. "Go and get the horses. The yellow-haired girl can ride Umi."

"Should I bring Panini? He's wild; she might be thrown."

"That's what she ordered. Maybe she can ride him; she's a good horse-woman."

The sour-faced old man named Ikua spat on his whetstone. "Too bad she's not a good wife."

I was shocked. I wanted to come to Leslie's defense, but bit back words which would betray my comprehension of their comments. I glanced at Leslie but she didn't know what they were saying; she only sensed it. She slipped her arms into Don's jacket as if it offered double protection, and folded the cuffs back carefully at her wrists.

Mahoe adjusted his currycomb and returned to the horse, which stood with a hip dropped in relaxation. As he curried, he muttered in pidgin to the other Hawaiian, words which perhaps he wanted us to overhear: "I t'ink Karl too much worry now. Else he no was'e time wit' dis Kolea—he kick his *okole* to hell outta here."

I put on Leslie's jacket and moved away to take a look at Alohilani while we waited for horses. Behind the ranch house a rose-covered stone wall enclosed gardens where paths led to flower beds, fish ponds, groups of gardenia and *plumeria* trees, big purple mangoes. A venerable monkeypod spread green shadows over table and chairs, tall cypress and eucalyptus which had twisted and groaned during the storm now swayed serenely in the freshening wind. On the slope several hundred feet behind the stables were scattered cottages of the *paniolos'* families, while, as far as one could see, rolling pastures and paddocks enclosed white-faced Herefords and the sleek horses which Don Farnham prized. Alohilani supplied beef to local markets and thoroughbreds to lovers of fine horseflesh the islands over. It was a valuable property, not on the vast scale of other ranches in Hawaii, but still an important source of food for the islands.

Remote as it was, Alohilani functioned necessarily as a world to itself, generating electric power, growing food, providing shelter for its people, independent of the rest of the island. This was a way of life suited only for certain individuals; to most modern girls it might offer isolation and monotony. I wondered, aside from her affection for Don, what it meant to Leslie.

I became aware that she was at my side. She stood with head back, her eyes moving over the land, resting finally on Haleakala, which brooded, lonely and mysterious, far in the distance. She took deep hungry breaths, as she became aware that I watched she said softly, "Three weeks is a very long time to be away . . ." and I knew that to Leslie it wasn't monotony or isolation, it was magnificence and grandeur. She had made it her home by right of immediate and passionate love. How could these Hawaiians treat her as an outsider? I glanced back at them but they weren't watching us; the two older men sat talking with heads together, their faces were grave. I saw Kolea then leading our horses out of the corral; I touched Leslie's arm and we walked back to where he waited.

I was busy for a while after we started, getting the feel of the gray horse, hoping he wasn't going to be too lively. Finally I decided that Umi was not temperamental and I could count on staying safely aboard, and I turned with some concern to Leslie. She rode a big sorrel with black mane and tail; he danced circles, he reared and then jumped stiff-legged when she tightened the curb, but Leslie sat at ease in the saddle, she laid a hand on his neck and spoke to him, and presently he settled to a running walk, tossing his head as he went. I coaxed the gray to her side and we rode in amber sunlight across green slopes.

"That's a magnificent horse," I said. "He's the exact color of your hair."

She was pleased. "You're very observant, Janice. That's why Don gave him to me."

She looked almost happy as she spoke. Now, I decided, was the time to ask one question which had been on my mind.

"Leslie," I said. "Why did you leave Don?"

She glanced at me, distress on her face. She nodded, reminding herself of something, and said, "I can see now that everyone's wondering about that. The cowboys, Karl's wife—they all blame me for going away—but not half as much as I blame myself—" She steadied her voice and went on more calmly, "There was an emergency in my family. Illness. I had to go—at least, I thought so."

"Oh," I said. "I'm sorry." I hesitated to ask why some other relative could not have gone to San Francisco in her place. "Was it serious?"

"It is still serious," she said. "But I'm beginning to realize there is nothing I can do about it. That's what Don tried to tell me. That's what we quarreled about."

"You quarreled?"

"Yes," she said. "We had a terrible quarrel. And I ran away."

She seemed relieved to have a confidante, for she began to speak rapidly. "It's my sister; she's nineteen, five years younger than I. She was a student at the school where I was teaching, I paid her tuition from my salary. I've always taken care of Peggy; when our parents died I promised to help her finish college. But last winter she eloped with her roommate's brother, a boy from San Francisco; they found an apartment there. With Peggy safely married, I decided to come to Honolulu. I'd always wanted to, and couldn't afford it before."

Leslie's horse shied suddenly, then went into a series of gyrations which took all her attention. I held on to my placid gray and jogged along until she could calm the big sorrel enough to continue talking. Hers was a familiar story, a family situation which often seems trite—except to those who are in it. I was glad that Leslie had had her vacation, her chance to meet Don. And at the thought that she might have been his wife for a tragically short time, that she might never see him again, I felt cold. Perhaps it was the chill wind which swept down from the mountain; I buttoned the suede jacket and was glad of its warmth. Leslie hadn't rejoined me and I looked back to see where she was.

The sorrel was jumping and tossing his head; she was holding him on a tight curb, trying to read something on paper which she held in her right hand. She looked toward me, pulled her horse to a stop, and slid off, calling, "Janice! Can you come here?"

I wheeled Umi toward her. Leslie looked up from where she stood and said in a queer voice, "Will you hold Panini?"

As I dismounted she shoved reins at me and held together sheets of paper which had been torn down the middle. Her hands were shaking.

"What is it?" I asked.

"It's a letter. From Don. I found it just now in his pocket." She started to read, hungrily.

I stood and waited, letting the reins slack so the horses could crop grass at our feet. Beyond the ranch buildings sea and sky seemed to curve together; behind us clouds veiled the mountains in blue distance; the whistle of plover sounded overhead and grasses rustled and bent under the wind as if caressed by an invisible hand. I tried not to stare but my eyes went irresistibly to Leslie; she looked up, then offered the letter to me.

"Read it, Janice." I wound the reins around my wrist as I took the typewritten sheets and fitted them together to read what Don had written.

My darling Sorrel-Top,

It seems eternity since you've gone. I've spent these hours regretting what I said and wishing I could put my arms around you and apologize. I still think your sister is selfish and spoiled and has no right to make further demands on you. Appendicitis isn't that serious, and she's adult and has a husband, even if he is in the army. But I shouldn't punish you for being the loyal person you are, for having the very qualities which made me love you in the first place. I should have answered your cables—stubbornness and hurt pride kept me from it. I'm answering now, and I'll call your hotel tonight and tell you in person. There are a lot of other things I want to tell you which I can't write or say over a telephone.

Everything seems to have happened at once. In addition to my miserable state of mind since you left, I've run into a grave situation which may change life here at the ranch for us. And today I had a row with my cousin Howard—he and Edith are two people I most detest and you'll never see much of them if I can help it.

Excuse me if this sounds incoherent, I'm sort of thinking out loud now, and I've had a shock. I've just been informed of something going on here which is so monstrous that I hardly dare believe it's true. You remember Eole; his father was my *paniolo* when I was a little kid and the boy is as close to me as a younger brother. Eole's been exploring around here, spending some time with a guy who calls himself Desmond, and the boy has discovered something I dread to contemplate.

I can't take any steps about this until I'm sure what Eole says is true—and if it is true I've got a very serious problem because the worst disaster I can think of is for even a hint of this to leak out to anyone. Remember what I told you about inheriting patriarchal responsibilities when I took over the ranch? This is a time when I feel scared instead of proud of being *alii*. And Eole is terrified half out of his wits.

We've arranged to meet tonight on my boat—I'm to pick him up after dark at a place where no one can see him come aboard and we'll talk this over where we can't possibly be overheard. I wish you were here. I just looked at the clock and I've got to get started. I'll finish this tonight when I get back; in fact, I'll telephone and tell you this letter is on its way. If you want to bring Peggy back with you to stay until her husband gets out of the army, please believe I'll welcome her here. We can talk about it tonight—

I handed the sheets to Leslie. She folded them carefully and put them into the pocket of Don's jacket. As we started on our way again she said thoughtfully, "He decided not to send the letter; he was going to telephone me instead. That night."

After a while she added, "Janice, if it hadn't been for you, I might not have found his letter."

"What do you mean?"

"I was so confused and frightened—you reminded me that I had to fight back at those people and that's why I had them moved out of our room—"

"You mean, if you hadn't ordered Don's clothes put back where they belonged, you wouldn't have worn his jacket."

"Something like that. You see, when Don didn't write, when he didn't meet me, I felt—well, we haven't been married long enough for me to feel—"

"You felt as if you didn't really belong here? That's what the Farnhams hoped you'd feel."

"Yes. I know."

I waited for her to add something else she knew, of which I was now certain. If Don's boat had sunk, it was not an accident.

She said nothing more. Leslie seemed dazed with relief now, while I, not involved emotionally with Don, felt more apprehensive than before. Let her have this brief happiness at reassurance that Don loved her and had written to tell her so. When she came back to earth again she would remember other things besides reassurance in his letter and she would begin to be more afraid.

Eole's father was on the lanai of his cottage; he straightened and gripped the arms of his wheelchair when he saw us. I remembered John Kuneo. When I visited the ranch as a child he had been foreman for Don's father, an intelligent and educated man who rejected political office in the nearby village to live and work on the land he loved. Leslie had explained that six years ago he had been injured by a wild steer; Karl's tenure at the ranch began after John's retirement. Eleven-year-old Eole had been riding his first roundup with John when it happened; his phobia about horses dated from the day he witnessed the accident which crippled his father. As we dismounted and tied our horses to the hitching rail near the lanai, the white-haired man waited, granite-faced.

Inside the house someone was sobbing.

We sat on the wooden steps and Leslie introduced me to John, who nodded and said, "I remember when you came here a long time ago. And we heard about what you did this summer for the Hawaiians at Wainiha. Emmett Cameron would be proud of his daughter."

I probably gaped slightly. There were only two white people in Honolulu now who knew what had happened at the little native village on Oahu—Steve Dugan and myself. I marveled again at coconut wireless; probably more Hawaiians knew about that episode than I would meet in my lifetime.

Leslie looked puzzled. As no one explained, and the old man lapsed into silence, she finally said, "John, I am so very sorry about Eole. I came as soon as I could. You know that we were the ones who found him last night."

His deep-set eyes turned to her. "Yes. Karl told me when they brought my boy home." His face worked, he said gruffly, "Karl said he might have been drinking. That is not true. Kolea was the one who brought whiskey to the stables. When I was boss nobody dared bring liquor here. Eole was not drunk. Sick, maybe, sick from worry, but never—"

She said gently, "We know that, John. Karl was mistaken."

"Karl did not like my son, because he refused to work with the stock, but Karl is a hard man, a man without patience, he did not understand the reason for Eole's fear. Don understood. That was why he promised to help my boy. Now Don is gone, and Eole is dead, and his mother cries because I will not let her make a spectacle of our dead son by holding a wake in this house. Eole will be buried with a Christian service, in the churchyard."

He tightened gnarled fingers around the arms of his chair and sat straight and proud as an ancient chief who has issued an unalterable edict.

There was silence. Leslie looked distressed and at a loss what to say. As the sobbing continued inside the house she rose. "May I go in and talk with Kaiulani? Perhaps there is something I can do—"

He nodded. She opened the screen door and went into the house. There was a fresh outburst of sobbing, then incoherent words which became less audible as John's wife led Leslie to the rear bedroom.

I moved closer to the wheelchair.

"John," I said, "can anyone hear us? I want to talk to you."

"No one can hear. His mother weeps, she hears nothing but her own sorrow."

I began to speak in Hawaiian, partly out of deference to John, and partly to develop confidence between us.

"Eole was not drunk, John. He went into the stall to quiet the stallion because he feared the horse might injure himself in his fear of the storm." I hesitated and then added a lie. "Eole told me this when I spoke to him."

The white-haired man relaxed his grip on the chair. "It was a brave thing my boy did, then, for he was much afraid of horses." His voice softened, he added, "Thank you for telling me."

"Eole spoke to me before he died, John. He tried to tell me something," I improvised carefully. "Something about Don. Do you know what he wanted to talk to me about?" I sat very still, waiting for his answer.

John shook his head. "I knew Eole was worried. When I asked him why, he said he knew a terrible secret, a secret of the *alii*, he must talk only with the *alii*. Don," he reminded me, "was our chief, as his father was before him."

"Tell me everything you can remember of what Eole said."

He looked down at clean dungarees which covered his useless legs, and began to speak slowly. "The night Don went away Eole came home late, he came through the banana grove to the side of the house. He was afraid, he shook with his fear. After that he never left his room, he said he was sick. He lay on the *punee* all day looking at the wall, saying nothing. But yesterday the sampan arrived from Molokai—you know about the fishing boat Don was going to buy for him?"

"Yes, Karl told us."

The old man smiled. "Eole was a child of the sea, not of the land, he was happy only near the water. It was because of this that Don promised to buy him a fishing boat, so that he could earn a living at something he liked—"

"Yes, John, I know. So the boat arrived yesterday and Eole went to the pier to look at it. And it was when he reached the house that he heard Leslie was coming home? Is that right?"

"That is correct. First he spoke to the other Farnham—the bad cousin— about money to pay for the boat. You know about that?"

"And Howard Farnham refused to give it to him. Yes."

The white head nodded. "At the house Eole was told that Don's wife was coming home. And he heard Mele talking on the telephone to the woman from the newspaper. Eole knew what she had done to help our people at Wainiha, he knew she could be trusted. He called her." He looked at me. "Was that how you happened to come here last night?"

"Yes. She couldn't come, she sent me instead."

I watched a lizard which lay in the sun by my boot, motionless except for the twitch of its tail. I was afraid to tell John that Eole had gone to the stables to meet me; he might realize that our rendezvous was the cause of his son's death—as I was more and more certain it had been. I didn't know what attitude he would take toward me if he knew.

He went on, speaking with effort. "Eole came home then. He ate some food and told us he was going to meet Don's wife, to talk to her about the sampan. He would wait at the stables, he said, until he saw the lights of a car, then he would come out and speak to her."

It must have been a terrible secret indeed. The boy had not confided even in his parents his real reason for going to wait at the stables. Perhaps his mother, chatting with another *paniolo's* wife, had mentioned his intention. And who could guess how many others knew before darkness came, before the storm brought howling wind and rain which kept all except the search party indoors, which made perfect cover for one who needed to silence Eole. The boy had not gone voluntarily near that screaming stallion. Had he been hit on the head, perhaps, and then dumped into the horse's stall? I stared at the lizard and wondered.

As silence lengthened between us I began to feel uncomfortable. I shrugged away tightness in my shoulders and rubbed prickles in the back of my neck. The lizard twitched and darted into a clump of ginger by the steps. And some atavistic perception quickened my pulse, my flesh crawled with awareness.

Someone was watching us.

I turned quickly toward the banana grove at the side of the house. Tattered fronds there were parted by brown hands like claws. From between them stared a face which was all eyes, cavernous eyes which burned with fixed malevolence. Then the face vanished and I was looking at banana leaves which writhed in the wind.

"Who was that?" I whispered.

"That was Kaula."

"Who is she?"

"Did you never hear of her? She is Mele's grandmother. She raised Mele from a child, until the girl was sent to the nuns in Honolulu. Kaula is very old. Many fear her. That is why they call her Kaula."

Kaula. One who foretells the future. In ancient times *kaulas* were believed to possess more power than any other class of *kahunas,* or witches, and their prophecies were called *wanana. Kaulas* were strange people, who lived apart and fraternized with no one.

Eole's father was saying, "Kaula remembers things which we ordinary Hawaiians have long forgotten, she has much dark, forbidden knowledge. Mele was taken from her because people said she was training the girl in secret arts."

"You mean Mele King, Karl's wife?" Mele seemed a typical convent school product, in her starched uniforms, her common-sense shoes. It was because of her training, then, that she made such an excellent housekeeper.

But—Mele trained in witchcraft? I found that incredible.

"You did not know Mele as we did, before she settled down and married Karl," John Kuneo reminded me. "She was a wild one, in spite of what the sisters taught. When she finished school she went to live with her grandmother on the land her family has owned since any of us can remember. Kaula has her own place deep in the valley and never comes out. Except today she has come to talk to my wife. She says that Eole violated a *kapu* of the gods, that is why he is dead, with his neck broken. I do not believe such things. I know it was the horse."

I jerked from the half-mesmerized state in which those burning eyes had left me. Sharply now, I was aware of what Eole's father had just said.

"His neck was broken?"

"Yes."

"How do you know that? Because Kaula says so?"

"The doctor was here, before breakfast this morning."

The old man's eyes closed, two tears slid down his cheeks. I could not let John know what his words had just told me; it would only add torture to grief, for he was helpless to avenge the death of his son.

I looked up then and saw Leslie standing inside the house watching us through the screen door. She came out onto the lanai, giving me a curious look. After murmuring further inadequate words of sympathy we made our departure.

As we rode back toward the ranch she said, "Where did you learn to speak Hawaiian?"

"From my father. He taught at the University of Hawaii."

"You understood what those *paniolos* were saying today. What was it?"

"Nothing important. They were worried about letting you take your horse out. One of them said Panini was wild, he was afraid you might be thrown. The other said you were an expert rider."

And a poor wife for Don. I'd find out what that meant; it was a clue to their hostility.

"Is that all?" she asked. Panini had begun to jump crazily, she was having difficulty restraining him.

"That's all," I said. "Leslie, don't dawdle along here because of me. Your horse wants a good run; why don't you let him have it?"

She smiled. "Okay. See you at the house." She loosened the curb and bent over his neck, saying something to him. He leaped as if catapulted, and I watched her race ahead of me, sitting easily in the saddle with the sun shining on her bright hair which matched the color of the big sorrel. Umi started dutifully to follow and I held him back to a more sedate pace while my mind plunged deep into confusion.

It seemed that I knew something of which nobody else was aware.

Eole had lifted his head when I first knelt by him on the stable floor. *A man with a broken neck cannot lift his head. So* the injuries he received from the horse might not have been fatal, might have been, in fact, no more than broken ribs and some bad contusions. The boy had been killed *after* we found him. Any question of accident was completely out; I knew now beyond doubt that Eole had been murdered.

CHAPTER SEVEN

LESLIE REACHED the stables some time before I did. When I arrived I saw her horse already loose in the corral, kicking and rolling to get rid of the itch of his sweaty blanket. Kolea appeared, carrying Leslie's saddle and bridle; when he saw me he dropped them and started forward. He was a magnificent fellow and he knew it; probably every *wahine* for miles around knew it too. Virility poured from him as the sun pours from the heavens; his bold dark eyes met mine, his smile flashed the unmistakable message by which male tells female that he finds her good to look upon. He gave me that Hawaiian look called *makaleha* which is used in the *hula:* a widening of the eyes, a sideways glance accompanied by a lift and slight twitch of the brows. Any woman under ninety probably found that message from Kolea irresistible, and I was no exception. I smiled at him.

Mahoe had been watching this byplay; he jumped forward with an exclamation of disapproval, but the young Hawaiian ignored him as he reached for my bridle. I dismounted and stood near the smithy while Kolea sauntered toward the corral with the gray horse. Mahoe had picked up Leslie's saddle; he brushed dirt from it as he started toward the tack room, glowering and muttering comments on worthless ranch hands who had no regard for good leather. Ikua never moved from the doorsill. But we all turned at the sound of pounding hoofs.

Karl came galloping toward us on a sweating black horse. He pulled up at the corral gate and shouted, "You, Kolea! Get on that gray and come with me. I need you!"

Kolea obeyed. As they started in the direction Karl had come from, Ikua called, "Wassamatta, Karl?"

Karl yelled back without slackening pace, "Pua's about to *haanau* and she's gone spooky. I need somebody to hold her while I get the colt out."

The two men pounded off in spurts of dust, Kolea riding with his legs dangling past my stirrups, getting speed out of Umi which I hadn't imagined possible. I perched on a mounting block with the air of one prepared to spend the day, and lighted a cigarette. Ikua stiffened; when Mahoe appeared he sent him a glance. Mahoe detoured to retrieve Leslie's bridle; he headed back to the tack room wiping the steel bit with a handkerchief. I smoked and waited. Silence. Ikua needed something to occupy his hands, to give him an excuse for not looking at me. He took off his straw hat and used his freshly sharpened knife to trim ragged edges from its brim, turning it slowly. Exhausting this, he reached into his shirt pocket for cigarettes, and finding none, began to pat himself, dismay on his face.

I held out my package. "Smoke?"

He hesitated, while I continued to offer cigarettes, then took one and said grudgingly, *"Mahalo.* Thank you."

Now we had made contact. I said in Hawaiian, "You are most welcome."

He looked up quickly, and as Mahoe returned just then, still voicing profanely his contempt of Kolea, he cautioned, "Dis *haole wahine* speaks Hawaiian."

"That's right," I said amiably. "I speak it as well as you do."

Mahoe gave me a slow, appraising look. Presently a smile quirked the corners of his wide Hawaiian mouth; true Polynesian that he was, he appreciated a joke even at his own expense. "You *kamaaina,* huh? Where you learn Kanaka talk?"

"Same place you learn," I gave him back in matching pidgin. "From my papa. He long time *aikane* [very good friend] all Hawaiian peoples."

Ikua asked sharply, "Wot name he got, dis *aikane?"*

I told him. Mahoe looked puzzled but Ikua said that now he remembered my father and me from our visit years ago. I began to speak in their mother tongue, reminding them of Emmett Cameron's friendship for Hawaiians, his lifelong efforts to help them preserve their culture, his collection of folklore, genealogical chants, and place histories which—since early Hawaiians had no written language and such knowledge was handed orally from one generation to the next—might otherwise have been lost. The emotion with which I spoke of my father was something they expected and understood, since Hawaiian mores approve of pride in one's progenitors. It was a relief to discard Caucasian false modesty.

When I finished, Mahoe stepped to my side. He bowed gravely, then took my hand and pressed it to his brow in salute. I felt embarrassed, for this gesture is only for the great chiefs. When I protested Mahoe said, "To your father."

Then he leaned against the wall of the smithy and asked, "Why do you come to this unhappy place?"

Barriers were down at last.

"I came because there is trouble here for my friends."

"She is your friend?"

A nod toward the house.

"Yes. She, as well as Don. Why do you dislike her? What has she done?"

Ikua and Mahoe exchanged glances. No answer.

I went on. "She has great trouble. She needs your *aloha.* Why don't you like her? Why did you say she is not a good wife to Don?"

Ikua's face grew stern again. Mahoe looked uncomfortable. Finally he said, so low that I could barely hear his words, "She has a bad *mana.* She brought misfortune to Alohilani."

I was appalled. This might be complete stalemate, for we were on most delicate ground. Mahoe had mentioned to me, with great reluctance and then only because I was Emmett Cameron's daughter, something which a *haole* is never told. I dared not even hint that the belief in *mana*—spirit power—is superstition and no more. My father taught me that none of us should presume to ridicule the beliefs of another. Man, he had said, is an obtuse creature groping his way through life with only a pitiful minimum of his potential and his perceptions realized, and beyond doubt these qualities are more developed in some than in others. There might be, for all I knew, such a thing as a bad or good *mana* which could be attributed, as Hawaiians believe, to some individuals. But that was something which could not pertain to Leslie. Someone had deliberately tried to create ill feeling toward her.

I thought of those malevolent eyes peering through the banana leaves. I said carefully, "Do you believe this?"

Ikua looked down at the earth between his worn boots. Mahoe's shoulders moved uneasily against the wooden side of the building.

"She loves Alohilani as much as you do," I insisted. "How could she bring bad luck?"

Ikua said then: "After Don brought her here everything went wrong. The fair-haired man came back to Auohe, he bought Hawaiian land. . ."

Came back to Auohe? But I didn't dare interrupt.

". . . the worthless Farnham people came. Trouble began, Don was worried. Don went out on his boat, the boat disappeared. Then the day *she* came back, there was the big storm. And Eole was killed."

"But she wasn't here when all these things happened!"

Mahoe shrugged. "No, she was not here. What kind of wife is it that runs away when her husband needs her?"

I feared then that there might be little I could say in Leslie's defense which would change the opinion of these people—and that meant all of the island. Alohilani wasn't too isolated for coconut wireless to operate with its customary efficiency. But I made an effort to get a truer version of the story into circulation.

I drew a breath and began to talk rapidly, giving the two old *paniolos* a highly dramatized story of the illness of Leslie's sister and her call for help. Appendicitis wasn't enough—I made it a major operation. I suggested that of course they could understand how Don felt about being deprived of his bride—they nodded at this—and described their quarrel over her departure, concluding with an expurgated version of his letter of reconciliation which Leslie found in Don's jacket pocket.

When I finished, Mahoe's eyes showed a twinkle, and even Ikua's lined face seemed less sour. Mahoe said with a little chuckle, "I t'ink mebbe us plenty *huhu* because we no have *luau*."

Then he went on to tell me that the ranch hands had planned a welcoming feast for Leslie, which was to have been a surprise. The *imu* was dug, the pig dressed and wrapped, *laulaus* made, all the good foods ready—and they had worked overtime at ranch chores in order to take time off the following day. A delegation was to announce the *luau* early in the morning. And then, the night before, Leslie had telephoned for a taxi and left without a word . . . .

"Didn't Don explain anything?"

Ikua grunted. "He make dark face, don' speak. Too *huhu* for talk." He hesitated and then added with a grin, "Mebbe Don *hoolili*, eh?"

I agreed that naturally Don was very jealous because his bride went to her sister against his wishes. From the expression on Ikua's face I decided that he felt slightly complacent over knowledge that he had a wife who didn't have sick relatives two thousand miles away, who wouldn't dare walk out on him in any case.

"Don was angry when she left," I admitted. "But—don't you remember now? What happened here began *after* she had gone. Leslie didn't cause any of it. Perhaps she took Don's good *mana* with her."

"Perhaps," Mahoe agreed politely. Ikua said nothing, but I hoped, watching him, that I'd presented a new angle to consider.

I didn't mention Eole or the three who had moved into Don's house, because I didn't know what to say. I slipped off my perch and said I was glad we were going to be friends, I counted on them to be friends with Don's wife. We parted amicably enough, and I walked to the house hoping that Mahoe and Ikua would talk to the other *paniolos,* that their antipathy toward Leslie would change to sympathy. Now that they had begun to have confidence in me, perhaps someone would volunteer additional information. What was happening here was Hawaiian in nature—it pertained to the ranch. Someone might know something—maybe someone would talk.

Leslie came to my room as I finished pinning up my hair. She had changed to a blue piqué dress, she had put on lipstick and a touch of powder. It couldn't conceal deepening shadows under her eyes. But her chin was up again, her voice was firm enough as she said, "I'm going down to the pool to talk with Edith Farnham. Would you like to come along?"

I wouldn't have missed it for anything. I stuck a final pin into my upsweep and picked up Leslie's suede jacket as we went out.

Tawny sunlight lay over the land, a brisk wind tossed our skirts as we went slowly across terraced rock garden, then down the sloping path toward the swimming pool. Far below us cobalt waters moved; white spray flew up from rocks at the island's edge. The awkward-looking craft which tugged at its mooring alongside the little dock must be Eole's sampan; it was painted the color of the water and had an eye on each side of its prow, since every Japanese fisherman knows a boat must be able to see where it is going. The outboard tied alongside it looked toylike in comparison; if it belonged to Denis no wonder he had been drenched traveling through the rain.

I stopped to shake crushed coral from my sandals, and Leslie halted beside me, looking out over the ocean as she waited. She said, as we resumed our pace, "Have you ever seen this place very early in the morning?"

"No. I was a child when I visited here, my morning memories are of a maid bringing hot cereal to the table and Hong standing at the kitchen door hissing at me to eat it all up, it would make me big and strong and then he would give me candied ginger. Hong—I suppose he went back to China to be buried."

"No," Leslie said. "He's still here. Don says he's the best cook in Hawaii."

"He must be a hundred years old. Why did you ask about early mornings at the ranch?"

She said, "I was just remembering my first morning here. Don and I got up at five and came down this path; he wanted me to see the dawn arrive, so I could understand why his grandfather chose this site for the house. That's where the name of the ranch—"

"Of course!" I exclaimed. "I never thought of it before. Alohilani—do you know what it means?"

" 'First light from heaven at sunrise,' " she said softly. "The Farnhams built their house to face that morning light."

We walked on. Presently Leslie said, "Do you believe that things which happen in our lives fall into a pattern?"

"I don't know. I'm not sure what you mean."

"I'm not quite sure, myself. I was thinking about another ranch, the place where I grew up. In Wyoming. We never saw the ocean, of course; in fact I never dreamed that any cattle ranch could be as beautiful as this! But the Triangle-T was ours and we loved it. When Dad got sick, Mother mortgaged the place and we tried to keep going. He died, and we lost the property, and then Mother—" She was silent.

"I was thinking," she resumed, "about losing Alohilani, about how Don would feel. That's not going to happen if I can possibly—" She didn't finish, because we were stepping onto the concrete terrace, and Edith Farnham's feet had swung down from the chair.

Edith pushed the umbrella around and said, "Good morning. How do you feel today, Leslie?" As she spoke she opened a magazine and laid it face down across some papers on the table before her.

Leslie said coolly, "Good morning. I'm perfectly fine now. Where is your husband?"

"He and Denis went to the village. Oh, by the way, we've invited Denis to stay here a few days, until his house in the valley is fit to live in. He got rained out last night. Hope you don't mind."

It made no difference to her whether Leslie minded; the words were token courtesy. Leslie said nothing.

Edith added, "Howard went to meet the steamer; we've sent for some divers from Honolulu. They're going to the place where that fisherman saw the explosion."

"Good. I hope they find—" Leslie stuck on the words.

I tried not to think of what they might find, a body trapped, perhaps, in a small cabin— Leslie began to talk in a higher voice, rather fast, possibly to shut out the same picture.

"Your things have been moved to a guest room. I hope you will be comfortable. Perhaps you did not know that the rooms you were occupying belong to Don and me."

The other woman sent her a quick look. She shook a cigarette from a pack before her, lit it, and glanced with satisfaction at the square-cut diamond on the hand which laid the match down.

Then she said, "Howard will be annoyed about your moving us, I expect." She kicked a chair toward Leslie. "Why don't you sit down? Cigarette?"

"No, thank you." Leslie seated herself at an angle from Edith Farnham, while I pulled another chair close to the table. I meant to have a look at what was concealed under that magazine if I could manage it.

"As for me," the woman went on, "it doesn't matter. We don't expect to live in the main house, anyhow. The foreman's bungalow is large enough, and when the place is remodeled, with some decent modern furniture—"

"Karl's house!" Leslie's face began to grow flushed. "What on earth made you think—" She stopped and began again, with obvious effort at calmness. "Mrs. Farnham, let's be realistic about this situation. You evidently consider that all you have to do is move in here and take over, no matter who protests. I'd like to know how you ever conceived such an idea."

Howard's wife flipped her cigarette into the swimming pool, then skidded her chair around to face Leslie more squarely.

"Why don't you relax for a moment? Now, I'll explain in a few words what you were evidently too confused last night to understand. Howard is the owner of this property—no, let me finish—and we're going to stay here."

Not a syllable of sympathy, not a word of hope that Don might still be found. Leslie's hands made two fists in her lap; she looked down at them.

I inched closer to the table and started to put an elbow on the magazine. Edith Farnham flicked a glance at me and slid the papers out of reach. She was enjoying this.

"As I said, we're going to stay here. But we have no intention of rusticating the way Don Farnham did, or going around smelling like cattle. There are more pleasant ways of making money. This place is going to be converted into a dude ranch—it's perfect for the business. The main house will be dining room, lounge, and bar; those cottages the cowboys live in will be guest houses, and we'll build more of them. We'll probably have to enlarge the swimming pool"—she waved toward it—"and of course the dock down there—"

At this point Leslie's control broke. "Do you imagine," she demanded, "that I'm just going to sit helplessly and let you perpetrate such a—such a thing? Even if Don were dead—and I know that he is not!—I would never, never—"

A jeweled paw waved at her. "Don't get hysterical again, Leslie. You have nothing to say about this. And neither, for that matter, have I."

She sounded amused, then, at her own words. "Howard is a very determined man, my dear, and the best way to get along with him is to let him do as he chooses." Her mouth curved slyly. "I manage to have my fun, too, as we go along."

Her voice became more crisp. She looked at Leslie and said in a businesslike tone, "You are probably thinking that if Don's body isn't found it will take several years to prove his death. That is not so—in this case. And if you want technicalities, see a lawyer. Howard's had expert advice, he knows what he's doing. It's only a matter of a short while now until he can go ahead with his plans."

Leslie leaned forward, breathing fast. "But it takes a fortune for a development like that, and Don told me—" She left the implication in the air.

"We'll manage. Howard's had an offer for the land."

"It can't be sold! Your husband said so last night."

"It can be leased. And this is the time, with Honolulu overcrowded and neighbor islands getting so much promotion. A place like this has everything to offer: riding, swimming, hunting, fishing trips—we're working out an arrangement with Denis, too—"

Leslie put both hands on the table and pushed back her chair. "I've seen honest working properties converted to dude ranches before, self-respecting cowboys turned into flunkies for a lot of tourists! I won't let you—"

"Don't get yourself all worked up," Edith said. "It won't do any good. And you have more important problems. I hope for your sake that Don left some insurance."

Leslie sank into her chair again, while color ebbed from her face.

Edith said then, in a more pacific tone, "Let's don't fight about this. I'm not responsible for it any more than you are." She included me in her smile. "Since we're the only three women on the place, we might as well be agreeable."

There must have been two dozen women at least; wives of the *paniolos*, housemaids. I said, watching her, "How about Mele? She's a woman, she and Karl are friends of the family."

"The housekeeper?" Edith Farnham laughed. "She certainly is a woman, and a damned disturbing one. Did you know she was once in love with Denis? That's why he bought the valley land—because he used to live there with Mele. No wonder Karl is furious. That respectable pose of hers can't fool me; if Howard wasn't so busy right now I'd certainly keep a sharp eye on him when she's around."

She lit another cigarette and leaned back to regard Leslie curiously. "Didn't you ever wonder what used to happen between Don and that piece of female dynamite, alone here together for days at a time while her husband was off somewhere with the cattle? We thought that might have been why you took off for the mainland so soon after Don brought you here to live."

"You thought that?"

Leslie stood up, moving away from Edith Farnham with an involuntary gesture of revulsion. Apparently nothing in her experience had prepared her for contact with the older woman's kind of mind. I thought of a critic's comment about the mind of Molly Bloom in Joyce's novel: a cesspool, he had called it, of forty years' accumulation.

Edith saw what Leslie was unable to conceal; her face became ugly with anger. Before she could speak a foot scraped on concrete behind us; Edith hit the umbrella furiously so that it swung around to reveal who stood there.

It was Mele.

"Excuse me, Mrs. Farnham." Edith half rose, and at that moment I saw my opportunity. I laid both hands on the magazine as I pushed my chair back, and shoved everything across the metal table to the floor.

"How clumsy of me!" I said, and reached for sheets of paper. Before I could touch them a shoe came down on my hand, hard.

"Oh. So sorry." Edith lifted her foot at the same time that she bent and swooped up the letters. All I saw was a gaudy orange letterhead: *"—icana Hotels, Ltd.,"* and a New York address.

She slipped the papers into the magazine and held it in her lap. "Yes, Mele. What did you want?"

Mele ignored her. She was speaking to Leslie. "You had a telephone call. The operator will ring the ranch again in thirty minutes."

"Thank you, Mele. I'll go right up." Leslie started toward the house without a backward glance at the woman under the umbrella. I followed, rubbing my right hand, which bore the imprint of Edith Farnham's shoe.

Leslie glanced toward Mele once or twice as we went toward the house; she looked as if she wanted to apologize for suspicions she had never entertained, an insult she had not offered—but didn't know how to begin. Mele's frozen expression forbade approach.

It didn't forbid me. I caught Mele's arm, forcing her to walk by my side while Leslie went ahead. I kept a firm grip on her while I muttered in Hawaiian, "You should be ashamed of yourself for the way you are treating her! She's frightened and in trouble—she needs friends. She's Don's wife, she's fighting to keep his land for him. She loves this place as much as you do—maybe more—for you sold your land, the land that was your birthright and the home of your people—"

She stopped. She turned to face me. The mask was gone and her face was convulsed with an emotion I could not read. She said in a shaking voice, "You meddling fool! You don't know what you're talking about. Let go of me and leave me alone!"

She twisted her arm free and went swiftly ahead of us, up the path to the house.

CHAPTER EIGHT

THE PHONE WAS ringing as we stepped into the hall, and Leslie started toward it. Haru pattered from the dining room and picked up the instrument; as Leslie reached her with a "Thank you, Haru," the maid shook her head. "No, missus." She nodded at me. "Somebody talk you."

It was Lily Wu.

"Janice? I'm at the hotel. Can you come down here?"

"I certainly can." I let out a sigh of relief at the sound of her light voice. "Where are you? In the lobby?"

"No, I have taken a room. I'll explain when you arrive." She mentioned the number. "Come directly here so we can talk."

Leslie was standing by the window; I said for her benefit, "Did you bring me some clothes?"

"I brought clothes, and the galley proofs, in case you decide to stay on the island for a while."

I had forgotten the galleys, and the fact that publishers expect corrected proofs returned by a certain date. "Thank you so much," I said with sarcasm.

Her laughter tinkled over the wire. "You are most welcome. I shall expect you this afternoon."

I explained to Leslie, "It's the friend I spoke of, Lily Wu. I'm to meet her in the village. Is there a car here that I can use?"

"There's the station wagon—" she began, and Haru interrupted from the dining room: "No stop. Othah mans take." Leslie frowned, then said, "We have a jeep; it's rough riding but you're welcome to it."

"Okay, thanks; I'll manage."

Haru asked, "You *kaukau* now?"

We looked at the clock, which said noon, then at the dining table, set for five. Leslie said in a low voice, "I don't want to eat with—"

"Neither do I. It would spoil my appetite."

She turned to the little maid. "Can you give us lunch in the garden?"

Haru bobbed and smiled. "Okay. I fix."

We ate under the monkeypod tree; Haru had scattered salmon-colored hibiscus in the center of the peel table. It was cool there in the shade, where perfume of gardenias and plumeria mingled with steaming curry; our plates were piled with rice while side dishes held chopped peanuts, grated coconut, and mango chutney.

I was very hungry. Between mouthfuls of curried shrimp I said, "Don is right. Hong must be the best cook in the islands."

Leslie nodded with an abstracted look on her face. She was tense; she barely touched her food. When a car skidded to a stop on the driveway at the side of the house she jumped and dropped her fork; she half rose from her chair and then sank back, waiting.

The car door slammed and someone walked across the lanai and into the house by the side door. Then we heard Howard Farnham's voice inquiring of Haru when lunch would be served.

Leslie slumped; she made no further pretense of eating. "You can have the station wagon now."

I nodded as I lit a cigarette. "It's your car, isn't it?"

"Yes."

"Then if I were you I'd take the keys out. There might be a time when you'd want to use it in a hurry."

"Yes," she said.

Someone came from the stables toward the garden, whistling; it was Kolea sauntering toward us. He gave Leslie a respectful smile and asked, "You got a key to the medicine chest in Don's office?"

She laid her napkin on the table. "Yes, I have Don's keys. What's the matter—did something go wrong with Pua?"

"No. She got a fine colt, black like Pilikia. It's Karl's horse—he's foundered. Karl wants the bottle of founder medicine."

"I'll get it right away." She hurried into the house, and as soon as she had gone Kolea dropped his respectful dignity and flashed a smile at me.

"What's 'foundered'?" I asked.

He shrugged broad shoulders under the bright flowered shirt. "When a horse runs too hard, cools off too fast, he goes lame. Legs swell, he can't walk." He held out a pack of cigarettes. "Smoke?"

"Thanks, I have one." I picked it up, saw that it had gone out. He lit it for me, bending so close that I could smell the roses around his hat. As he held the match his eyes met mine and said that there were things much more interesting than sick horses which we might consider. I couldn't let this go too far.

I said, "This foundering. Is it serious?"

He took off his hat and twirled it as he leaned against the monkeypod tree. "Might be," he said. "Karl's mad like crazy."

At that moment Karl appeared in the stable door and bellowed, "Kolea, what th' hell's keepin' you? God damn it, I want that medicine! Get it and rattle your hocks back here, *wikiwiki!*"

Leslie arrived then with a box which she gave to Kolea. "Here it is. I'm sorry I kept you waiting." He took it and went toward the stable. Leslie said, "My phone call just came. It was a Mr. Murchison; he's a lawyer. He asked me to come to his office this afternoon." She sighed. "At least I'll be doing *something.*"

I was relieved to hear that. She needed to see a lawyer.

Neither of us mentioned the divers who were probably already at work somewhere out there in that deep blue water. We went upstairs together and headed for our rooms to prepare for the drive down to the village.

When Leslie stopped the station wagon at the first gate Denis Desmond rose from the shade of a *kamani* tree. "Let me do it," he said, and swung the gate wide. As she drove past he signaled her to wait, then came to the door and asked, "Can you give me a lift? I have to go to the village, and it's a long trip with an outboard."

"Certainly," she said politely. He had just come from there—why was he going back? Had he been sent by the Farnhams to spy on her, or did he come of his own volition?

I moved over so he could sit in the front seat with us, and he said as he closed the door, "Thanks a lot. I did so much running around with Howard this morning that I forgot my own little affairs."

He was uneasy in Leslie's presence; he seemed self-conscious, almost apologetic. And well he might; he must be aware that he was neither Don Farnham's friend nor Howard Farnham's guest by virtue of Howard's right to offer an invitation. In the city it might be a simple matter to get rid of him, but here things were different, and I could understand Leslie's predicament; ranch hospitality was traditional.

Leslie drove without speaking, her eyes on the road. I also kept silent, rather enjoying manifestations of Denis' mounting unease. He kept looking at the two of us, squirming on the leather seat, then turning to stare out the window at cattle who raised their heads and watched with calm eyes as we went by. There was no calmness in him; eventually he had to break the silence.

When he did, his first words were a surprise. "You're curious about me, aren't you?"

Leslie didn't answer; I gave him a reserved smile.

"No doubt you think I'm peculiar for living alone in the valley," he blundered on. "Or"—he shot Leslie a glance sideways—"perhaps Don told you—"

"Yes," she said.

"He told us about you." I added significantly, "Quite a lot, in fact."

He said hastily, "That's all over, you know. Mele doesn't mean anything to me now. She's married, our little affair is forgotten, even if I did buy the place where we shacked up—" He gulped back the rest.

So Edith Farnham had told the truth. I remembered what Eole's father had said about Mele's "wildness," in spite of what the nuns had taught.

Since neither of us made any comment, Denis seemed compelled to go on. He said heavily, "A lot can happen in seven years."

We made no response to that brilliant observation. He squirmed. He took cigarettes from his shirt pocket and offered them to us.

"No, thanks." Leslie was curt. I felt slightly annoyed at her—didn't she realize that the way to get information from this man was to give him a little encouragement? Then I remembered that once I had been much like this girl, until I encountered circumstances where candor was synonymous with disaster. At the same time, fortunately, I met Lily Wu, and began to take lessons in dissembling from a ruthless little expert. There simply wasn't any guile in Leslie; she was as uncompromisingly honest as the man she had married.

I accepted a cigarette from Denis and said, to soften her refusal, "Leslie doesn't smoke; she's a swimmer." I added in a chatty tone, "I swim a bit, too, but I don't have her will power."

She wasn't so obtuse as I had thought. She made an effort. "It isn't will power, really. I lived in a women's college until a few months ago. Physical education teachers weren't supposed to smoke."

We had reached another gate. While Denis was out of the car I said, "Let's try to keep him talking—maybe we can find out something."

We started again, and Denis reached for the dashboard lighter. As he held it I steadied his hand with mine on his wrist, and saw the anchor tattooed inside his forearm.

"How long were you stationed here during the war?" I hazarded.

That took the lid off. Words began to pour out of him.

"Four months. The happiest months of my life. I was born in North Dakota—ever been there? Well, you haven't missed anything. Cold weather begins about Labor Day, and the snow lasts until—well, you think you'll go nuts. It's twelve above in my home town this week—think of it! And here I am—" He gestured toward sun-flooded land around us, he took a dramatic breath of wind which was bringing the smell of cattle, of pastures springing from warm, rich earth.

"I never left that lousy little town," he said, "until I went into the navy. You've heard about the lure of the tropics, how these islands bewitch you and you can't forget them, can't be happy anywhere else—" He looked at us as if afraid he sounded too emotional.

Leslie helped him. "I come from Wyoming," she contributed. "Blizzards—wind which cuts like a thousand knives . . . if you felt anything like I did, after being away from here only three weeks—" She didn't finish.

Apparently he was too absorbed in himself to feel any twinge of guilt at this reminder of her present unhappiness—or his part in it. "It took me seven years to get back," he told us. "But I made it!" A kind of incredulous triumph rang in his words. Then his voice hardened. "And I'm staying here, no matter what—"

Leslie had stopped for the next gate. The lock was difficult and as Denis worked at it I reflected that much of what he said sounded true; it is a common story in Hawaii today. The islands were flooded with people just prior to and during the war; hundreds of thousands of servicemen, construction workers, convalescents from the Pacific battle areas—inevitably some fell in love with the islands and wanted to stay. No discomfort of crowded housing could alter the perfect climate, the beauty of lunar rainbows, of beneficent blue skies and sunshine which keep the land perpetually green and brilliant with flowers. Many who were sent back to mainland homes managed to return; they found some kind of shelter, took any kind of job, brought over wives and children. The resulting population increase is still a major island problem.

So Denis was one of them. I studied him while he held the gate and waited for the car to pass. He wasn't wearing Don's clothes now; one of the servants must have laundered his cotton suntans and blue T-shirt. He was a good-looking man, his blond hair shone in the sun, his skin was tanned. Seven years ago he would have been more attractive, before that subtle slackness developed, a flabbiness of personality more than flesh, although physical signs were there: a sour droop of the mouth, pouches around the gray eyes, the first thickening of the waist. Mele might have loved him seven years ago—could it be possible she loved him still? Was that why she let him have her land?

But he was involved in something far more grim than a sentimental return to the islands or a resurrected love affair. I remembered that as he came back to the car. So, apparently, did he, for the moment of honesty had gone, his bearing had changed.

"It took time, liquidating my holdings, turning responsibilities over to others," he informed us. His tone was false, the words slid out glibly. "But the simple life is what I want. Like that guy Walden, you know. Used to read his books over and over, when I was in college."

Now I was certain he was a fake.

I asked, "But what do you plan to do, isolated in that little valley?"

He waved a hand; I stared at it, fascinated.

"Oh, I'll loaf a little, explore the country, probably finish writing my book. I'm doing a history of Polynesian culture—early Hawaiian customs, you know. Archeo—I mean, folklore, has always been a special hobby of mine. There are some interesting ruins right near my house."

I looked at that hand, resting now on his knee. It was square, thick-fingered, with ridged and broken nails rimmed with black. A hand which worked with machinery or tools, which had no acquaintanceship with pen or typewriter.

"But how are you going to live?" I pursued.

"That's the least of my worries," he proclaimed airily. "I have some income—from real estate. And in a place like this, living doesn't cost much. I can raise a garden, pick bananas off the trees, catch all the fish I need. Eole was teaching me to fish Hawaiian style, with a spear. He used to hang around a lot—" He stopped abruptly.

"Did you know him well?"

"No," he said, and was silent for the rest of the trip..

The village was crowded; it was steamer day. Leslie cruised the main street looking for a parking space. We passed the business section and rode under poinciana trees spreading over a stream which flashed past wooden houses half smothered in ginger. She turned and started back; we crawled behind a Model T (there must be more of them left in the islands than any other place in the world) which sagged under its load of three fat Hawaiian women and at least a dozen children. One of them yelled to a thin-legged Japanese girl in short cotton dress, clacking along on wooden *geta:* "Amy! Wassamatta you no go school?"

The girl grinned and yelled back, "We got new baby our house! To-day no school." She held up a silver quarter. "I go Krass fo' buy present. Where you goin'?"

"We go boat-side. Sell *leis.* Mebbe make plenty money—buy somet'ing fo' baby!"

"You come our house toni'. We got *chimaki, haskiwa mochi,* bottle of *sake."*

A Hawaiian woman in the back seat laughed until the basket of *leis* almost shook from her lap. "You papa-san get plenty drunk, I bet!"

Leslie managed to squeeze past the Model T and we found ourselves behind a truckload of Filipino plantation hands headed for the sugar mill which rumbled at the edge of the town. I began to perspire, for the air was warm, heavy with the odor of molasses, flowers, and people. At the end of several blocks where there were no parking spaces Leslie said, "I'll have to try a side street."

As she turned, Denis opened the door. "I'll get out now. Have to go see someone. How about a ride back? Suppose I meet you in front of the lawyer's office?"

Neither of us had mentioned that Leslie was going to see a lawyer.

She said, "I don't know when I'll be finished."

"Then maybe you'd better pick me up at the ho—" He changed his mind and substituted, "You're bound to be through sometime around four. I'll wait in front of the office until you come out."

She agreed. He got out of the car and walked away, and as she turned up the next street I craned around to watch him. He headed toward the center of town, then cut across the street and started back in the opposite direction. He had started to suggest that Leslie pick him up at the hotel—that must be his destination.

Leslie found a parking place and we sat a minute and discussed our respective activities. She intended to order ranch supplies; Hong had given her a grocery list. I was going to see Lily Wu. We agreed to meet at the lawyer's office at three; I would bring Lily with me. I left Leslie locking the doors of the station wagon and started to the hotel, walking on the opposite side of the street from Denis. I glimpsed his blond head turning in toward the old-fashioned wooden building while I was still half a block away; when I got there he was nowhere in sight. I stood on the lanai glancing down the row of chairs, a few of which were occupied by hotel guests, then decided there was no use trying to find Denis; I'd go to Lily's room.

As I started into the lobby I heard a familiar voice: "Miss Cameron!" and saw a plump, smiling woman rising from a fan-backed chair near the door. She murmured something to the person sitting next to her and came toward me eagerly. It was my recent traveling companion, Mrs. Bessie Watson.

I was in a hurry, she was the last person I wished to see at that moment, but I had to be civil. I'd made a bond of sorts between us by giving her that *lei* the night we arrived; it would have been graceless to refuse her opportunity to thank me properly. I stopped, I said how nice it was to see her again, and how was she enjoying the island?

"Oh, I'm having the most wonderful time!" She matched her step with mine as I walked into the lobby, and while I looked around for Denis she chattered about the village, the friendliness of the people, about places she had seen and other trips she intended to make—I listened with half attention because I had glimpsed a figure in tan cotton pants and blue shirt going along the rear lanai. Could that be Denis? I nodded and smiled absently while I hurried through the lobby toward my quarry with Mrs. Watson prattling beside me. At the edge of the lanai I halted and ground my teeth with frustration as I watched the blond head disappear into a double bungalow which was one of a group of guest cottages in the hotel gardens.

Mrs. Watson was saying, "—do hope you can have lunch with me. I never did have time to say *mahalo nui*—see how I'm learning?—for your kindness. Or if you haven't time today, perhaps you'd call me—I'm in one of the bungalows—"

I whirled. This was too good to be true. "One of the bungalows? Which one?"

She looked surprised, then said, "Number Three." It was the one Denis had entered.

I grasped her arm and steered her behind a potted tree fern. "Mrs.
Watson, I'm going to ask a favor of you. And you'll have to trust me
because I don't have time just now to explain. I want to go into your
bungalow."

She opened her pink mouth to ask, "Why?"

"Because I'm following someone who just went into the other half of
it, and it's important to me to find out what he's doing there."

"But—I don't—"

"I haven't time to be polite or make long explanations. All I can tell
you is that a friend of mine, the girl I am visiting, is in serious trouble and
I'm trying to help her. The man I'm following has something to do with
it. Can you trust me enough to help me get into your rooms without being
seen, and then not ask questions?"

She gave me a long, searching look. As I met her eyes I recognized
that for all her innocent enthusiasms Bessie Watson was no dope. She
said quietly, "All right. I'll go and talk with my neighbor—her name is
Mrs. Dumke—and while we're talking you go into my side of the house."

I nodded and she turned immediately and went along the curving
path to the screen door of the bungalow and knocked. When no one answered she knocked again, then opened the door and walked in. I ducked
behind some hibiscus bushes, made my way through them to the bungalow, and got inside as quickly as I could.

The cottage was as thinly built as I had expected, and when I leaned
against the inside wall I could hear:

Mrs. Watson: "—was just wondering if you'd like to stroll down to
the docks with me. The steamer is arriving pretty soon and it might be fun
to watch."

Mrs. Dumke, in a thin, almost childish voice: "I can't, thanks just the
same. I got company. Some other time."

"You have company? I'm so sorry for interrupting. I'll just run right
along."

Steps tapped over the wooden floor and a screened door opened and
shut, while from the shadowy room where I stood I watched Bessie Watson walk back toward the hotel building. Heels tapped across the floor
again and the childish voice called, "You can come out now."

Someone walked out of the rear bedroom. Denis' voice said, "Who
was that?"

"The lady next door. She wanted me to go with her to see the boat
come in."

"Where did she go?"

"Back to the hotel. Don't act so scared, Denis—nobody can hear as."

I heard chair springs squeak. Then he demanded in an angry voice, "Now, what's this business about sending me to jail? Who the hell ever put that idea into your head?"

"It ain't me, Denis, honest. It's Pop. He's so mad—I'm afraid he'll do it, too. That's why I borrowed the money from Elsie and come over here."

"Nobody can put me in jail! I didn't steal anything."

"Sheriff Baker says he can arrest you. Because of the money you owe. And because of—of desertion. The people you did that radiant-heating job for—the fella's wife is Sheriff Baker's cousin. You owed over two thousand for materials, and the supply house slapped a lien on the property."

The chair squeaked again, then I heard Denis begin to stride up and down the room.

The girl's voice grew more shrill. "Denis, how could you go away and leave us like that? Every day somebody comes with another bill—payments on the car, the furniture, on the house—you never even paid your helper the last three weeks before you left! And the baby's been sick; he's had chicken pox, and I've almost gone out of my mind, worrying!" Her voice broke on the last words and she began to cry.

"Not so loud, Cora, for God's sake!" His steps halted and I pressed close to the wall, straining to catch his low-voiced words.

"—told you I've got a deal on here. It'll take time. As soon as—give you enough to pay—some left over for yourself and the kids. There's no use—to jail—it won't do anybody any—"

Her sobs drowned out the rest of what he was saying. I heard nothing then except the sound of her weeping, his deeper voice in expostulation and, eventually, anger. At this climax he went to the screened door and unlatched it. The girl ran after him.

"How much longer do you think I can wait?" she cried. "Elsie won't keep the children forever, she's got her own to look after. And I can't stay on here—it's costing me so—"

"You had no business coming here in the first place."

He opened the door and went outside. She followed.

I tiptoed to the front window. She was very young. She wore a black-and-cerise rayon jersey dress and stilt-heeled kid pumps which turned sideways with every step. Her body was thin as a child's, her black hair was frizzed from a cheap permanent, and her skin was sallow. She reached for Denis with arms thin as two sticks, she clung tightly.

"Denis, we don't need all that dough you're talkin' about." She pulled on his arm, and there was desperation in her voice. "We was gettin' along fine before you—you got this crazy streak. The business is good—why, you got more jobs than you can handle! Denis, it's not too late to go back. Pop will square things with Sheriff Baker, you can take up right where you left off, and we'll all be—"

He jerked away with an exclamation of disgust. He looked down at her and said, "Listen, Cora, and listen hard. I'm telling you this for the last time. I'm here, *and I'm staying.* Oh, you can queer everything for me if you want. You can even have me arrested, drag me home. But it won't do anybody any good, because I can't pay bills when I'm in jail—and if you make me go home I'll rot there the rest of my life before I pay a dime! I told you this before—you gotta believe me. If you're smart you'll take what I offered and make the best of it."

She started to speak, then she looked into his face. Her arms dropped to her sides and her thin shoulders sagged. The man shrugged; his gesture was the essence of finality. "Cora, I can't give you anything more."

She moved back a step, then said in a low voice, "All right. What do you want me to write to the folks? They're waiting to hear from me. Pop sent a list of what you owe, including payments on the house and car and all, plus the bills you left. It—it comes to around fourteen thousand."

"You write and tell your old man I'll pay every cent of it."

"But—when?"

"I can't make a move until—" He moved closer and his voice dropped. "Everything depends on who has control of the property. There's a lot of things going on—that's why I hung up on you, and couldn't call back until late last night." He scowled. "Say, how did you find me, anyhow?"

"I saw you on the street with a fella, in that station wagon with the name of the ranch on it, and I asked Information."

"Well, don't try to call me again—I won't be there. You sit tight. I'll get in touch with you—"

"When, Denis? *When?*"

"Maybe tomorrow. Maybe the day after, I'm not sure. But soon."

He turned without further word and went quickly toward the hotel. The girl watched until he disappeared into the building, then opened the screened door; I heard her beginning to cry again as she walked toward the rear of the bungalow. I got out of there fast.

So that was how he delegated responsibility, turned his holdings over to others! I was boiling. But uppermost in my mind was knowledge that I'd been right about those hands of Denis Dumke, calling himself "Desmond"; they belonged to a plumber, not a scholar. Those hands might have twisted Eole's neck until a vertebra snapped. He was cruel enough. And he certainly had enough at stake.

CHAPTER NINE

"WELL, MISS HAWKSHAW, it's about time you turned up." That was Steve Dugan, greeting me from her position by the window of Lily's second-floor hotel room.

"I watched you pussyfooting in and out of that bungalow," she explained. She flopped into a chair, swung her feet to the bed, and began to wiggle her toes. Steve's number nines, as usual when she was inside a house, gaped on the floor beside her.

"If I'd been the hotel detective," she said, "I'd have nabbed you long ago. You look guilty as hell."

I couldn't respond to her good humor. "I don't feel guilty. I'm mad, damned mad. That vulgar, sneaking, hypocritical—trying to pose as a glorified beachcomber when he's deserted a wife and children—" I stopped for breath.

"You do feel guilty, Janice." Lily spoke from the bed where she lay stretched like a lazy little kitten. "We know how you hate spying. Why not start at the beginning and tell us what this is all about?"

I turned on her. "You and your eternal perceptiveness!" I began, then shrugged and let it lay. "Well, this man, Denis Desmond, as he calls himself—"

"That's not the beginning. Start from last night, when you boarded the plane with Leslie Farnham."

I almost did a double take at that. Last night seemed such a long time ago. I sighed, and dropped into a chair.

Steve said, "If I'd dreamed how much worry it would involve, I wouldn't have roped you into this. You've got your own work to do, without taking on a load like—'"

"Worry for me! Load!" I practically snarled. "Leslie Farnham's the one who's got the load. That girl is in desperate trouble: I hate to think what might have happened to her if some sort of friend hadn't shown up! Stop talking like an idiot, Steve."

Steve grinned. "Well, let's have the details. And *wikiwiki,* baby. I have to leave here in twenty minutes. I'm supposed to be interviewing another herd of cattlemen at Waikiki. Joe Kunimoto's doing my stint for me, but I've got to get back and edit his copy before press time."

"Is there news of Don Farnham?" Lily asked.

"No. They've got divers looking for his boat now."

Steve's eyes grew worried. "Any idea what happened to him?"

"No. Except that I'm sure it was no accident." I took time out to light a cigarette and continued: "There's something very nasty going on at that ranch. Don's wife is a bewildered and frightened girl—and they're doing their best to keep her that way."

"Who's 'they'?"

"Howard Farnham and his wife."

Steve scowled and started to say something, but Lily spoke first. "What did you find out from the Hawaiian boy?"

"Nothing. He was killed. Before he could tell me anything. Remember what he said over the phone last night? Something dreadful is going to happen— Well, so far as I know, nothing's been done to stop it. I've had my hands full taking care of Leslie, and trying to get some kind of cooperation from the Hawaiians. They're against her too—somebody's planted the idea that Leslie brought bad luck to the ranch."

Lily and Steve absorbed this in silence. Steve scratched under her bun of ginger hair and looked worried. Lily's perfect little amber face was blank with concentration. Finally she said, "Are you sure that the Hawaiian boy was murdered?"

"Yes, I'm sure." I explained why.

As I spoke, Steve swung her feet to the floor. She said, looking at me as she felt with stockinged toes for her shoes, "Talk fast, Janice. You say Don's cousin is there with his wife. Are they in this?"

"Up to their necks."

"How do you know that?" Lily asked.

"Because they were on the scene immediately before Don disappeared. Don said so in his letter to Leslie."

"Letter?"

"Leslie found a letter Don had written and decided not to send. They'd had a fight, over her trip to California, and—"

Steve interrupted. "Just a minute. How about these Farnhams? What are they up to?"

"They want the property. Howard's going to turn the place into a dude ranch."

Steve had leaned forward to pick up a shoe. She rammed her foot into it, hard. "Oh, he is, is he? What else do you know about them?"

I went back to our arrival, their treatment of Leslie, what Howard and Edith had said and done. I included all the details I could remember: the envelope I saw under Howard's shirts when Leslie took them from the

bureau drawer; the letterhead Edith Farnham had hidden under a magazine on the table by the swimming pool.

Steve made notes, and I knew that if she had to canvass every office
building in Honolulu she'd find out which firm was corresponding with
Howard.

As she scribbled Lily said, "If you need any help, Steve, call the
Chuns; they have many connections."

"I'll do that."

Lily looked at me. "Who else is involved?"

"The man who calls himself Desmond."

"Is he that handsome blond character you were following a while
ago?" Steve asked. "What's his racket?"

I told them as much as I knew. I finished with an unexpurgated expression of my opinion of Denis Dumke-Desmond.

Lily raised her brows. "Are you sure you aren't being a little bit of a
snob, Janice, because he's a plumber? Not everyone can have a famous
professorial father."

"Don't be ridiculous!" I snapped. Then, as I so often do when I talk
with Lily, I thought a little deeper. "You may be right," I admitted. "But
I'll do my personal soul-searching later. Right now I'm disgusted because—well, if you'd heard the way he talked to that wretched little wife
of his—Lily, they've got two children, and one's a sick baby—"

Steve flapped a hand at me. "*Malama, malama!*"

Take it easy. I needed that reminder. I subsided while she put on her
other shoe and stood up.

"I'll do some thinking about Howard Farnham," she said. "Maybe I
can fix his little wagon. And I'll check the desk downstairs for the Dumke
family; his wife probably registered from their home town. Now, if I can't
make it back here by tomorrow, one of you call me and we'll compare
notes by telephone."

At the door she stopped. "So Eole's neck was broken. And the guy
named Denis was in the navy. That means he probably had judo training.
Janice, don't you think we ought to get the police in on this? How about
asking Kamakua to pay a visit to the ranch?"

I said uneasily, "I'd have done that myself, if it weren't for what Don
wrote in his letter. The worst thing that could happen, he said, would be
for the slightest hint of this to reach anybody. It's something to do with
the Hawaiians. And where those *haoles* come into it, what they're trying
to pull off, I haven't figured yet."

"Kamakua's Hawaiian. And he can be trusted."

We three knew that from experience, since Kamakua had helped us, in a most unorthodox manner, to expose a vicious murderer in Honolulu. Very few suspected what really had happened at Wainiha, and Kamakua's part in it was never entered on departmental records.

I repeated that I was still reluctant to ask for his help, since Don's anxiety had been so great, and since we had entered the situation uninvited by either Don or Leslie.

"Let's wait just a little while," I said, "at least until we get a report from the divers."

Steve agreed. "Call me immediately if anything happens."

As soon as the door closed I turned to Lily. "We haven't much time. We're supposed to meet Leslie at three, and we'd better start. I'll brief you further on the way."

Lily got up and slipped a white silk dress over her head, belting it with green straw which matched her sandals. She glanced at the mirror and slid another pin into the coil of black hair at the back of her neck. She snapped the locks on a shagreen overnight case and said, "I'm ready. That's your bag there."

I picked it up. She hadn't packed all her clothes. "How about the room? Aren't you going to check out?"

"No. It may be useful to have headquarters here. I don't like the idea of being tied too closely to that isolated ranch. And Steve may want to use the room."

When we reached the lobby I made a little tour in search of Bessie Watson. She wasn't around, and I scribbled a note of thanks for her help and gave it to the desk clerk.

As we walked along the hot street I gave Lily a sketchy outline of what had happened since I started on that stormy flight to Don Farnham's ranch. Lily listened without speaking; she seldom makes interruptive remarks.

When I finished she offered no comment on anything I had told her. She said instead, "The character of Leslie Farnham seems an important element to consider. What sort of girl is she?"

"I don't really know. It's hard to judge anyone who's under such a strain. At first I thought she was unsure of herself, rather easily intimidated. But I didn't know then about the quarrel she had with Don. Yet, even before she found his letter—" I became silent, rearranging impressions, trying to analyze and sift facts more carefully.

"I remember now that Leslie showed some spirit even before she found Don's letter," I resumed. "At first she was completely stunned. I gave her a little pep talk, and she took it very well. When it came to a preliminary showdown she didn't hesitate to put the Howard Farnhams out of her rooms, and to let the servants know who was mistress of the ranch."

We detoured past a Japanese family who were ambling, phalanx-fashion, toward the dime store. The tiny mother carried a jet-eyed child in her arms, and the eldest girl wore a very fat, very new infant strapped to her back, bending slightly under her human burden. There was a strong smell of fish from the market we passed, mingled with soya and peanut oil from a Chinese restaurant next door. I looked at street numbers. The building we sought was in the next block.

As we regained a place on the sidewalk Lily returned to the subject of Leslie Farnham.

"And this display of courage came before she found her husband's reassuring letter," she said. "That is good. But aside from her worry about him, the strain she is enduring, what sort of person do you think she is?"

"Well, I suspect she's a bit ladylike, or at least has pretty rigid moral standards. Maybe I got this impression because she taught in a private school, and she doesn't smoke or drink."

"Yet she is superior at sports. That requires stamina and discipline," Lily commented. "She came alone to Hawaii this summer, so she must be fairly independent. And you said she went into the stall with that stallion—"

"You're right," I agreed. "But why are you so concerned about Leslie's stamina?"

We were at the curbing. As we waited for a passing truck loaded with brown sugar bags for the steamer, Lily said, "I have been thinking that the amount of courage Leslie Farnham possesses may be important. It is difficult to imagine a more unnerving experience for a girl to face: returning to an unfamiliar home to find her husband disappeared, probably dead, possibly murdered, and a group of strangers trying to intimidate her so she cannot fight for her rights. How she reacts to this pressure may—"

We had crossed the street. I said, touching Lily's arm, "You'll have a chance now to judge for yourself. There she is."

Leslie was waiting for us in a doorway at the foot of some stairs which led to the lawyer's office. I introduced the two girls and they murmured conventional acknowledgments; as we began to climb Leslie sent a shy glance, which held both curiosity and admiration, toward Lily Wu.

Lily smiled and said, "Did Janice tell you we are sisters? There's not much resemblance between us, is there?"

At Leslie's puzzled look I explained, "We're foster sisters. That's her weird Oriental humor."

Leslie laughed, and when she looked at Lily again some of the shyness was gone. Her face sobered and the strained look returned as she grasped the knob of the door to the lawyer's office. We followed her inside.

Andrew Murchison was a small, bald-headed man with cold gray eyes and a precise manner of speaking. He brought a chair to add to the two already before his desk and waited until we had seated ourselves. He looked at Leslie and said, "I regret, Mrs. Farnham, that our first meeting must be under such distressing circumstances."

Leslie murmured something, and waited.

"I presume you've had no word of Don?"

"There are divers now looking for his boat. Nothing yet." She folded brown fingers around her purse. "What did you wish to see me about, Mr. Murchison?"

He glanced at Lily and me and coughed delicately. Leslie said, "Please speak freely. These are my very good friends."

He cleared his throat and began. "Howard Farnham has requested an audit of the ranch books. I thought it best to discuss this with you personally rather than by telephone."

Leslie sat a little straighter. "An audit? Why?"

He put veined hands together and began to explain. "Howard claims that he heard your husband and the foreman in a violent quarrel the day that Don disappeared. He believes it was over mishandling of funds, possibly money received from the sale of beeves while you were on your honeymoon."

"Do you think this is true?"

"I have known Karl King since he came to work here. Although he is not island-born—I believe he comes from somewhere in Texas—there are few better foremen in the Territory. So far as I am aware, he has no debts, and certainly he and his wife could not ask for a more pleasant life than they have at Alohilani. Also, Mele King has just received three thousand dollars for her land—"

"Three thousand dollars! But Don offered her—" Leslie didn't finish.

The bald head tilted. "You were about to say . . . ?"

"Nothing, Mr. Murchison. It doesn't pertain to Karl, at any rate. Please go on."

He smiled, showing a yellowish denture. "On the other hand, it will do no harm to make sure that the accounts are in order. And you need feel no awkwardness with Karl, because this is not of your doing. Howard Farnham has demanded it."

I said, "What right has he to make such a demand?"

He blinked at me. "Because, my dear young lady, if Don's boat is found—" He stopped and glanced at Leslie.

"Go on," she said. "If Don's boat is found—then what?"

"Then Howard will take the evidence to court and have his cousin declared legally dead. You see, the ranch is a business which must be competently managed at all times. It is not like other types of property which can stand idle while an estate is being settled. Alohilani is almost an industry, and as such must be in continuous ration. That is why—"

"But, Mr. Murchison," she burst out, "Howard doesn't intend to raise cattle! He wants to turn Alohilani into a dude ranch, a place for tourists!" All the contempt of the born rancher vibrated in her voice.

The old man smiled. It was the smile which tolerates emotionalism. Dude ranch or cattle ranch were all the same to him. The dreams, the long struggle to develop the land, breeding fine strains of stock, of building the home destined to shelter generations of one beloved family, were inconsiderable, if indeed they were even realized.

Seeing this, Leslie stiffened. The lawyer's smile disappeared; he became precise. "Howard has made no announcement of any proposed changes at the ranch," he said. And I knew by his tone that he was informed of what Howard planned to do, and not unwilling to become the local legal representative of such a profitable development.

He said casually, "You know the terms of the will, of course?"

"It was explained to me. The land is called a life estate and can't be sold. But it can be leased." Her voice rose again. "And that is what Howard is planning to do!"

He looked resigned. He tilted back in his chair to wait until she could control herself. I wanted to pick up the heavy glass inkwell and throw it, at least splatter enough of its contents on that narrow gray face to change its expression.

Lily Wu leaned forward from the straight chair where she sat. "Would you review the terms of the will for us?"

He regarded her with a frown which asked what business it was of hers. Lily said, "If you please, Mr. Murchison. We should like to know precisely what those terms are."

He turned to Leslie. She seemed puzzled but repeated, "If you please, Mr. Murchison."

His chair snapped forward. He picked up a sharpened yellow pencil and began to tap the blotter. "Legal phraseology is rather unintelligible to those unacquainted with it—"

I produced a simper and stuck my oar in. "Do go ahead, Mr. Murchison. When you come to a word we girls can't understand, we'll ask you to explain for us."

He stared at me, uncertain whether I was trying to make a fool of him. I couldn't help batting my lashes a couple of times.

Gray lips folded over the yellow denture. He turned directly to Leslie, speaking in a curt, refrigerated voice. "The terms of the will, in essence, are these: Don inherited the land for the duration of his life. In case he should die without issue—that is, if you and Don have had no children—the ranch goes to the next of kin. Howard Farnham is the son of Don's father's brother, which makes him a first cousin. He is therefore the heir."

"But, Mr. Murchison," I said, "Howard Farnham can't become the heir overnight. That kind of legal procedure takes months."

"On the mainland, possibly. Here in the islands we do things differently. In a case of—er—urgency such as this—" He tilted his chair again and tossed the pencil onto the desk.

Of course, I thought. If the hotel chain that wants Don's land has enough money behind it—no wonder Howard was so sure of himself.

The old man was speaking to Leslie. "It is rather unfortunate, Mrs. Farnham, that you and Don have not been married two years, instead of only two months. The situation might then—er—have been different."

"Thank you," Leslie said wearily, and stood up. "Will you arrange for some auditors to check the books, please? They can start in the morning."

The gentleman didn't rise to show us out. We heard him cough as we closed the door of his office and started down the stairs. Denis' head appeared just before we reached the exit; he studied Leslie, and satisfaction showed on his face before he composed it and stepped forward.

On the way back to the ranch I tried to relax by tuning senses in to the rhythm of the evening. The islands, I reflected, pulse with vitality, they seem to breathe, perhaps because land and sea breathe in turn. During the day there is a sea wind bringing a briny tang; at evening the earth breathes toward the water, when the land breeze rises. I watched it coming, rustling through pasture grasses, bringing the smell of mountains and rich jungle growth. I had an impulse to share this thought, but checked it. Denis and Lily, in the back seat, were exchanging stereotyped comments on Hawaii, Leslie drove with a set look on her face and her eyes straight ahead.

When we rolled onto the driveway she stopped the car with a jerk and fumbled for the door handle. She got out without speaking, and by the way she headed blindly toward the house I knew she'd had enough and wanted to be alone. Denis opened the rear door for Lily, then went along the driveway toward the front of the house, probably hunting for the Farnhams. Seeing that Leslie had forgotten the keys of the car, I slid over and took them from the ignition, then pulled on the emergency brake.

While I was doing this Lily followed Leslie up the steps to the side entrance. I reached them in time to hear Lily say in a quick low voice, "Leslie, we know how you feel, but you cannot let go of your feelings now. You must not. Let us go to your room where we can talk. There is something I want to say to—"

Leslie tried to be polite. "Please," she said. "Please—not now. I—"

A crash echoed through the windows of a room just off the lanai. A man's voice—Howard Farnham's voice—shouted, "You'll do as I tell you, Karl—or I'll have you thrown off this place!"

"Don't bust up the furniture, Howard." Karl's deep tones weren't angry; he might have been talking to a child in a tantrum. "I'll do as I know Don wants me to do. This was ordered and it's going to be shipped and paid for."

"And I'm telling you it is not! I won't accept delivery. And what's more—"

By then Leslie was inside, Lily and I behind her. A few steps beyond the entrance was Don's office, which I had not seen before. Howard and Karl were there; Karl was picking up a chair which the other man had slammed against the wall. They both looked startled as we walked into the room.

"What is this?" Leslie demanded.

Karl spoke first. "We just got word that the Santa Gertrudis bull Don ordered will be shipped next week. C.O.D. Howard has asked me to cancel shipment."

"I asked nothing," Howard said. "I'm *telling* you what to do!"

Leslie stepped toward him. "You are?" she said. "By what authority?"

He straightened and rammed his hands into the pockets of his tweed jacket. "By my own authority—as owner. I don't intend to buy any more stock for this ranch."

"When did you acquire ownership of Alohilani?"

"The day Don died."

She flinched as if lashed by an invisible whip. Then her chin went higher. "And what day was that?"

He didn't answer.

Leslie went on: "You have no authority here, and you know it. Until Don returns I am in charge—and Karl takes orders only from me."

She turned to Karl. "How much will the bull cost?"

"Six thousand."

"How does Don generally pay for a C.O.D. shipment?"

"He pays by check, Leslie." Karl nodded toward a small safe in the corner of the room. "The bankbook's in there. I haven't got the combination."

"I have it," she said. Her eyes went toward the desk. Both men regarded her with surprise. "But I can't sign checks. I'm not sure just how—"

Karl grinned. "Don't worry about money. I've got enough stashed away to carry us till Don comes home."

"Karl!" She put out a hand, let it fall. "Will you cable asking when we can expect the bull to arrive? And—thank you—"

He went to her and put a big arm around her shoulders. "Don't give it another thought, Leslie." When she turned an anxious face up to him, her eyes asking the question she didn't dare articulate, he said, "No, nothing yet. Hang on to the curb, girl. Maybe tomorrow—"

He went to the door, gave her a half salute, and departed. She turned to the other man.

"Now, Howard. Let's understand each other. If you continue trying to interfere with the management of this place I'll have to ask you and Edith to leave. Please remember that you are my guests. *Guests only.* In Don's absence, no one gives orders here except Karl and me."

Howard straightened and took his hands from his pockets. He smiled, as if he were about to announce something unpleasant which he would enjoy telling.

"All right, Leslie," he said. "Now—"

"Howie!"

At the sound of that husky voice we all turned. Edith Farnham stood on the lanai outside, with Denis beside her. I was near the window, and I saw how her hand clung to the hand of Denis, fingers curling in his palm. "Howie!" she called again. "Come and have a drink with us."

It was more than an invitation.

"Howie" went to join his wife. I watched through the screen and saw that she released Denis' hand only when the door opened. Then her fingers went into the curve of her husband's arm, and the three walked out of sight, leaving me wondering uneasily what Howard had intended to reveal.

CHAPTER TEN

LESLIE'S perplexed expression indicated that she was also wondering about Howard. She made a gesture as if dismissing it from her mind, and sank into the chair before Don's desk. She took a notebook from a drawer, read some figures, and put it back again.

"I have to open the safe in the morning," she explained, then bit her lip. "Oh—I forgot to tell Karl about the auditors. I must do that before tomorrow."

"Isn't a desk drawer a rather obvious place to hide your combination?" I asked.

"Don doesn't keep much money there, except on payday. The safe's for ranch records, in case of fire."

Lily took the chair recently picked up by Karl. "You feel better now?"

Leslie looked surprised. "Yes, I do."

"Adrenalin," Lily murmured, "is sometimes a great help."

I sat down by the window. I was tired. "I could use a good fight right now," I announced. "Or—a good drink."

Leslie rose immediately. "I'll see Hong, he's an expert bartender. And I'll send a message asking Karl and Mele to eat dinner with us." She hesitated. "Is there something you prefer to drink, or will you leave it up to Hong?"

"Hong?" Lily looked interested.

"He's the cook," I told her. "He's a thousand years old but he makes the best curry in the world."

"Then whatever he gives us—"

While we waited I glanced around Don's office. It had the air of a place where business was efficiently conducted, while it also bore the imprint of time and Farnham personalities. The desk front was polished from the oil of many hands, the cowhide seat of the chair before it curved from the weight of masculine *okoles.* On the walls were pictures of horses and of Farnhams: Don standing with the Maui polo team, mallet in hand, Don's father erect on a big black horse, eyes smiling into the camera, Don's mother in a white dress, sitting in the garden with flowers in her arms.

There was a shelf of reference material pertaining to ranch management: books on animal husbandry and veterinary pharmacology, bulletins on agricultural subjects; next to it was a glass-floored locked cabinet which contained medicines and ointments. Branding irons hung on the wall, and beside them hung other articles which made me remember the bawling of outraged bull calves I'd heard when we visited the ranch during a roundup long ago.

Lily had picked up something from Don's desk; she showed it to me. A picture of Leslie and Don riding a surfboard; it had been enlarged from a snapshot and put into a leather frame.

"So this is what she's like, normally," Lily said, and I detected a note of worry in her voice. She studied the picture and I looked at it a second time, trying to see what Lily saw there. Leslie looked different—balanced with arms outstretched, she was laughing at a wave which crashed toward them as if she felt secure in her element. Don's tanned face was serious under its smile; he had placed both hands protectively on her shoulders .

What Lily meant, I decided, was that Don's wife was not the kind of person who could bear up well under tragedy; it devitalized her. Lily was concerned over Leslie's stamina . . . I lost the thought because she returned then.

Hong was with her. He stuck his head in the door and looked at us with beady eyes from a saffron face, wrinkled as dried lichee. He regarded Lily with interest and said something in Chinese to which she replied briefly. The old man scowled and went away.

Leslie said, "Would you like to go upstairs? Hong will bring the drinks up."

I left the two girls in Leslie's room exchanging get-acquainted remarks and took myself to my own quarters. The drink which presently arrived was wonderful, concocted with *okolehau,* a Hawaiian liquor distilled from ti-root and possessed of wonderful properties and a name that cannot be translated into polite language. I drained the glass, wished for another, and decided against it. I undressed and showered and did some female puttering, enjoying the luxury of being alone and quiet. This enjoyment was heightened by distaste for the prospect of dinner, when we would have to sit at table with the Farnhams—and with Denis, if he hadn't taken himself off yet—and act civilized, knowing that those were Leslie's enemies, they would welcome the news which she dreaded, news which might be announced at any time now. I wondered briefly what Lily was talking to her about and dismissed it, knowing I'd find out soon enough, and for the time being could put Leslie from my mind with certainty that she was receiving shrewder counsel than I'd have been able to give her.

Eventually I got around to thinking of what to wear; I opened the bag Lily had packed for me and found my dinner dress was wrinkled. I belted a kimono around myself and took the dress over my arm and went down to find someone to press it for me. At the door of the kitchen I halted.

Lily was there, seated at a long wooden table and—I gaped at this—she was shelling peas. Lily, who never goes near a kitchen except to open the refrigerator! At her elbow sat Hong, a wizened figure enveloped in white apron, and while Lily prepared vegetables he rapidly brushed Chinese characters onto a tablet, touching his brush occasionally to the ink pad between them. It looked almost like a game of tick-tack-toe. First Hong would make characters and hold them before Lily; she would read and nod comprehension while her fingers split green pods and peas rattled into a bowl. Then she would take tablet and brush and make a few strokes. Once when she tried to put aside the vegetables Hong looked at the clock by the big kitchen range, muttered something, and scowled. Lily quickly went to work again, pushing the tablet toward him. Apparently they had made a bargain; if she would help prepare dinner he would take time out from his duties to tell her something she wanted to know.

They sensed my presence and looked up. Lily said, "We communicate by writing. Otherwise we cannot understand each other. Hong speaks Cantonese."

And Lily spoke Mandarin. I had heard these different dialects often on the streets of Honolulu. I hadn't before realized that for purposes of conversation they are about as similar as Greek and Gaelic. Fortunately for Chinese communication, there is only one written language.

I held out the dress and said to Hong, "This I wear tonight. You find somebody to press for me?"

He nodded. "Shuah. You leave dless heah. Somebody pless."

He picked up the brush and drew some word pictures for Lily. She looked at me and asked, "Do you know somebody here by the name of Kolea?"

"Yes. He's one of the *paniolos.* I met him this morning."

"He is leaving the ranch. We just saw him enter the stables. Can you find an excuse to go and talk to him?"

"I guess so. What for?"

She glanced at the tablet covered with black characters which the old man had drawn. "The *paniolo* knows something about the Hawaiian boy, Eole. Last night while the men were out on that searching party Kolea stayed here. He was drinking in the stable. Hong gave him a hangover remedy this morning, and Kolea hinted that he saw something last night. Go and talk to him, if you can, before he leaves."

I laid the dress over a chair and went out. Before I had left the kitchen Hong's and Lily's heads were together and the tablet was in his hands again, the brush was moving quickly over white paper. I went to my room and put on a dress and some lipstick. Then I started toward the stable, trying to saunter as if I had nothing on my mind except a sight-seeing tour.

The stallion's stall was empty. Other horses were in various loose boxes; they raised their heads and one of them whoofed oats at me as I walked past. Doves cooed on the roof, a night breeze riffled through the place, stirring the smell of hay and animals and manure. In the middle of the long building was an open door which led to the corral. A figure appeared there and someone said, "Hello."

It was Kolea. The bright shirt was soiled now, the roses on his hat were withered. But the charm was more evident than ever; his direct look showed that he had discarded all vestige of phony subservience which he might previously have felt his job necessitated.

"Did you come to say good-by?" he asked.

"Good-by? Are you going somewhere?"

He grinned. "Yeah."

"I'm sorry. I didn't know that. I came to see the horse. The one that's foundered."

"In here." He went to a box stall near by. A brown horse stood there, his front legs wrapped in wet burlap, his forefeet deep in a trench of mud.

"That's to cool the fever," Kolea explained.

"Is he better?"

"He's all right. We gave him medicine."

I didn't know what to say next. Let him make the move. I looked at Kolea. He flashed that special smile and said, "I'm leaving the ranch. Going back to town." He shrugged and laughed, moved closer and said in an intimate voice, "Tonight there's gonna be a party—at my sister's house. We go for broke. Celebrate Kolea's no more *paniolo*—he's a free man."

He slapped the pocket of his dungarees. "I've got money. We'll have a good party." His dark eyes dared me. "Mebbe 'letta go da blouse' a little. You want to come?"

"Yes," I said.

I could talk to him then, when he was in his own background. Especially when he'd had a few drinks.

As he gave me his sister's address his smile was a bit complacent; it said that girls were all much alike, even blond *haole* girls who came from a big city like Honolulu.

A car honked, and I saw a jeep with a Hawaiian at the wheel, waiting by the corral. Kolea went to the door and called that he'd be there in a minute. He took a paper-wrapped bundle from a feedbox and went to the tack room, letting me tag behind. He reached under a pile of saddle blankets and brought out a half-empty bottle of Bushmills. "My private safe," he said, grinning. He unwrapped paper from a wad of soiled clothes and folded them around the bottle, retied it and gave it a pat, smacked his lips. "Good stuff!" He jerked a thumb toward the ranch house. "They got plenty in there. I take this home—tonight we share it, eh?"

After the jeep had gone I went back to the house wondering what I was getting myself into. Kolea was the bragging type; he'd no doubt boast to his friends of this newest conquest. He didn't feel sufficiently loyal to this place to care about either Eole or Leslie, but I might get him to talk-with enough stolen Bushmills in him. I sighed at thought of another long drive to the village, but I had to go if I intended to find out anything from Kolea.

Lily came to my room while I was dressing. She wore the kind of clothes she puts on when she chooses to be unnoticed; a Chinese panel dress of severe black, very little makeup, and her everyday jade-threaded gold ear hoops. I was disappointed, but brightened as I saw that she hadn't been able to resist wearing the twin bracelets Henry Leung had recently given her. Flawless jewel jade and pearls of a quality to make any connoisseur drool; beside them, Edith's entire collection would look like carnival prizes. Aside from the bracelets, the personality Lily was assuming made her look all of fourteen, about as formidable as a child just wandered out of the family courtyard.

I raised my eyebrows at her, and she gave me that limpid expression which she can summon at will. "Did you have your talk with Leslie?" I asked.

"Not yet," she said. "But now I know her better. I'm afraid she's as much of a lady as you said."

She took a cigarette from my purse, sat down, and tapped it on her thumbnail. "There are times," she said reflectively, "when being a lady isn't enough. I wish—"

She stopped to light her cigarette and changed the subject. "Did you see the *paniolo*?"

I moved so that I could talk to her reflection in the mirror while I did my hair. I told her about Kolea's invitation and my acceptance. She looked pleased. "Leslie will probably lend you the station wagon. Is there another car here—in case it should be needed?"

She meant in case they found Don's body and called Leslie to come and identify it. I shivered.

"There's a jeep, but it's gone. I'll try to get a taxi. Did I tell you about the driver who brought us up here last night? He was afraid of the ranch."

I repeated the old man's talk about *alii* rain which falls only when a chief dies. "Lily, that means the Hawaiians think Don is dead."

"But Karl does not?"

"No. He insists Don is alive. Maybe that's because he isn't really close to the Hawaiians, in spite of being married to one. There are barriers: he wasn't island-born, and he's in a position of authority here. Karl's pretty tough with the *paniolos.*"

"Perhaps it is fortunate for Leslie's morale that he doesn't accept native superstitions."

"I suppose so." I wondered uneasily how Leslie would react if she knew all that we had discovered. *The coffin is almost ready.* Had Eole been talking in symbols?

Lily was still considering the Kings. "Is Karl's wife very friendly with these Farnhams?"

"Oh no."

She looked thoughtfully at her cigarette. "Hong told me she is the one responsible for their being here."

"What?"

"She telephoned Honolulu the day before Don disappeared and asked Howard Farnham to come to Maui. Hong beard her make the call."

"Mele? Mele did that?"

Then I said, "No wonder the Hawaiians don't confide in Karl. They must be aware that his wife is working against Don's interests. She refused to sell him her land, then sold it to Denis at what I'm sure was a lower price than Don offered. But, Lily, I can't figure why."

"Maybe we shall find out," she said. "Shall we go and see Leslie?"

We went across the hall and knocked. Leslie opened the door and moved back to let us enter, then waited for comments.

I said, "Congratulations, Leslie. It's perfect."

She was wearing a *holoku,* or run-stand, as the Hawaiians named it when the first missionaries persuaded a magnificently naked chieftainess to cover herself with the garment. The original import was a shapeless bag with a long starched collar which hung like armor over some of the voluptuousness which so horrified those Puritans. What the Hawaiians did with it is characteristic. They shortened the ugly bertha to a frill which draws attention to breast and arms, they added a ruffled train which slips across the floor behind its wearer like the feathers of a peacock.

Leslie's *holoku* was a Farnham heirloom. Of sheer white batiste, lace-trimmed, it fit close to her waist and fell straight in front, its train rippling and flowing as she moved. Wearing it, Leslie acquired stature; her cheeks were pink, and her eyes, in spite of shadows beneath them, shone with pride and memory of recent happiness.

"This belonged to Don's grandmother," she told us. "I wore it to dinner on our first night here."

"It is beautiful," Lily said, and I echoed her approval, silently applauding Leslie's gesture of wearing such a symbol of her status in this house. But as we followed her down the stairs, leaving room for the lacy train, I reflected that Lily was right. Leslie needed more than symbols.

Her entrance made the effect she desired. Howard rose involuntarily, straightening his white linen coat and swatting at his hair. Edith stared, she opened her mouth to make comment, drained her cocktail glass instead, eyes narrowed behind their little black fences of mascara. Denis, who sat at the side of the room near Mele, still in the clothes he had worn to the village, rose also, belatedly, watching Howard for his next cue. Mele stiffened, she fixed her eyes on a point past Leslie's shoulder. Karl turned from the bar with a delighted smile and strode across the room.

"Girl, you look wonderful! Won't you have a drink with us?" As she refused, his eyes shifted to Lily and me; he said, "And you two—what would you like?"

I introduced Lily Wu; earlier in the day Howard and Karl had been too engrossed for such amenities. We found chairs and Lily and I accepted cocktails. Leslie sat opposite Don's relatives and said politely, "I hope you find your room comfortable."

Edith didn't answer; she was looking at Lily with covert speculation.

Howard said automatically, "Yes, thank you," remembered how he happened to be in a back bedroom, and added, "For the time being."

Leslie ignored this, she turned to Karl with a question about the new colt which he had delivered. Howard and Denis sat down, and various lopsided conversations began.

Anyone glancing through the window might have found us an attractive picture, a gathering typical of the rich social life of the islands. A handsome Hawaiian woman and her big, affable husband; a fair-haired man with tanned skin and casual clothes, a blond, brown-eyed girl in nylon frock and high-heeled sandals, a demure little Chinese in the dress of her people, a tall thin man wearing tropical white linen; the overdressed woman beside him who might be a visitor from the mainland—and the slim girl in white *holohu* who was obviously hostess to these agreeable people. Logs blazed in the fireplace, throwing shadows on white plastered walls; lamps shone on carved ivories and silver polo cups, on bowls of flowers, bright covers of new books and magazines.

A charming tableau—and completely misleading.

We were the opposite of congenial, and everyone was pretending. Karl cast uneasy looks at his rigid wife while he talked with Leslie about ranch affairs. The Farnhams spoke in low voices, but Edith was inattentive. She had switched her speculation from Lily to Denis; her painted eyes looked feverish as they watched his brown throat above the knit shirt. Denis ignored this and tried to talk to Mele; he got no cooperation since her attitude said plainly that she was here only because she had to be. Lily, of course, did nothing but sat with a sweet, empty expression; I knew she wouldn't miss the flicker of an eyelash anywhere in the room.

Leslie attempted the most difficult pretense of all. She had no cocktail, she had no cigarette with which to make the meaningless, nervous social gestures common to most of us. When Karl went to the bar again and she was momentarily alone, her face showed strain. She simply could not smile, she could not manage any superficial flow of conversation.

I tried to help. "What is the wonderful fragrance in here?"

Lily sniffed. "Sandalwood?"

Leslie glanced up at huge beams which spanned the ceiling. "Yes. Don's grandfather chose the trees himself when the house was built, and had them cut and brought down from the mountain."

"They're probably full of termites," Edith's voice interjected. "These old buildings generally are." She looked at the ceiling as if deciding whether to leave it intact when she started to remodel the ranch.

Leslie started to make a retort; I forestalled her by commenting on how comfortable the overstuffed furniture was. She gave me a grateful glance. "Yes, I like it too. Don says I can replace anything I wish, but it's well made, and it fits here." She brightened. "Let me show you—" She went to a corner table and returned with a package which she unwrapped to disclose a bunch of fabric swatches.

"I got these in San Francisco," she said animatedly. "Haru's going to make slipcovers for me"—she looked defiantly at Edith—"when I decide which I prefer."

She moved around the room in the trailing white dress, laying colorful squares of material on various pieces of furniture. Edith's diamonds flashed as she jerked away from the arm of the sofa. Leslie laid flower-printed linen where her hand had been.

"I rather like this, don't you? Of course, colors look different at night—I may change my mind when I see it in sunlight tomorrow." She picked up her train and went back to the chair, leaving pieces of fabric where she had placed them. She sat down, and for a moment her pose slipped; she looked haggard, spent by her effort.

Lily came to the rescue. "What are those odd-looking things over the fireplace?"

Again Leslie picked up her cue; she glanced at crossed weapons which were bolted to the chimney, spears of polished *kauila* wood tipped with sharp ivory barbs.

"They're old fighting spears. Don says they're made of human bone. We don't mention them in front of the Hawaiians—" Here she faltered and sent a quick look at Mele. Karl's wife stared at her lap. Leslie continued: "—because once some *paniolos* left the ranch when they heard about them." She turned to me. "Isn't there some sort of belief—"

"Well—" I tried to quote my father's notes on the subject. "Early Hawaiians believed that if they could use the bones of their enemies—or the ones they loved—they would derive more power." I finished lightly, "They're probably wild goat or cattle bones, Leslie. But it makes a good story."

Edith Farnham looked at Leslie with a faint, goading smile. "There's a man in Wailuku—fellow named Barnet—who wants to buy stuff like that. He's making a collection of Hawaiian relics, and he's got plenty of money. They'll probably be worth five thousand to him."

Leslie gasped. Before she could speak Karl went to her side. He said, seating himself so that his bulk was between Leslie and Edith,

"Had to fire one of the hands today. Fella named Kolea. He's been here a week on trial, but he don't belong in our stable—feels his oats too much." He leaned closer, trying to lower his big outdoor voice to a confidential note. "Yesterday he got drunk on the job—had a bottle stashed somewhere, even though the damned fool knew our rules about liquor. I paid him off and told him to rattle his hocks outta here."

Leslie said, "Does that leave us shorthanded?"

"We'll make out all right."

She bent toward him. "Karl—have the divers—have they found anything yet?"

He gave her a worried look.

"Karl!" she said. "What—"

He said reluctantly, "Nothing definite, Leslie. I talked with one of the men a while ago, he said they've located the boat. They'll start again early tomorrow."

She put her head back in the chair, breathing shallowly. Edith and Howard watched her. I thought again, looking at Edith over my glass, that she couldn't have been more out of place anywhere than she was here. The sequin-trimmed dress she wore was an unfortunate choice; it made her overripe figure appear in glaring contrast to Leslie's youth. I came to the conclusion that Edith, stripped of jewels and expensive clothes, would fit best into the atmosphere of a River Street bar, the type frequented by the rougher class of sailors and longshoremen.

At that point Haru came to the door and beckoned to Lily. There was a phone call, she said. Lily went into the library, and as she began to talk, conversation lagged. Over the telephone came a long crackle of words; Lily answered in a few staccato sentences, none of them intelligible, since she spoke Chinese. She listened awhile, then said in English, "Thank you very much. Yes, we will be there. And please give my respects to your honorable grandfather."

Dinner was announced as she hung up. She waited until I reached her en route to the dining room and said, "My cousin who lives in the village has learned that I am here, and called to invite me to her grandfather's birthday party. You are also invited, Janice."

I knew that Lily had relatives on Oahu and Kauai, but this was the first I'd heard of any on Maui. I said, hoping for clarification, "Good. I wouldn't want to miss it. How will we get there?"

"Someone is coming for us."

We went into the dining room.

Leslie sat at the head of the table, and from the unhappy expression on her face as Karl pulled out a chair for her, I decided she was wishing desperately that Don were sitting there instead. The meal began with awkward dribbles of conversation; Karl was the only one who made continuous effort to inject warmth into an atmosphere of tension and hostility.

Howard put an end to this effort. We had started the second course when he laid down his knife and said portentously, "Well, Leslie. Did you order the books to be examined?"

Instant silence, while faces turned to her. Leslie saw only Karl's face, she winced visibly at the shock in his eyes which had so recently regarded her with affection and sympathy. Food dropped unnoticed from Karl's fork while he looked at her, waiting. Her face was miserable with guilt as she answered, "Yes. The auditors will be here tomorrow."

Under Karl's mahogany-colored skin dull red was rising. "Auditors?" he repeated. A vein at his temple began to swell. "What auditors, Leslie?"

"Mr. Murchison—he's the lawyer—advised it, Karl," she stumbled. "He said that at a time like this, with Don absent—"

Karl put both hands on the table. "I see," he said. He shoved back his chair and stalked from the room.

She rose to follow him, but before she had walked five steps the outer door slammed. She stumbled over her train as she returned to the table. Her face was whiter than the lace which framed it; she looked sick. Howard smiled, glanced at his wife, then picked up his silver and began to eat with hearty appetite. We finished dinner in silence.

At Lily's signal I lingered so that we were the last to leave the dining room. She walked close to my side and whispered, "That was a message from Steve. She can't leave Honolulu, but is sending someone to the hotel. I shall go there while you are at Kolea's party."

"I hate to go to that party alone."

"I will join you there as soon as I can."

She had steered me into the hall. I stopped. "A taxi can't get here for at least an hour. What's the hurry?"

"You told me that the Hawaiian left here with a bottle of whiskey. There will be drinking at the party. You shouldn't waste any time."

"I don't want to ask Leslie for the station wagon, she may need it. I left the car keys in her room." I finished obstinately, "We'll have to wait."

We had reached the foot of the stairs. Lily said in an urgent voice, "We needn't wait—we can leave now. Hong told me that Eole's father refused to permit the customary Hawaiian wake here for the boy. He is to be buried in the churchyard tomorrow morning. And Karl ordered the hearse to arrive after dark—and to leave while people were at dinner."

"Lily!" I shuddered. "No!"

Lily looked at me. After a moment I started for the door. She caught my arm. "Go up and get our coats and purses. I'll ask Hong to call a taxi for us; we can save time if we meet it halfway down. The other car is waiting."

When I came downstairs I heard voices in the living room, the sound of music from the radio. I longed to return to lights and fire, to living people, no matter how alien. Leslie was alone with them; she needed a companion. Second thought reminded me that Leslie had greater need of the kind of help I could give by pumping Kolea for information. I went out to the lanai.

A long dark car stood at the side of the house. Someone opened a door and I climbed in; Lily came next and then a man who took the outside position. The car rolled down the sloping drive, and as it turned onto the road I looked back.

A figure stood at the rear of the house, silhouetted in light from the kitchen. A tall woman with gray hair—unbound for mourning—hanging to her waist. As I watched, she lifted a handful of hair and covered her face.

"Aauuuuuweeeee!"

That moan rang in my ears as we started silently, without lights, on our journey with the body of her murdered son.

CHAPTER ELEVEN

WE WERE FOUR in the front; if Lily hadn't been so small we could not have managed it. She sat on the edge of the seat, braced by my shoulder. The Portuguese driver on our left smelled of stale sweat; the fat one by the door was a cigar smoker. Hunched between them, I felt a nervous urge to talk, and could not. Nobody said a word. After we reached the road the driver turned on the lights and we rolled along in silence unbroken except for the crackle of tires on hard-packed dirt, the boom of surf against the coast. The air was so still and close that I welcomed sudden rain which spattered on the car—until I remembered Kolea's party. A storm might spoil everything.

"Do you think we're going to have another Kona?" I asked anxiously. The driver grunted. I repeated the question when the second man returned from closing a gate. "This only a shower," he said gruffly. "Watch your dress, miss."

Lily didn't need that reminder; her Chinese dress was bamboo-slim. I couldn't reach my skirts, she pulled them away from his wet leg. He said something in Portuguese to the driver, which brought another grunt. Neither looked at us but I was sure we were the subject of comment. Useless to explain that we had asked for this ride neither from indifference to the burden they carried nor from a desire to save cab fare. I sighed and put my head back. Once when we hit a bump I cried out, almost warning the driver to be careful. Was Eole strapped to a stretcher, I wondered, or did his body—I gritted my teeth and told myself to stop that nonsense. Eole could not care how rough the road was, he could care about nothing. The hearse was big and shining, I thought irrelevantly of ebony tassels I had glimpsed, frozen at the corners of its tonneau. Like a package, I thought, and puzzled again over what Eole had said. Was it his own coffin he had referred to?

"Janice," Lily said. As her voice brought me back, I heard my own tremulous sighing.

"All right, Lily."

I looked at the road ahead and saw that we had reached the top of the grade and were starting the long, twisting descent to the village.

The downpour stopped, island-fashion, as if someone had turned a faucet. Mist began to rise from cane fields we passed, the atmosphere grew thicker. My hunched shoulders ached, and my clothes felt sticky. Just as I was wondering how I could possibly manage a cigarette, lights flashed around a distant curve.

"That's our rent driver," Lily said. "Stop, please."

The chauffeur braked the heavy car, the other man got out and helped us to the road. They started again without acknowledging our thanks or waiting to make sure this was the taxi we expected. We picked our way to the center of the wet road and waved as the car approached. Fortunately it was our taxi, and when it stopped we explained to the driver, climbed into the rear seat, and settled back while he turned the car and headed in the direction from which he had just come.

We laid coats and purses on the seat between us and lit cigarettes. I said, "That was a lot of telephone talk you listened to a while ago."

Lily finished winding down a window. "Steve asked a Chinese friend to call for her, so that no one could eavesdrop at the ranch. He relayed some information about the Farnhams which she thought would interest us."

"She did a quick job," I said. "What did she find out?"

"She has seen the Farnhams around town for a long time. She had a sort of hunch about Edith which she never bothered to verify. They aren't important people. Most of their friends are tourists, or the hard-drinking service element. Occasionally they are invited to dinner with one of the old island families who knew Howard's parents. These invitations now come seldom."

Lily laughed softly. "I can imagine some of those dinners; their hostess chattering about Hui Manu or the Academy of Arts, while their host eyes Edith uneasily and wonders whether he dares tell his wife not to invite them again."

"Edith? Why not?"

"Do you remember yesterday Steve was joking about the woman who offered to sell her 'house' on River Street?"

My mouth opened slightly. "Do you mean . . . ?"

"Yes. Edith's place of business was on Pauahi. She sold it at the right time—just before Pearl Harbor—and became respectable."

Lily was watching me; her eyes glinted with amusement. "Shocked, Janice?"

"Well—a little," I admitted. "But I decided earlier this evening that she belongs in a certain background, the sort preferred by sailors and longshoremen."

"Janice!" she said. "Don't be a tiresome little snob. Anyhow, sailors and longshoremen don't have a monopoly on women of Edith's type. Steve could tell you that many gentlemen of our best families know their way along those streets. You grew up here—don't you ever remember seeing those inconspicuous doorways where a green light burns all night?"

"Yes," I said. "But I never gave it any thought. Besides, I thought it was red lights."

"The green light indicates a prophylactic station. For any serviceman who needs it."

I began to laugh. Lily said, "What's so funny?"

"I was thinking of those Walkatours for tourists—to picturesque sections of the city. Some bright person could make a fortune by organizing Strollatours, to places which aren't on Walkatour itinerary."

I sobered then as I considered the dissimilarity between the Farnhams, both of the same blood. The healthy, well-balanced one had fallen in love with Leslie. His thin, inhibited cousin had found Edith.

I said, "Does Howard know about this background of hers?"

Lily tossed her cigarette out the window. "Did you see a recent story in—" she mentioned a popular picture magazine, "about the son of a prominent mainland family who married a woman notorious as owner of a San Francisco house?"

"I remember it. There was a picture of her former establishment. The story said she had retired with a fortune."

"Howard was a regular caller of Edith's for some time. After she sold her business he married her."

"I wonder why?"

"Possibly because he loved her. Or because she has the drive which he lacks. Also—she had quite a lot of money."

"You used past tense. Are they completely broke?"

"They've had no income for ten years. Their house is heavily mortgaged. Howard is supposed to be an insurance broker, but he makes about enough to pay office rent. They owe a lot of money, and their credit has been cut off."

"So those clothes and jewels are a front."

"Yes. They're desperate. Possession of Don's property means a chance for them to recoup."

"And their proposed use of it fits the picture. Howard hasn't got brains or ability to make money, but Edith has."

"That is right," Lily said. "The ranch is Howard's last asset, and his wife intends to make use of it."

"I can picture what she'll do to Alohilani," I said bitterly, "and the type of people she'll attract there. It makes me simply wild to—" I stopped because the car had stopped. We were in front of the hotel. Lily began to gather up her things. I hated to see her leave.

"Whom are you going to meet?" I asked.

"A girl by the name of Rose Wong. She works for Weldon & Company, a firm with offices in the Dillingham Building."

The envelope I'd seen under Howard's shirts. Lily stepped out of the car and as she did so a plump Oriental girl wearing glasses and a tan linen suit rose from a chair on the lanai and moved forward. Lily waved to her as I closed the door of the car. She repeated Kolea's sister's address, said good-by, and started into the hotel. I watched the two girls greet each other, feeling very much alone.

The hotel was brightly lighted, people in evening dress drifted about, I heard an orchestra playing dance music. I wanted to go in and mingle with them; I wanted to sit at a table with a frosted glass and an agreeable escort; I wanted to laugh and enjoy myself like everybody else.

Not quite everybody else. My eyes focused on a familiar figure, seated apart in a reed chair. Mrs. Bessie Watson, wearing a dinner dress of lace—probably because "it travels so well"—watching other hotel guests. Someone moved toward her and the plump figure leaned forward; at a word she would smile, would say how much she was enjoying this wonderful vacation. They passed, the eagerness drained. She could fill her days with sight-seeing and exploration and chats with strangers; nights were different, they belonged to friends, family, or lovers, and she had none. I wished that I could do something to change that situation for Mrs. Bessie Watson.

Her eyes turned to mine; recognition made her face eager again. She hurried toward my taxi, and I wanted to tell the driver to move on, and hadn't the heart. She came to the door of the car and said, "Miss Cameron! I was wishing I knew where to find you. There's something—" She hesitated and looked embarrassed.

"Yes," I said. "What is it?"

"Well, I assure you I never did anything like this before, but after I met that poor girl today—" She looked over her shoulder.

I leaned forward. "Go on, Mrs. Watson."

"We had dinner together this evening. She told me quite a lot about herself, how she happened to come here. Honestly, I never felt so sorry—"

"Mrs. Watson," I said, "I have to apologize again for being in a hurry. I owe it to you to explain, but at this moment—"

She smiled. "That's all right. This is what I wanted to tell you. This morning, before I knew who he was, I saw Mrs. Dumke's husband sitting in a car talking to another man. I was walking past and heard something they said. I might not have been impressed, except that such a lot of money was mentioned. Sixty thousand dollars!"

"Who was the other man?"

"I don't know. He was driving the car. I noticed Mr. Dumke because of his hair, and he sat near the sidewalk. Then, the mention of so much money—"

She looked earnestly at me. "His wife told me—"

"Yes," I said. "I know about it."

"Do you think I ought to mention it to her? I hate to do anything like that."

I patted one of the plump hands which lay on the car window. "No, don't. But if you see him here again, or the man who was with him, will you call me?" I gave her the ranch phone number.

She nodded, still wearing a distressed expression. I wanted to stay and ask more questions but didn't dare. I said good night and watched her go back to the lanai and sit down.

Sixty thousand dollars. I'd think of that later. At this moment I had a job ahead and had better get there soon, or Kolea's celebration might be too far under way for my purposes. I hadn't any idea what I'd do when I got to the party, but knew one way to make myself more welcome. I asked the driver to stop at the nearest liquor store, and didn't look back at the cheerful lights of the hotel as we started.

Kolea's sister lived in a dilapidated old house on the outskirts of the village; some distance away I recognized my destination by the lights and music. The driver let me out at the edge of the street and I made my way through a grove of mangoes and then over a plank bridge which spanned a stream. I walked carefully in the dark since I carried breakable packages: a gallon of wine and three quarts of liquor. One was Canadian Club, because I knew I had to do some drinking and I don't like Irish whiskey. Kolea could finish the Bushmills alone—if he hadn't already done so. At this thought I quickened my pace.

Laughter and voices reached me, and music from stringed instruments—sounds of a Hawaiian-style party. I could feel myself smiling, then I remembered this was one occasion where I couldn't let go in natural enjoyment. I was coming not in friendship but as a spy. I slowed my pace, reminding myself of why I was there, erasing guilt by that reminder. I put on another smile as I reached an area where an electric bulb, shining through a Japanese paper lantern, shed pinkish light on glossy foliage and glinted on the stream which curved around the property.

I knew better than to go to the front door. I walked along the side of the house, then stood a moment watching the people, waiting for someone to notice me and come forward. Standing there, I realized too late that I hadn't had enough time or forethought to dress properly; in powder-blue nylon and high heels I looked more like a tourist than an ordinary island girl who might be a little bit smitten with a good-looking *paniolo*. How could I have been so stupid?

There were about twenty people on the ragged lawn behind the house. Searching for Kolea, I saw men in khaki pants, T-shirts, *mokus* and *aloha* shirts of bright patterns and colors; I saw girls and women in cotton dresses, in skirts and blouses and printed *holokus,* most of them wearing grass sandals or with bare feet. There were Portuguese and Oriental and Hawaiian faces, all with dark eyes and black hair—I would be the only blonde at this party.

I waited, holding my packages. Eventually a handsome Hawaiian woman in red-and-white *holoku* turned in my direction. She came toward me with unfailing Polynesian courtesy and said, glancing only briefly at my unsuitable dress and embarrassed expression: "I am Lala, Kolea's sister. You his girlfriend, eh?"

I answered yes. I didn't offer my packages and she ignored them. I said in Hawaiian, "I am away from home and lonely. I am glad to be here."

She looked at me, her smile broadened into something more warm and friendly. "*E komo mai,*" she said. "My home is yours."

My high heels were sinking into the soft ground, but I felt better. I said, "Kolea—where is he?"

Her smooth face puckered slightly, and I wanted to tell her that she needn't feel worried. She shrugged a brown shoulder. "Kolea? He's like his name—the bird that flies away." She looked at me and asked, anxiety trickling through, "You a special friend of his?"

"Only to have fun together," I said in her language. My choice of words has more than one translation. I let her see that I knew this; I imitated her shrug, and smiled. She looked relieved.

"Kolea went to get *laulaus* from the store. That Kolea! He comes home, says he quit his job, we'll have big celebration. On such short notice there's no time to cook. Come. He will be back soon."

I followed her into the clearing, found a wooden chair under a papaya tree, and set the packages at my feet. Eventually someone might be interested in their contents. The Canadian Club I laid behind me for a reserve.

The crowd was already warming up under influence of various bottles which sat at the end of the table. Music came from the usual volunteer instrumentalists: two men with ukuleles, one with a guitar across his knees, and a very short, fat Hawaiian behind a tall bass fiddle, slapping it amiably as if they were old friends. I lit a cigarette, smiled at anyone who looked in my direction, and tried not to look self-conscious. I didn't know them well enough to help set the table, but it was important to get into the swing of the party somehow. When one of the players laid down his ukulele I walked over and picked it up, then followed the others into the melody of "Alekoki." They didn't stop their music but they did smile; as I began to play with them they grinned and nodded. I soon forgot my unsuitable frock and upswept blond hair. We played haphazard choices, choruses from modern songs, Hawaiian melodies, a mixture of everything; people wandered by with assorted glasses of wine or whiskey, they stopped briefly to sing a measure or ask for a song. We were having a jolly time when Kolea arrived.

He gave me a smile which was half surprised, half complacent; this was accompanied by a shrug and a gesture which said he'd be with me as soon as he could manage it. He carried an enamel dishpan filled with steaming *laulaus*, and he was accompanied by a harem. Three girls followed him, and one was outstanding. She had a heart-shaped face and the slightly oblique lids which said Oriental-Hawaiian, a blood mixture which often produces breathtaking beauty. Her full figure was Polynesian, her eyes were big and dark, and the hot look they sent me said that she didn't like me at all.

Kolea set down his burden with a flourish while a shout went up; women shuffled paper plates and began laying out food: *laulaus*, baked yams, chicken stewed in coconut milk, bowls of *poi* and raw fish.

"Kaukau!" Lala called.

We finished our song, the fat bass player leaned the big fiddle against my chair and wiped his wet face. "You pretty good on ukulele," he said. "How's about little drink fo' us musicians, eh?"

"I brought something," I offered, and pointed to my packages. He got them and brought them to the table, where they were unwrapped and set with the rest of the liquor. Somebody opened the gin and a thin old woman poured a jelly glass full and drank it down straight. Others sampled whiskey and wine. I accepted whiskey from my genial friend and sipped.

Suddenly warm fingers closed around my arm. "Hello, yellowhead. How do you like my party?"

As I had expected, as soon as Kolea saw me with another man he was able to get to my side quickly. I looked up at him with a smile. "I like it fine."

His fingers slid down to my wrist, loosened with reluctance. He said, "Maybe you better tell me your name again."

"My name is Kulolo."

My fat friend laughed. "Kulolo. Dat's not *wahine* name. It's food—we got some here."

I explained that my father had given me the name because I'd been so greedy for *kulolo* when I was a child. He reached for a hunk of the pudding—made from coconut and sweet potatoes and taro baked to caramel consistency—and handed it to me. I took a bite, said, *"Ono!* My favorite kind!" and people nearest us laughed. The ice was broken.

I ate with the fiddle player on one side and Kolea on the other. The pretty girl, Nani, sat at Kolea's other elbow, so furious that she made bare pretense of eating. I couldn't reassure her that my interest was for the evening only; I had to play up to Kolea. When we were half finished he bent to my ear and said, "How about that drink with me? I saved the bottle."

I nodded and we left the table together, followed by the jealous eyes of Nani. Kolea had hidden the Bushmills in a basket of orchids which swung near the steps of the lanai. I retrieved my own bottle on the way, explaining, "I'm afraid of Bushmills—it's too strong for me. I brought this."

He laughed. "Okay. It don' matter." Kolea was slightly drunk already. "Just so we drink together."

He poured drinks into two cheese glasses; we touched them together and drank. I set my glass behind me and shuddered as fire reached my middle. Kolea lit cigarettes for us and we sat with shoulders touching.

"It's too bad you won't be at the ranch any more," I began. "I'll miss you."

He looked sideways at me. He had probably heard that remark so many times he'd lost count of the girls who had said it. "You come down to see me," he said.

"But you'll be busy, working somewhere—" I put distress into my voice.

"Not me!" he said. "I don't need a job. I got plenty money." He pulled a wad of bills from his pocket. "See? Almost a hundred left."

I moved closer. I reached for the glass behind me and reluctantly poured Canadian Club into a potted begonia. "Where did you get so much?" My heartbeat quickened.

"I didn't get it for taking care of horses." He stuffed the money into his pocket, gave himself another drink, and filled my glass. He drank, wiped his mouth with the back of his hand, and said, "I got it for sleeping—in the stables. And next week, if I still keep my eyes closed—" He put back his head and laughed.

That laughter was too much for the tormented Nani, who had been watching us steadily. I saw her speak to the fat bass player, then the two left the table and came toward us. The fat man said, "How's about we make more music, Kulolo? Nani's gonna do a *hula*." The girl gave me a strained smile; I went because I had to. We played a modern fast-style *hula* for her. When she finished she joined Kolea, who had gone back to the table, and I couldn't quit playing because Lala rose and began to dance. Nani sent me another smile; triumphant this time. Kolea stayed by her side; she urged liquor on him; presently their heads leaned close together.

I had to do something. I said to the guitar player, "Do you know a song called 'Kolea'?"

He shook his head. "That's a very old *hula*. I don't know the melody."

The old woman who had drunk the glass of gin moved closer. She grabbed his guitar and nudged him to rise; she sat down and laid the instrument on her lap with its back up, then began to beat with her hands, chanting softly. Her white brows rose inquiringly; I nodded.

She said, "You're supposed to do this sitting down. Without music—only the chant."

"I know. But I'll do my own version."

She grinned at me. She began to beat more loudly; a few people looked in our direction. I took off both slippers and raised my arms, ready for opening gestures of the story about Kolea the plover, the bird that flies away.

The old woman grinned again, slyly this time. "Very ancient song. You know the words?"

She wanted to know if I knew what their secret meaning was. I gave her a wink. I hummed the more recent melody which has been added to the song, and presently one of the musicians followed with chords of music.

A ripple went around the group at the table. I lifted my arms, moved forward swaying, and cried "Kolea!" as I began to dance the almost forgotten intricate steps.

Kolea's eyes were on me. Nani was forgotten. When I reached the verse which says:

> *"Mala 'ele 'e he ala,*
> *Nou a ka lani.*
> *Puili pu ke aloha,*
> *Pili me ka'u manu,"*

his smile widened to a delighted grin; he started to make accompanying movements with his hands. I finished; there were loud cries for more. The musicians began again:

> *"Nancy, letta go your blouse,*
> *Hemo la, hemo la,"*

and somebody shouted, "Kulolo! *Hemo la!"*

Take it off. I stopped to unfasten a stocking, peeled it from my leg amid laughter and shouts of approval. I started to dance again.

"Hemo la!" they shouted.,

I peeled off the second stocking, flung it at Kolea. He caught it and wrapped it around his neck like a *lei*.

I had stopped near the musicians. I asked them to play "Malua," and they grinned and changed the music to an old and beautiful courtship dance, the man-woman *hula*.

I moved toward Kolea and began to invite him with feet, hips, eyes, outstretched arms, and beckoning fingers. He raised slowly from his chair, stood swaying. Then he gave an exultant cry and leaped toward me.

He was boneless, all fluid grace, weaving slim hips and bending knees until he almost touched the earth, curling upward as a wave rises. He took leadership and I followed his steps; Kolea's brows rose, his mouth curved in a smile, as we danced back to back, hips brushing briefly, then knee to knee, bodies touching and moving apart, circling and retreating. Kolea wasn't a shallow, conceited fellow any longer; he was a laughing satyr. And I wasn't the daughter of a scholarly college professor, I was the calabash child of Makaleha, the woman I loved, who had taught me the dances of her people. The music grew louder, the beat more insistent, my pulses raced and I forgot everything except the joy of dancing with a perfect partner.

The music finished. Kolea stopped in front of me, panting; his face was flushed and his eyes were dilated and brilliant. He laughed low in his throat, swung me into his arms, and ran toward the stream, brushing under thick oleanders into the shadows. I heard murmurs of approval behind us; for an instant, then, I was afraid. Kolea's tribal memory wasn't so distant in time as mine; in his early culture the dance we did was prelude to coupling. He laid me on soft grass in a little clearing where pinkish lantern glow reflected on the water. I knew Kolea was going to kiss me, and I didn't want to make love; I wanted to find out what he knew about a murder. When he leaned forward I felt a moment's panic.

He changed his mind. He seemed hot, he breathed heavily; instead of kissing me he bent and bathed his face in the stream.

"*Auwe!*" he gasped. "That feels good!" He wiped his face with his hands and said, "My throat's so dry it hurts. Let's have a drink."

"A drink?"

"Yeah. I hid the bottles here while Nani was dancing. She's a devil—she'd break 'em if she could."

He searched the grass behind him and brought out the Bushmills. There was a couple of inches in it; he tipped it to his mouth for a long pull. While he drank I took cigarettes from his shirt pocket and lit two; as he inhaled I began again to ask questions.

"Kolea, what did you mean a while ago? You said you get paid for sleeping. I'm curious—I don't understand."

Kolea was scowling. He looked at his cigarette with distaste and tossed it into the stream. "I went to sleep in the stables. I woke up when the horse screamed."

"Did you see Eole go into the stall?"

"No." His voice was thick. "But I saw your car coming."

"Where were you?"

"In the tack room." He added with effort, "On—the—cot."

"You saw us come in. Then I went to the house to get help." I thought quickly; I didn't dare ask what he saw. I said, "What did you do then?"

"Before the car stopped—" He swallowed, frowning. "I went—into—an empty—stall." He put a hand to his throat. "I saw somebody—who—somebody—" He got unsteadily to his feet. "Excuse me," he said thickly. "Back—in—minute." He reeled off along the edge of the brook.

He was going to be sick, I thought. Too much liquor and food followed by strenuous dancing. I let out the breath I had been holding, and leaned against a tree. I heard him stumble some distance away, then heard sounds of retching, and a groan. I wondered whether I should offer to help, decided it would be humiliating for him, and wished for another cigarette while I waited for Kolea to return.

After a while I began to wonder whether he was coming back. I half rose, and made a startled cry as I heard someone behind me. It was Nani. She looked half ashamed, half stubbornly determined.

"Where's Kolea?"

I pointed. There were sounds of someone being very sick. She glared at me. Then she went swiftly along the stream bank until she reached him. I heard her voice in low entreaty, his muffled reply. She came back and said, "He wants to be alone."

She stood over me, waiting for me to rise. I got to my feet self-consciously. "You go back and play the ukulele," she said. "Leave him alone!"

I hesitated, took a step toward the stream. She barred the way, raised brown hands with fingers curled like talons. She had long fingernails. I decided not to follow Kolea.

Salvaging as much dignity as I could, I reentered the clearing with Nani stalking behind me. I rejoined the musicians and, as we played and sang, kept watch on the path by which Kolea would return. He must have passed out, I decided; he didn't appear.

Lily Wu arrived instead. I went to greet her, and as I took her to our hostess I explained the situation in a few words. We waited for perhaps twenty minutes, then at a moment when Nani was not watching, we edged our way out of the group and started to search for him.

Beyond the radius of light from the party, we followed the path by using matches. At one point we saw where Kolea had vomited. At another he had fallen; grass there was flattened in a wide area as if he had thrashed around on the ground. When Lily saw this she walked faster. We reached a clump of broken ginger where he had turned in a circle and started back toward the house. We followed crushed ginger to where we found him.

He lay on the damp ground in a strange position, with knees drawn up to his chin, and he was breathing stertorously. I touched his shoulder. "Kolea!" He didn't respond. Lily struck a match and held it close to his face. She dropped it and handed the book of matches to me; I lit one for her. She bent over Kolea and pulled back his eyelid. His eyes were fixed, the pupils were dilated. The sound of his breathing was awful.

Lily stood up, she caught my arm and held tight.

"Janice," she said, and her voice was unsteady. "We must get him to a doctor. Quickly."

CHAPTER TWELVE

WHEN I TRY TO RECALL what happened immediately after that, it comes to memory with a sort of nightmarish quality and without continuity. I remember faces: solemn and frightened faces of the men who carried Kolea to a car; one of them staggered and regained his balance with a shamed expression. Lala's eyes looked blank; she kept insisting that her brother had only drunk too much, he would be all right tomorrow. Nani's pretty features were blotched by tears; she punctuated her violent sobs with curses at me, the one who was somehow to blame for disaster.

I ignored her; I began hunting for my slippers. I wanted to get out of there.

I remember the way the lawn looked, littered with dirty plates and crushed cups, the fluttering paper tablecloth scattered with faded flowers and food remnants, stained where drinks had been spilled. Musical instruments lay on chairs where players had been sitting; the bass fiddle had fallen to the ground where it looked ridiculously helpless.

And the people, who such a short while ago had been laughing and singing, now huddled together watching with scared eyes while Kolea was taken away; one woman crossed herself as the men stumbled past her with his body sagging between them. My own eyes widened in a sort of incredulous horror at my nylon stocking which still dangled from his neck. When it caught on a croton bush and pulled free I gasped with relief.

I found one slipper and picked it up, continued walking mechanically around in search of its mate. Lily emerged then from the direction of the brook, with my silk jacket over her arm. She looked at me. I held out my lone slipper, she pointed under the table and I knelt and took it from between the feet of a mongrel which was snuffling for food scraps in the grass. I balanced against a tree and forced my muddy feet into linen sandals, retrieved my purse from under the chair I had used earlier, then followed Lily's small figure toward the street.

Lily had rented a U-Drive sedan, and it was in this that we followed two shabby cars—one carrying Kolea and his family, the other filled with various friends—to the plantation hospital. A young man in white duck pants, stethoscope dangling over his pajama jacket, met us as we stepped inside.

"Which of you was with him?"

I identified myself. He said, frowning, "The man's in a coma now; he's been poisoned. We're doing what we can, but it's important to know what he drank. Can you describe his symptoms?"

While I told him, Lily removed my jacket from over her arm and held out Kolea's bottle. There was a half inch of whiskey in it. "He drank from this," she said.

The doctor snatched it from her, sniffed, scowled in concentration. He went to a door and called to a nurse who was hurrying down the hall with a covered tray, "Amylnitrite, Eunice. And prepare a strychnine injection." He turned to us, said, "I'll keep this—it has to be analyzed," and started to follow the nurse.

"Is there anything we can do?" I asked.

"No," he said. "You staying on the island?"

"At Alohilani Ranch."

"Okay, you can go. Someone will get in touch with you."

There was nothing more that we could do. Lala's eyes followed us as we started out; her arms tightened around the sobbing Nani. We passed the silent little group in front of the hospital, got into our car, and started back to Alohilani.

Neither of us said anything until we were on the ranch road; I was too tired and confused to talk; Lily was busy with the car and her own thoughts. A half-moon had risen in the east, the tranquil ocean was enameled with silver. I leaned my head against the door of the car, taking deep breaths as we climbed to a higher altitude and the air grew cold and fresh with the smell of forest and pasture lands.

After a while I looked at Lily and said, "Do you think he'll die?"

Lily said, "I do not know." After a minute she asked, "You're not reproaching yourself for what happened, are you?"

"No-o-o." I was remembering the eyes of Kolea's sister. "If he had only told——" That was useless. I began again. "Somebody was paying him to keep quiet, Lily. He admitted it."

"Of course. That is what his murderer counted on. That, and the fact that Kolea thought no one knew where he hid his stolen whiskey. We will find out from Leslie what drugs are kept at the ranch. Light me a cigarette, will you?"

I gave her one. She inhaled, and said, "We must also talk to Leslie about something else. But first let me tell you what I learned tonight from Rose Wong."

With memory of Kolea so sharp in me it was difficult to concentrate; gradually I was able to absorb and consider the additional information she had obtained.

Briefly, it was this: Howard and Edith Farnham were negotiating with a representative of Tropicana Hotels, Ltd., a chain which was searching for a location for a dude ranch. Howard had engaged an engineering firm in the Dillingham Building to make preliminary designs for converting Alohilani, to be submitted with a cost estimate. Rose Wong, who had been sent to Maui by Steve, was employed as secretary to the head of the firm. She told Lily that the staff had been under pressure for three days, all other work put aside to finish this job for Howard Farnham; the rush was because he knew Tropicana was also interested in another property. The latter did not have the advantage of proximity to the ocean, since most cattle ranches are situated on higher land, farther from the coast. But it had another advantage which Alohilani could not offer: the second ranch could be purchased outright instead of leased. Howard had been needling Rose Wong's boss for completion of his plans; they were to be delivered the following afternoon.

"And by tomorrow Howard expects to be certain of his inheritance," I said. "Lily, things just aren't done that way!"

"If he finds evidence that Don was drowned he can start legal action immediately. The court will appoint him executor until a decision is reached. Howard was born in the islands, he knows people here. Don't forget that it means money for local merchants to have an influx of tourists."

"Leslie's a newcomer. She doesn't have a chance."

"As soon as Howard moves in he can begin making changes, under pretense of improving the property. The Tropicana people have their own crews of workmen. They will be flown here immediately."

"But that's not legal! He'll have no right to sign any lease until his title is clear."

"There are generally means of getting around such technicalities. Especially where powerful interests are involved."

"The ranch hands will be fired, their families evicted—Lily, what can we do?"

"We must discourage the Tropicana agent."

"But how?"

"This may work: tomorrow Rose is to finish typing the letter which accompanies the preliminary plans. She told me it is five pages long. She will make two copies of the sheet which contains the figures; the extra copy will increase the estimate by thirty thousand dollars. Her boss will check it, of course, and sign the last page. When he gives it to her to hand to the messenger, she will substitute the false figures, which appear on page four."

"She'll lose her job!" I said. "What persuasion did you use, Lily—did you bribe her?"

"Not exactly. I told her what Howard is trying to do to Leslie, and she is willing to help. Rose is an intelligent girl. She wanted to be a laboratory technician, but had to take a job after she finished high school. We may find some way to make her education possible."

I thought of how it could be done. I knew most of the university board of course, through my father's work there. Lily's uncle and his wife were both doctors; they could help the girl later—

"You see," Lily was saying, "the vital element here is time. If we can postpone this deal the hotel chain may buy the other ranch. They want to start as soon as possible, in order to be ready for the spring tourist season."

"It won't take long for Howard to find that there's been an error, and to produce a corrected set of figures."

"That is true. But a mistake of that nature creates confusion—and sometimes distrust. Steve is also working on another angle. She has an appointment tomorrow for a luncheon interview with the Tropicana representative. She is going to drink too much. She will then indiscreetly let slip a rumor she's heard about Alohilani."

I almost laughed at that picture. Steve's alcoholic capacity is a source of marvel, even to those who know her. Then I remembered Don's anxiety about publicity.

"She won't talk about the trouble there?"

"Of course not. She has heard that Don was having difficulty with his

water supply—remember he tried to buy the valley in order to pump water up for the cattle? Suggestion of such a possibility will necessitate a
thorough survey before any work can be done. Or—it may be the final
factor to influence a decision against the property. We'll hope for post-
ponement—for the time being."

I marveled, as I often do, at the thoroughness with which Lily functioned. And Leslie, how helpless she would be if she had to use the kind
of subtlety which to Lily was practically instinctive—

As if reading my thoughts, Lily said, "There is still a third stratagem
and it is the most important. Leslie must become the key figure. She can
help now."

"Do you think she will?"

"She must. You have been protecting her because of the emotional
strain she is under. Now her stamina will really be tested. We must tell
her everything. Tonight."

As we approached the ranch I thought I saw a light on the lower floor.
We turned a curve, I looked again and blinked, decided I must have imagined it. The building was dark.

Leslie was not asleep. She responded instantly to a tap on her door.
"Yes? Who is it?"

She switched on her bedside lamp as we entered; she sat up straight
and asked in a voice which was thin with alarm, "What is it? Has something . . . ?"

"Yes," I said. "We want to tell you about it."

She threw back the sheet and I handed her the lilac silk kimono from
the foot of her bed. As she put her arms into it I noticed how sharp her
collarbones were, how the lilac accentuated purple hollows under her eyes.
She said, looking from my face to Lily's, "What has happened?"

I began. "We didn't spend the evening with Lily's relatives, Leslie. It
was quite another kind of party—"

When I finished, Leslie put a hand to her head dazedly.

"But why should the Hawaiian man—I'm not sure that I—"

"Leslie," Lily interrupted. "What kind of drugs are kept here? If we
can let the hospital know in time, it may save Kolea's life."

Leslie took a key ring from the top of the bureau. "I'm not sure I
remember. Let's go and look."

We went down to Don's office. She unlocked the medicine cabinet
and studied its shelves. "Here's gall cure, linseed oil, creolin for cuts and
bruises, carbolated vaseline, picric acid for saddle sores—that's all, I think.
No, something's missing—the founder medicine. I gave it to Kolea this
morning for Karl's horse. It's probably still in the stables."

"What kind of medicine is it?" Lily asked.

"Tincture of aconite. It's used to reduce fever in a bad case of founder."

Lily was at the telephone on Don's desk. "Dr. Foyle? This is Miss Wu calling, in regard to the man who was brought in a while ago. Oh. I am very sorry. Yes. No, we don't. Yes, we will be here. We are most anxious to know. Thank you."

As she hung up I asked, "He's dead?"

"He died half an hour ago. They are sending the whiskey to Honolulu to be analyzed."

Leslie said, "But we already have a pretty good idea—"

"Yes. And if I told them so, they would send the sheriff here immediately. It is preferable to keep local authorities out of this. The sheriff cannot help Kolea."

Leslie blinked. "But if it's murder. The police—"

I explained to her. "We're on an island, Leslie. They know we can't go anywhere. And Kolea was not rich or prominent. He was a Hawaiian ranch hand."

Two Hawaiians dead in two days . . . and both were young. Eole, who loved Don, who wanted to be a fisherman. Kolea—in his exultant masculinity he had been more alive than most men would ever be. I felt a little bit sick. Vaguely I was aware of Lily explaining that since we were trying to respect Don's wishes that Alohilani be given no publicity . . .

Leslie nodded, still with that dazed look; her eyes wandered, then she exclaimed, "Look at the safe!"

The thick door was slightly ajar. She knelt and examined its contents. She turned to look up at us, saying, "Everything looks the same as it did earlier this evening. I came in here after dinner and opened it—there was nothing except some insurance papers, the ranch books, and—" She looked back at the little shelves. "My letters!"

"What letters?" Lily asked.

"The ones I wrote to Don while I was away. He had put them in the safe . . ." Her voice trailed off and she rose to her feet.

"What was in your letters?" Lily asked.

"Just news of my trip, and about my sister, and—and personal things."

"Then we'll worry over it later. You'll know about the books tomorrow when the auditors finish. Let's go to your room, Leslie. Many things have been happening here which you don't know about. It is time for us to start at the beginning and tell you."

That was an exhausting session. I began by telling Leslie of the conversation in Honolulu which resulted in my boarding the plane that brought her home to Alohilani. I told her what happened when I spoke to Eole as he lay on the stable floor, and went on to add what I had concealed from her before: how Eole's father had unknowingly told me that his son was murdered. When I came to the interview which had taken place while Leslie was inside the house, I remembered Kaula, Mele's grandmother, who watched from the banana grove.

At that point Lily interrupted. "You didn't mention her before."

"I forgot it. There was so much else to tell you."

"And the old woman lives in the valley which Denis bought from Mele?" she asked. "Does he know her?"

"I haven't any idea." It was the first time I had thought of any possible connection between them.

"Go on," Lily said. "Tell Leslie what you heard in the hotel this afternoon between Denis and his wife."

"His wife?" Leslie looked more dazed than ever. Her mind was so filled with worry over Don that she was finding it almost impossible to assimilate this information. I went on talking. Lily sat in a chair with her feet tucked under her; Leslie had gone back to bed, and I lay on the twin bed beside her, propped on one elbow. It felt good to lie down.

I was relieved to stop talking and let Lily take up the story. She added an account of Steve's activities in Honolulu, and further details which Rose Wong had brought to the interview in the hotel room. Lily's voice is light but low-pitched; her speech has an almost indefinable cadence which indicates that the first words she learned were those of an Oriental language. I slumped and listened, and found myself unable to suppress a yawn. Sixteen hours of almost uninterrupted activity were dulling my faculties; I yawned again and languor spread over me. The last words I remember were: "—and now let us go back to your interview with the attorney. According to the terms of Don's father's will—"

I was awakened by a gentle touch on my shoulder. I opened my eyes reluctantly and saw Lily bending over me.

"Wake up, Janice. You'll sleep better in your own bed."

I got to my feet, steadying myself by the bedpost. "Excuse me," I apologized to Leslie, "I've had a day, what with horseback riding and dancing and driving all over the island—" I stopped because Leslie obviously didn't care. There was no longer a dazed look on her face. Color burned in her cheeks, her eyes were wide and very bright. But her gaze was fixed as she considered some inner problem and tried to make a decision.

I followed Lily, too sleepy to ask what she had said to Leslie. I'd find out tomorrow. From the door she smiled at Don's wife. "Good night. Try to sleep now."

"Yes. Thank you, both of you. Good night."

My good night was lost in a prodigious yawn. I stumbled to my room and took off my wrecked blue dress and tossed it on a chair. I got into a nightgown and wondered whether I had energy enough to clean my face, decided I had not. As I pulled the sheet over me I remembered that I hadn't washed my dirty feet. It didn't matter; I turned out the light and slept.

I awakened next day with a start, immediately certain that the ranch was deserted. The way my nerves tightened with alarm at prospect of being alone in the house told me how tense I had grown in the past two days. If I, with no personal stake involved, could feel like this—how about Leslie? I grabbed my kimono and rushed to the hall. Leslie's door was open, her bed unmade. Swift survey of other bedrooms revealed similar emptiness and lack of order. Halfway down the stairs, I stopped, immensely relieved to hear voices in Don's office. Auditors were human and normal. I went back to my room.

But as I stood by the window, brushing my hair, I looked in vain for other living persons. There were signs of activity; a horse neighed and stamped in the corral; a rooster crowed, and from a lower pasture a calf bawled for its mother. There wasn't a ranch hand in sight, nor were there any women or children around the *paniolos'* cottages. I finished dressing in a hurry and went downstairs.

The living room was empty; flowers looked wilted and ashtrays were dirty. Leslie's swatches of fabric still lay over sofa and chairs where she had placed them the night before. Puzzled, I went through the library and dining room toward the kitchen.

"Gar damn silly langlage you talking!"

I pushed the swinging door and saw Hong and Lily again at the table. Hong's saffron face didn't match those words; his grin showed a gold-capped molar.

He looked at me and shrilled, "You want blekfast? Nobody stop now."

Lily said, "They've gone to Eole's funeral."

"Oh," I said. "Hong, if you'll show me where to find coffee and a toaster—"

He was already bustling around the kitchen, opening the refrigerator door, slamming pans on the stove. "Wot you want?" he demanded. "Ham? Eggies? Omletty?"

"Toast and coffee, and a piece of papaya if you have it."

He snorted at this inadequate breakfast and started preparing it. I sat by Lily and pushed aside sheets of paper covered with black Chinese characters.

"Did Leslie go?" I asked.

"Yes. She took Eole's parents in the station wagon. I loaned our rent car to Karl and his wife. The funeral parlor sent transportation for the others."

"How about the Farnhams and Denis?"

"Denis went somewhere in his boat. The Farnhams have gone to the village—"

"To the funeral?"

"She had an appointment at a beauty parlor. He—" She shrugged to indicate lack of information about Howard.

I asked, "What did you say to Leslie last night? She looked so strange after you talked to her."

"I suggested—"

She couldn't finish because Hong announced that my breakfast was ready. I wanted to eat in the kitchen with them but he wouldn't have it. He shooed me into the dining room and served my scanty meal with dexterity and grumbling. I tried to make friends with him but no dice. Hong would talk only to Lily.

I ate to the accompaniment of muted voices in the next room. It was when I finished coffee and went to ask Lily for a cigarette that I discovered they had disappeared. From the back door I saw them going up the slope toward the *paniolos'* cottages; Lily's skirt billowed in the wind and Hong's cotton blouse flapped as he trotted beside her.

"Hey! Wait for me!" I called. They didn't stop. I ran, and caught up with them at the steps of the largest cottage. Hong scowled; Lily said rather breathlessly, "I want to search Karl's house before anyone returns; Hong will be the lookout."

Island doors are never locked. We stepped inside, and my first impression was that we might be in a hotel room. It was meticulously neat, its simple furniture stiffly arranged, there were no books and few magazines. The only evidence of domesticity was a *lauhala* basket filled with mending and a rack of dirty pipes. In the bedroom we again saw evidence that these people had few personal interests, but to my surprise, for Karl seemed rather a crude, earthy sort, there were signs that the Kings were devout.

A crucifix hung over the immaculately white-spreaded double brass bed. On a small corner table stood an image of the Virgin before which a votive light was burning. The table drawer contained a worn prayer book; when Lily opened it several holy cards slipped to the floor. She picked them up, turned them in her fingers thoughtfully. "Religious objects are the only beautiful things in this house."

She put the prayer book away and went to the dresser. "Help me search these drawers."

"What are you looking for?"

"The letters from Don's safe. When I touched the lamp on the desk last night it was still warm. Someone left the office in a hurry when we returned—that is why the safe wasn't closed."

I hadn't imagined that light in the house.

"Why do you think it was Karl? How about the rest of the household?"

"I've searched the other rooms and found nothing. Except—the Farnhams had a letter from Mele suggesting that they contact the Tropicana representative about leasing Alohilani."

"You mean—she knew Don was going to disappear?"

"The letter wasn't dated. Take the bottom drawer, Janice; we haven't time to talk now."

We found nothing. The clothes closet contained breeches and boots, starched uniforms and oxfords, other personal garments. Mele didn't possess a hat, while Karl had two: the usual straw worn by the ranch hands and a big gray Stetson of the type called ten-gallon. When Lily asked to see it I handed it to her from the shelf which she could not reach. She turned the big hat and glanced at the sweatband. "It's practically new. From a store in Brownsville, Texas."

"That's where Mr. Murchison said Karl came from. He probably keeps it out of sentiment."

Hong muttered something from the front door and Lily said, "He wants us to hurry."

I was glad to close the door of the cottage and step into sunlight. "I don't like snooping," I complained, as we started back to the ranch.

Lily gave me a sharp glance. "Do you think I enjoy it?"

"I'm sorry, Lily."

She smiled. Then she sobered and said, "I keep wondering who opened the safe last night—and what for. Karl and Howard were the ones who saw Leslie indicate the location of the combination—"

"Edith and Denis stood by the office window," I said. "But Howard's the one who hates Karl." I thought of what a girl named Rose Wong was doing in Honolulu—possibly at that moment. "Howard might have altered some figures in Don's books. Or, if Karl is really a thief, as Howard claims, he could be the one—"

Lily nodded, but from the way she looked into space I knew she was preoccupied with some other conjecture. I've learned from her example to ask direct questions as rarely as possible, so I didn't ask what that conjecture was. "What else did you find out from Hong?"

"He described the activities of these people on the day that Don disappeared."

"And—"

"Howard was out hunting for wild goats. His wife was in town. Karl rode to one of the upper pastures to repair a water trough. Denis—he didn't appear until the night Leslie returned. He claimed that the roof of his house leaked, and asked shelter from the storm. Mele never left the ranch during the day."

"Then she's the only one we can be sure of." I made that concession with reluctance.

"Hong told me he heard something strange that night, Janice. He heard drums beating."

"Drums?" I thought instantly of Mele's grandmother in the valley. I chewed a finger while I tried to figure out why old Kaula should have been beating drums on the night of Don's disappearance.

"Lily!" I said. "She could have been sending a message!"

"To whom?"

"Obviously to some Hawaiian. I've been sure all along that Hawaiians are in this somewhere. I'll go and find Mahoe; maybe he'll talk to me. Maybe he'll remember drums too."

I started toward the front of the house and stopped. "Damn! He's not here. And so soon after Eole's funeral he may not talk at all."

Lily said, "I think I hear cars returning now." She went to the window, but I turned away. I didn't want to see those Hawaiian faces—especially not the faces of Eole's father and mother.

Leslie entered, wearing a black frock which made her look thin and colorless. Karl was behind her. As they reached the hall one of the auditors came out. "We're finished, Mrs. Farnham. " His partner appeared behind him, fastening straps on his leather briefcase.

"You'll find the books on the desk," the first man said. "Everything's in perfect order. Fortunately we were here in June for our semiannual visit; there weren't many additional figures to check."

"Thank you. I'm sorry this was necessary, but my husband's cousin requested it." She turned to Karl, who looked straight ahead, granite-faced.

"Karl," she appealed. "I've said I'm sorry. You know that I—" She faltered into silence.

He gave her a stiff little bow. "You don't need me here, do you? I've got work to do."

Lily and I had watched from the living room, where Haru was pattering around putting things to order. When Leslie came in and sank into a chair with the sigh of one who is bone-weary, Haru went to her with a square of coral and beige linen. "What kind this?"

Leslie said, "I'll take it, Haru." Then she withdrew her hand. "No. Put it back on the sofa."

I gave her a smile of approval. Leslie tried to respond; she put a hand over her trembling mouth instead.

Lily said, "Steady."

Leslie cried, "Oh, I can't—" She pounded clenched fists together. "It's this waiting, waiting to hear—"

"Mrs. Farnham." Mele stood in the doorway. "Someone is here to see you."

Leslie rose, took a step forward and stopped. "Is it . . . ?"

It seemed to me then that Mele's expression altered, for a fleeting second she looked at Don's wife with sadness and pity. It didn't last. She nodded stiffly, and walked out of the room toward the kitchen. I hated her. She didn't even care enough to stay and hear whether they had found Don's body.

Leslie was ashen; she swayed slightly and I thought she would faint. I started to her and she straightened, she said, "No. I'm all right. I'll go alone."

With a look of frozen endurance on her face, eyes straight ahead like a sleepwalker, she went outside to hear what the divers had to tell her.

CHAPTER THIRTEEN

SEVERAL *paniolos* were in the driveway, gathered around a gray sedan. They stood aside to let Leslie through. Howard was in the rear seat, leaning forward to talk with the driver; when he saw Leslie he sat back, waiting.

The driver got out and raised his hat. "Mrs. Farnham?"

"Yes."

"I am George Carvalho, of the Marine Salvage Company." He nodded toward his companion. "And this is my partner, Archie Olsen."

She looked at him. "You have found my husband's boat?"

"Yes," he said. "I'm afraid—"

Leslie seemed to become aware then of the spectators; she glanced around her and said in an expressionless voice, "Will you come inside, please?" Without waiting for an answer she walked back up the steps.

Edith and Denis were watching from the lanai. Leslie went past them into the house. She crossed the big room to the fireplace and turned to face the group that entered. The Farnhams were first; they had to be in at the kill. Then Denis, then Lily and I, then the two divers. I stood close to Leslie and could see her press back deliberately until lava rock cut into her shoulders, as if she wanted sharp reminder that she must take this standing. The two divers stood with hats in hand and told her what they had found. She thanked them and said they would receive payment as soon as possible. The men went out, and left silence in the room.

Howard had to break it. "Well—" he began.

Edith took one look at Leslie and called, "Haru! Mele! Anybody! Bring some ammonia, quick!"

Before anyone else could reach her, Denis poured rum into a shot glass and held it to Leslie's lips. She swallowed and coughed. When Mele came with a glass, she shook her head, still coughing, then said, "Thank you. I don't need it now."

She moved to the sofa and sat down. Howard went to stand in front of her and said, unnecessarily, "They raised Don's boat."

"Yes," she answered. "I am aware of that. It sank because of an explosion in the galley. They found remnants of the clothes he was wearing, and—and one of his shoes." Her eyes looked blind.

"You realize," Howard said, his tone strengthening, "that this means legal proof of Don's death."

She nodded. She looked up and let him have his say, as he began telling her of steps to be taken. The boat would be towed to the village, examined by experts, then held as evidence. The local judge was aware of the circumstances; legal processes would be expedited.

And so on.

Leslie said nothing. Mele stood with the glass in her hand, watching intently. Edith had found a comfortable chair; her eyes glittered; she dropped her lids and began to examine her new manicure. Denis was nervous; he fidgeted, finally he poured himself a drink from the glass he had filled for Leslie.

Howard finished talking. He waited for reaction: wild protest, hysterics, a storm of grief. Leslie did not move. She did not speak. Suddenly he snapped his fingers and started from the room.

Edith looked toward him. "Where are you going?"

"To send a cablegram," he called over his shoulder. "That bull is supposed to be shipped soon, and I'm going to stop it."

Leslie's shoulders went back; she sat straight. *"Don't do that,"* she said in a clear voice.

He stopped, he came back a few steps. "And why not? I haven't any use for a six-thousand-dollar bull."

"But I have," she told him. "He is needed to improve the strain of our stock."

Howard looked at his wife with an expression which indicated that he thought the girl must be temporarily unbalanced. Edith's shrug said, "Let's humor her—for a short time." Howard's smile was tolerant. "What do you mean, Leslie?"

She drew a breath and began in a steady voice. "I had not wanted to make this a public announcement—" She swept a look around the room and smiled faintly. "You can understand, I am sure, that I preferred to tell my husband first. But since he won't—since Don can't be here—I must explain."

Her hands had begun to shake. She folded one inside the other and fixed her eyes on her wedding ring. After a second she raised her head and looked straight at Howard.

"Edith asked me about insurance yesterday. I checked the papers in Don's safe to make certain that provision has been made for me. Don is insured for twenty thousand dollars, which will be payable when—and if—he is legally declared dead. Mr. Murchison explained the will to me yesterday, so that I am certain of my position."

She stopped and drew in another deep breath. With one finger she began to trace gold *mamo* feathers on her wedding ring. Without looking up, she said in a tender voice, "Don's land is safe. On his death it is inherited by his next of kin—only if he dies 'without issue.' I intend to continue management of Alohilani just as Don has done—for myself, and for the legal heir."

So that was what Lily had told her to say.

I glanced at my foster sister. She sat in a chair near Leslie, an expression of polite interest on her face. I had to look away quickly from that picture of Lily sitting so bland, so innocent

There was a gasp from Edith. She said hoarsely, "Do you mean that you're pregnant?"

Leslie looked at her with that faint smile.

Howard's jaw had sagged. His throat moved convulsively as he tried to speak, then finally shouted, "I don't believe it! It's a lie!"

Edith said, "You've only been married two months. That's too soon for any doctor to know."

Leslie met her glance. "I had an A-Z test. It was positive."

Edith sank back. Howard had listened to this, turning his head from one to the other. As his wife accepted Leslie's information he made an inarticulate noise. He started toward Leslie.

"Howie!" his wife called, and he jerked to a stop.

He looked wildly around the room, at the sofa, spears over the fireplace, the old-fashioned chairs, everything he had already possessed in his mind and contemptuously disposed of. He took another step toward Leslie, and she rose to face him. Howard's face twisted, his lips writhed in a parody of a smile while his eyes glared undisguised hatred. "My warmest congratulations!" he said.

"Thank you." She walked past him out of the room.

He stared after her, then went to the bar and poured a drink which he raised to his mouth with an unsteady hand. He looked at his wife then. The ranch was his last asset, their hopes were pinned on it; he was afraid.

So was I, watching her. She sat silent, studying her red fingernails. Then she said thoughtfully, without glancing up, "That damned little gook is at the bottom of this somehow. She was talking to Leslie in her room for a long time last night."

I said, "What is a gook, Lily? Do you know?"

Lily's voice held an overtone of amusement. "It is vernacular used by some of the uneducated classes to denote a member of a race other than their own."

Edith stiffened, but she didn't look at Lily. Subtlety was not her natural weapon, but I had the impression that she was sharpening it now. She said to Howard, lightly, "We'll know the truth in a few months."

Howard's answer was a shout. "You know damned well we haven't got a few—"

"Shut up, you damned fool!" He shut up.

She went on in a wifely tone, "You must get hold of yourself; the ranch isn't that important." She walked across the floor to him. "Howie, you know we have all the time in the world."

Howie gaped, he didn't know what to say. She slipped her hand through his arm and steered him out of the room. Denis followed and I heard Edith ask, "Staying for lunch with us?"

"No. I'm getting out of here. Now."

Lily came to my side and murmured, "That woman is up to something."

She walked with me toward the stairs. "From now on one of us must stay close to Leslie. I'm going to use the telephone in Don's office while I have this chance. You go upstairs, and don't let that girl out of sight for an instant."

That was all very well, I thought, standing outside Leslie's closed door, but I couldn't force my company on her all the time. As I hesitated, Haru came up the stairs with a covered tray. Her old-fashioned Japanese hairdo was mussed, her soft face showed signs of tears. She knocked and then went in without invitation. I glimpsed Leslie sitting by the window, staring out at the sea. She didn't turn around.

"You *kaukau* now?" Haru coaxed. "Hot soup, plenty milk, make strong."

"Thank you, Haru. Put it on the table."

Haru set down the tray, smiled, said timidly, "Me too glad you get *keiki* now. Bimeby big man like Don, you no lonely."

"I want to talk to Karl. Is he downstairs?"

"Karl no stop. He go long time." She urged, "Bettah *kaukau* now. Hot soup, glass milk. Then go *moemoe.*"

Leslie smiled politely. "Perhaps a nap is what I need. Thanks, Haru. Close the door when you go, please."

I went to my room, leaving the door open. If Leslie intended to rest for a while I'd have to stay there. I took a correspondence block from my bag and settled in position to see across the hall. The Farnhams passed, dressed in riding clothes; Edith's were tailored for bridle trail instead of open country. I noticed that without a girdle her behind wobbled. The house settled into quiet; I picked up tablet and pen again.

Some time later I grew tired of letter writing and wandered across my room to the window. I stiffened there; Leslie was at the stables, dressed in frontier pants, Mahoe was just leading out her saddled horse. I don't know when I've changed faster; I tossed garments in all directions and grabbed the jodhpurs I'd worn the day before and thrust my arms into a shirt. With everything unbuttoned and boot straps flapping at each step, I hurried down to the stables—in time to see Leslie riding at a canter across the hill.

I yelled at her. She heard me, turned and waved, and rode on. Mahoe was staring; I said, buttoning my shirt, "Get me a horse. Quickly, please!"

Mahoe didn't ask questions. He said okay and headed for the corral while I zipped my pants and bent to fasten bootstraps. He returned with the gray horse, and as he saddled him he asked, "You take care Don's wife, eh?"

I asked in Hawaiian, "Do you know where she's going?"

"She asked the way to the King's Runners' trail." He pointed. "You know John Kuneo's house, where you went yesterday? You'll see it there, past the banana grove."

"Thanks, Mahoe." I reached for the reins.

"Janice! Where are you going?" Lily called from the lanai. I beckoned and when she came out I explained while Mahoe tested stirrups for length. As I took the reins Lily said, "I'm going with you."

"But you can't ride!"

She turned to the old *paniolo*. "Will that horse carry two people?"

He looked her over. He said to me in Hawaiian, "She doesn't weigh as much as the saddle. Your horse won't like it but he'll take her. Do you want the Chinese girl to go with you?"

"Yes."

"She'll get sore legs without breeches.'"

I repeated this to Lily. "Help me up," she commanded, and Mahoe cupped his hands and boosted her into position behind the saddle.

As we started he called, "That trail is old, not safe. Be careful."

Lily's arms tightened around my waist as we started at a gallop in the direction Leslie had taken. She was out of sight by then, but when we reached the banana grove her blue shirt was visible, moving through the leaves. I called loudly, then called again. This time she waited, halting her horse in a clearing at the edge of the forest.

"Leslie!" I said. "Where are you going?"

She gave me a resentful look. "I'm going down to the valley, to meet Denis."

"Denis? What for?"

"He sent me a note."

Lily asked, "May we see the note?"

"I left it at the house. He said that after what he heard today, about my having a baby, he had decided to tell me something I should know."

Lily said, "You're not supposed to be riding now. What about Edith and Howard?"

"I waited until they left," she said, still resentful. "They rode in the other direction. If Edith says anything to me—" she shrugged. She didn't care what Edith thought.

"Hawaiian women ride horseback during pregnancy," I told Lily. "It depends on what you're accustomed to."

I turned to Leslie. "But Mahoe told me that the trail isn't safe."

She gathered reins together. "I'm going."

"May we go with you?" Lily asked.

Leslie hesitated. "If you wish," she said grudgingly. "But not to Denis' house. He asked me to come alone."

"We will wait somewhere out of sight. We only want to be certain that you are safe."

Leslie's resentment dissolved. "To tell the truth, I'm glad you're here," she admitted. "That jungle looks awfully gloomy."

As we entered the forest I decided I shouldn't want to be alone there, either. It was shadowy and humid; thick growth of *koa* and camphor trees stood tangled in vines and giant ferns which almost concealed the old cobblestoned trail. We ducked outthrust branches, vines which reached and clung with enough strength to unseat us. I had to watch the trail constantly for jutting roots and loose stones. Once I started violently and Lily clutched me tight as a brilliant bird whirred and flashed over our heads.

"How old do you think this path is?" Lily asked, after we regained our poise.

"Ancient. It means that a village once stood in Auohe. Hidden is a good name for it. The Hawaiians could pick off invaders before they got down to the valley. The trail was used by the chiefs' runners to carry messages and to collect whatever form of taxes the people paid."

"Taxes," Lily said. "Those were supposed to be the free days."

"Chiefs have collected taxes since time began," I reminded her. "The Hawaiians paid in various ways: weapons, food. Feathers, too."

"Feathers?"

"That bird reminded me. There were professional feather gatherers; they hid in these jungles with long gummed poles tipped with flowers. When the birds came to sip from the flowers they were caught. *Mamo* birds had only a few little golden feathers; you can imagine how long it took to collect enough for a chief's cape. Mele's grandmother could tell us plenty of interesting things about those days if she wished. She's probably custodian of a lot of unwritten history."

"Have you thought of visiting her?"

"It would be useless. She wouldn't talk. I suspect that she's the one who spread the rumor that Leslie is bad luck to the ranch." I glimpsed light ahead and said, "I'm glad we're almost out of here."

We emerged onto a sun-flooded plateau; rushing wind was cool on our faces. A few feet away the trail seemed to disappear into space. We dismounted and tied the horses to a tree, then followed cobblestones to the brow of the cliff. There I drew back involuntarily; the valley wall was almost vertical, the trail descended in a mad zigzag, partially eroded, offering a most precarious foothold. Far below a stream glinted; that meant a waterfall at the head of the narrow valley. I hesitated; I wanted to suggest that we go back and get someone to take us by boat to the seaward entrance which Denis used.

Too late; Leslie had already started down the trail, and Lily was close behind her. After another moment I followed. I caught my breath as I slipped on the first sharp-angled turn; I braced, fighting vertigo, resisting desire to retreat to the safe, level place we had just left. Leslie was descending without hesitation and Lily now had the advantage of us, dressed as she was in cotton skirt and crepe soles. I started again and followed them cautiously, down and down.

I reached the bottom a few minutes after the others.

The trail traced the valley floor in two directions; they had turned right along the stream toward the sea. I stopped for a moment to bathe my hot face in swift cool water; as I raised my head I saw near the edge of the trail a small mound of stones; on them lay some withered lehua flowers and a sweet potato. A quick look around disclosed yellow ginger growing on the other side of the stream; I crossed it and picked some blossoms to lay with the other offerings on the stones. Then I hurried after my two companions.

They had stopped to wait; Leslie kept glancing impatiently along the path toward the place of her rendezvous with Denis. We went swiftly, and came at last to the remains of a native village, a clearing divided by ancient stone walls. Taro still grew in one patch, irrigated by a man-made channel from the stream. Beyond the stream further on, bamboo made an impenetrable thicket; then we saw *kamani* trees, and finally a cluster of coconut palms which waved languorously in the wind from the sea, which sparkled not far away. The stream had widened into a lagoon, on the other side of which, facing the ocean, we saw a small frame house. We stood there wondering how to cross the lagoon without going back too far. Then we heard voices.

Leslie whispered, "He said he'd be alone!"

Lily caught her arm; the three of us crouched and moved backward until we found concealment behind the thicket of bamboo.

Palms clashed in the wind and then were still. In the interval we heard Denis say: "—no idea how I feel. Don't you realize that everything I dreamed of, everything I—" Palms rattled overhead and words were lost. Then he appeared, with a woman at his side. My eyes widened as I saw that it was Mele.

Not the Mele we knew at the ranch, aloof in starched blue cotton, her face a sullen mask. This Mele was barefooted, wet black hair streamed down her back, her superb body was wrapped in a sheath of scarlet cloth, tucked in at her breasts. She did not clutch Denis' arm as his wife had done; she walked proudly by his side, and she evaded his touch.

They stopped on the bank of the lagoon almost opposite us and Mele grasped the man's shoulders and turned him to her. "You can never realize that dream, Denis," she said. "It's too late. Go away. Give up this wickedness. You are mad to think you can succeed in what you are doing. Something dreadful is going to happen—leave this island, leave Hawaii, while there is still time!"

"Will you go with me?"

"You know that I cannot." She said it wearily, as one who has given the same answer many times.

"Then make Karl go. After all, that's why you sold me this place—for enough money to get away."

Mele began to walk back and forth, wringing her hands. "What a fool I've been! I wish my tongue had been torn from my mouth before I told what I did! If you only knew how I have argued, have gone on my knees and begged Karl to leave—"

"Then I'm staying too."

She stopped. They stood silent, in the attitude of fighters who have exchanged blows until they must stand exhausted and face one another, each hopeless of victory. Then the man said, "Mele, for the last time, listen to me."

She moved closer.

"If I can't have you—I'll have the next best. Money. A man with money can buy anything he wants."

"Except honor," the Hawaiian woman said. "That is why I must stay with Karl." Her head went up. "My people knew about honor. And I could never face them if—"

"People!" he shouted. "To hell with people! I've spent the last seven years doing what people want me to do—and it's no good! I'm not a man of honor. I'm flesh and blood."

He stared at her, his face working. "Christ!" he said. "I can't stand this!" He dropped to his knees and put his head into his hands, sobbing.

Mele watched. Her proud face softened into tenderness, she moved toward him, hesitated, moved again. Then she was on the sand at his side, her arms cradled him, her hair fell across his shoulder. He caught the long dark waves and pressed them against his face, murmuring incoherently. They clung together on the soft sand. And when the man's mouth sought Mele's throat, when his hand fumbled at the fold of cotton tucked between her breasts, she drew him to her.

Leslie stiffened beside me and turned her head away. She rose cautiously and retreated along the path toward the trail. I followed her. Lily stayed. That left me hesitating between the two girls; Leslie moving along the path, Lily behind the bamboo, watching. I waited for Lily.

When she finally joined me I said, "Did you learn anything you didn't know?"

She was oblivious to double meaning. "No," she said. "They won't be talking for a while." She was deep in thought. Leslie by then was far ahead of us and I forgot her as I walked slowly, matching my pace to Lily's.

She said, "Denis didn't send for Leslie."

"He could have. Mele's visit might have been unexpected."

"That is possible. Where do you think Mele has been? Her hair is wet."

"She used to live here with Denis. Perhaps she came back to swim in the lagoon where they used to—no, she doesn't have to make a play for him. He's no lost lover. He wants her to leave Karl and she's the one who refuses. She's urging him to get out of here."

I stumbled and regained my balance. "Lily, she said the same thing to Denis that Eole said to me: something dreadful is going to happen."

"There's money involved," Lily reminded me. "He promised to give some to his wife."

I told her then what Bessie Watson had said about seeing Denis with some man in the village. "They mentioned sixty thousand dollars. Denis could pay off a couple of wives—"

"Try to think, Janice: how could anyone get so much money from a place like this?"

"Well—there's been dope-running in the past. An isolated place like this valley would be useful, especially when only a few know how to get a boat through those rocks—" I stopped. "This isn't the way!"

We were on a path so faint that it was almost invisible; guava trees had grown over it. "Come on," Lily called, and ducked under an over-hanging branch. "Let's see where this goes."

We struggled through guava into a clearing. A grass shack stood there, weather-beaten and deserted, reminder of community life long past. We stepped closer and stooped through the doorway. The floor of the shack was covered with rotting *lauhala,* wind rushed through ragged openings and rattled dried palm leaves which formed the walls. Bright patches of sunshine served to accentuate shadowy corners; one golden shaft rayed like a spotlight over an object in the center of the floor.

"What is that?" I whispered.

A long box of black wood rested there across two wooden trestles. As I recognized its shape I drew in a deep breath. "Lily! It looks like—"

"Yes," she said. "It is a coffin."

Eole had said, *"The coffin is almost ready."*

For whom?

We moved closer. My foot struck something; I looked down at a hammer, screwdriver, pliers. In a corner was the tool chest from which they came. When we looked into the coffin we saw that it was metal-lined, with soldered seams. The soldering iron and strips of bright solder were in the center of the box.

Lily said, "How useful—Denis is a plumber."

A centipede slithered across my boot and I started back, stifling a scream. A big scorpion scuttled up the wall, there was a sound of scratching. "Let's get out of here!" I urged.

We stooped through the door and fled. Once more headed along the proper route, I began to hurry, looking for Leslie. Lily wasn't used to physical exertion; she would have to follow as well as she could. My breath hurt but I quickened my pace, stopping only when I reached the foot of the trail. From where I stood, the crazy footpath up the valley wall was barely visible. Leslie was on it, climbing steadily, she was already three fourths of the way to the top. I stopped to catch my breath before beginning the ascent behind her.

To my surprise I found Lily at my elbow.

There was a loud noise, which echoed madly from the walls of the narrow valley. Dirt sprayed around Leslie's head. The blue-shirted figure far above us jerked backward and slid from the trail with a cry. While we watched helplessly, Leslie began to fall.

CHAPTER FOURTEEN

A LANDSLIDE of rocks and dirt pelted us; we braced with arms over our heads and stood still. Once I was able to glimpse Leslie sliding down the face of the cliff, clutching desperately at clumps of vegetation. When the landslide stopped I saw that her feet had touched a narrow outcropping of rock; she flattened there, one hand grasping a bush just over her head.

I started up the trail. Lily said, "Let me go first," and pushed past me. She began to climb lightly, rapidly, making twice the speed I would have been capable of. But I knew that even when Lily reached the top she could not help; Leslie was far out of reach, and the valley wall offered no foothold other than those few inches of rock. Leslie couldn't hold herself there very long.

I called, "Leslie, hang on! We're coming!" and began to climb after Lily.

Leslie didn't try to answer. Once she moved sideways to regain the trail and slipped. She retreated to the rock and pressed against the earth. I climbed and panted, stopping with shoulders hunched as loose earth dribbled past and dust mingled with sweat trickling down my back. When I was only halfway up, Lily had reached the top and disappeared. By the time I joined her I found that she had taken the leather reins from the gray horse's bridle and tied them together.

"This thing," she said, tugging at straps of the cinch, "is it very long?"

"No. But the straps are." I went to the other side of the saddle and began slipping leather out of the cinch ring while Lily loosened her side. When we got everything tied together with the bit loop on one end, Lily went to the edge of the cliff and let the clumsy arrangement down gently to where Leslie hung. It reached almost to her head.

Lily lay on her stomach, looking for something to brace herself with—there was nothing but grass. She called to Leslie, "Put your wrist through the loop; it'll help support you." She lay flat and wound leather around her own wrist, then turned her head to me. "Take the other horse and go for help. I'll try to hold on here."

Leslie's black horse didn't like the idea of my riding him any more than I liked it myself. He backed and turned as I tried to get a foot into the stirrup; he started before my right leg was over; I pulled leather for all I was worth and got my balance with desperate effort, only to lose it again as he took me under the branch of a tree. Another time I might have been more frightened; I checked him and heard myself cursing; he steadied and went on. The bewildered gray floundered after us; he lost his saddle almost immediately, then plunged ahead through giant ferns and raced out of sight.

When I came out of the banana grove I saw the gray galloping down toward the stables; two horsemen who were riding in the opposite direction had halted to watch him. I waved and one of them wheeled his horse and began to race toward me. It was Karl.

"What's wrong?" he yelled. "Where's Leslie?"

"She fell off the trail—Lily's holding her—"

He didn't wait; he urged his horse into the forest and I reined the black around and followed him, crouching and clinging to the pommel and letting the horse take me.

When we came out onto the plateau I gasped relief to see Lily still lying there with one arm over the edge of the cliff. Karl hurried to her, looked over her head, and cried, "Leslie! Don't move! Hang on a minute longer."

He went to his heaving horse and unstrapped a coiled rawhide lasso from the saddle. He called down to Leslie, "I'm going to lasso you. Lean back a little, and don't jump when you feel the rope."

It whirled and settled over her shoulders; Lily dropped the leather strap and Leslie thrust her arms through the rawhide loop until it was around her waist. Then Karl pulled it taut.

"Now," he commanded. "Lean back at an angle and hold the lasso. Go sideways to the trail. Don't be scared if you slip—I won't let you fall."

She began to move as he directed, and then she was on the trail again and he was pulling her up. I turned my attention to Lily, who was sitting on the grass, rubbing her right arm where leather had bit into it. At my inquiry she said, "I'm perfectly all right."

I sat down suddenly. Karl was supporting Leslie with one arm while he brushed dirt from her shoulders and her hair.

"Thank God!" he exclaimed. "Girl, are you hurt?"

"No. My hands are scratched—" She swayed against his arm. "Karl! That wasn't any—" She went white and her knees buckled. Karl carried her to the shade of the tree where our horses had been tied.

As he put her on the grass another rider emerged from the grove behind us; it was Mahoe. "Everything all right?" he asked, reining his horse. I reassured him.

Karl paid no attention; his eyes were on Leslie, who was sitting up, brushing a hand over her dirty brow. He scowled at her. "You had a narrow escape, young woman. That trail ain't safe—it's more than a hundred years old. If these two gals hadn't been with you—you might be—" He swallowed.

He remembered Lily and me then. "You two all right?"

"We're fine," I said.

Karl turned back to Leslie. "Where were you? How the hell did you happen to be on that trail?"

She answered reluctantly, her eyes on Mahoe, "I went down to see Denis."

Karl stared at her, taking it slowly. His face darkened, his jaw thrust out. Leslie didn't say any more, she got to her feet and started unsteadily toward her horse. Karl said, "You can't ride—"

"I'm going to."

He made a helpless gesture. "We're short two horses; we'll have to double up." He untied the leather which Lily had knotted together and hung it over the pommel of his saddle. As he coiled his lasso he went to the edge of the cliff and looked down; when he turned back, anger glowed in his dark eyes and two harsh lines framed his mouth. Leslie watched as if she wanted to talk to him but knew this wasn't the time. We finally started back to the ranch, Leslie riding ahead of us on Panini, Mahoe taking Lily, Karl in the rear with me behind him.

When we passed John Kuneo's house I glanced toward it and then away—black crepe hung on the door.

Mahoe and Lily were ahead by then; Karl urged his horse to Leslie's side. She turned eagerly and started to speak, but Karl spoke first. "I'm going to turn Panini out to pasture." His voice was gruff, embarrassed. "You shouldn't be riding now."

Leslie averted her eyes. Her face might have revealed the guilt she felt—if Karl had been watching. He was engrossed in his own problems. He muttered, "I'm sorry about the way I acted over that audit. Just my damned pride, Leslie."

"Oh, Karl!" she said, turning to him. "I understand, I—"

He wasn't listening. He held out his hand. "Can't we be friends, like Don and I were?"

His use of past tense was unconscious. Leslie reacted as if he had struck her. She looked at him from shocked eyes, then with an exclamation that sounded like a sob, she spurred her horse ahead. When Karl and I reached the stables she had already disappeared. Lily was not in sight either; she was probably getting into a hot bath, which was what I wanted to do immediately. I went into the house and had one foot on the stairs when I heard quiet movement in the living room and turned to investigate.

Leslie was there, moving slowly around the room gathering up fabric swatches from the furniture. Her blue shirt was filthy and torn, there were scratches on her face.

I said, "Would you like me to run a hot tub for you?"

She didn't look up. "Please go away."

I went to my room and slumped on the bed, too tired and depressed for further movement. Lily arrived then and, as she entered, began in a thoughtful voice, "It is very interesting, Janice, that—"

"Very interesting indeed!" I exploded. "Leslie's the key figure now, just as you planned. She's target for another murder. That noise we heard just before she slipped wasn't any rock falling. It was a shot!"

Lily sat down wearily. "Where are your cigarettes?"

I shoved a pack at her. "You and your damned Oriental subtlety! Persuading her to tell a lie like that!"

She hurled cigarettes across the room. "You and your damn Occidental crudeness! Do you imagine you can bludgeon malevolence to the surface?"

"If you think—" We spoke simultaneously, stopped and glared at each other. Then we subsided. Lily's smile deepened the dimple in her cheek; mine was sheepish.

I said, "That was a relief."

"We needed it. We're both tense. Have a cigarette."

I picked up the cigarettes, held a match for her and then for myself. "That was some mountain climbing you did today. And I always thought you were such a silken little creature."

She tilted her head and exhaled, watching smoke rise and drift toward the window.

She said, "I have a friend who was at the University of Peking. She married another student and they joined the Eighth Army. During the Japanese invasion Kuei-tsu was one of the women who helped to carry a dismantled factory several hundred miles and then set it up again."

"You're sure she wasn't a cousin?"

"Not this one." She smiled.

"Well," I said, "now that we're safely out of that place, I'll admit that I'm weak. We might have been killed."

"No. Not us, that would have been too much. But if we hadn't gone with Leslie—"

"She was meant to go alone."

"And that shot was only to startle her into falling. She might not have been killed, but she would probably have had a miscarriage."

I said, unstrapping my dusty boots, "It has to be the Farnhams. Denis didn't know she was there. I don't think he sent her any note."

"Did you ask to see it?"

I told her about Leslie in the living room, and her state of mind.

Lily said then, "We're actually sure of nothing. Denis could have heard us and followed. And don't forget the old woman, Mele's grandmother. She doesn't like *haoles;* she lives apart."

"A gun wouldn't be her weapon. A spear, perhaps."

"She might have figured that herself, Janice. Chinese don't have a monopoly on subtlety. Karl—how close was he?"

"Nowhere near. Besides, Lily, Karl may be a tough character but it is obvious that he's trying to protect Leslie."

I said the last almost questioningly; I was tired and jittery and on the verge of doubting my own conclusions. Lily stubbed out her cigarette and pulled up her cotton skirt. She said, rubbing a bruise on the inside of her knee, "I think it was the Farnhams. They went out before she did."

I peeled off jodhpurs and shirt and began to pace the floor.

"What are we going to do about it? Sit and wait until the next attempt is successful? Why don't we tackle the Farnhams—or at least call Captain Kamakua and ask him to get over here in a hurry and put some pressure on them?"

"And how would you suggest tackling the Farnhams, as you call it? With what evidence? A bullet which might be impossible to find? A gun, rifle, whatever it was, which may be hidden somewhere on several thousand acres of land? And what could Kamakua do here, except put everybody on guard?"

She pulled down her skirt and stood up. "No, Janice. You said from the beginning—and you are right—that this mystery is Hawaiian in nature. Our trip to the valley was not wasted. We know now that there is somebody else besides Leslie who has reached a low point of the spirit. Mele—the Hawaiian."

I began to feel less depressed. "Remember, she said to Denis that she had betrayed her people, she wished her tongue had been torn out before she told what she did."

"That's right. She's terrified now, trying to stop something which she herself must have started. We will play on that terror and remorse. We will try to find out through Mele."

She glanced in the mirror and frowned at her dirty face. "I'm going to bathe; I suggest you do the same. By the time we're finished Mele may be back from the valley. I'll ask Haru to watch Leslie's room—"

"That's what I was doing today, and she got out without my seeing her. She used the door of that little sitting room."

"Haru can watch from the hall. And Hong will let us know as soon as Mele appears."

When I was dressed I went to Leslie's bedroom. She had not washed the dirt from herself; she lay on her bed staring at the ceiling with dull, dry eyes. I said, "Leslie. Could I see the note Denis sent you?"

"I tore it up." Her voice was flat. "It's in the wastebasket."

I found the note, torn into such small bits that it would take hours to piece them together. The message had been printed with pencil. I picked the pieces out and stuck them in my pocket. In the wastebasket I also found the swatches of material; I rescued them—gay splashes of yellow and aqua and coral—and tucked them under the cushion of the window bench.

Leslie's head turned. "It's a week today since Don's boat went down. They say—in Hawaii the sea gives up its dead in seven days. Is that true?"

I couldn't answer. I looked out the window at intense blue swells of the Pacific, barely moving in amber afternoon light. I couldn't tell her about insatiate marine creatures, vicious eels, giant crabs, sharks, which made ridiculous that superstition about recovering the drowned. I couldn't meet the eyes which questioned me.

I said, "Your face is dirty." I went to her bathroom and wet a washcloth, and wiped her cheeks and forehead. I found a brush and tried to smooth some of the dirt from Leslie's coppery hair. When a knock sounded on the door I dropped the brush and didn't remember to pick it up.

Lily came in, Mele behind her. Leslie looked at Mele and said dully, "How did you get back?"

Mele stood very straight by the bed. "I came with Denis in the outboard—it is quickest."

Mele's hair was braided tight again, she wore the stiff dress. But the hostile look had gone; she regarded Leslie with a shamed expression and with deep sadness.

She bent toward the bed. "Did you tell my husband what you saw?"

"No."

Mele's shoulders straightened. "Thank you. I can't talk here—this house is no place for secrets. But—" She started to turn. She took a breath and finished quickly. "Miss Wu told me what happened today. She has reminded me—you are young, you are going to have a child—"

She stepped close to the bed and finished in a very low voice, "I want to talk to you. Put on your bathing suit and go down to the swimming pool. If anyone asks questions, say you're nervous after the accident, you've asked me to give you a *lomi*, Hawaiian-style, out in the sun."

When she left her steps were silent. Mele had discarded her shoes, she walked barefoot again.

Leslie was off the bed before the door closed. She fumbled at shirt buttons, jerked her belt loose. Color had returned to her cheeks, her eyes blazed. None of us said anything. Leslie was afraid to put hope into words; Lily and I were relieved that she didn't try.

We went downstairs. Edith was on the lanai reading a magazine; she looked up curiously but we passed her without speaking. As we walked down the long path to the terrace Leslie said, "Those people must leave here. Tonight, if possible."

I hoped that they would leave in custody of the police.

Mele waited near the swimming pool, a towel spread on a bench there and a bottle in her hands. While Leslie stretched on the bench in the sun, Mele poured coconut oil into her palm and began to *lomi*, speaking rapidly in a voice which was barely audible.

Lily and I sat in chairs near by and listened.

"I have been a coward for too long," Mele began. "Two men swear that they love me, and for this love I have permitted a terrible thing. I have betrayed my people and have done a great wrong to you. Now I must—" She grew silent as steps scraped on the walk. She said to Lily and me from between her teeth, "Keep that woman away from here."

Edith joined us. "I ache all over from that damned horse. How about a *lomi* for me, Mele? I had no idea you were such an expert."

"My grandmother taught me," Mele said. "If you'll wait until I finish—"

"Come over here with us!" I called to Edith. "We're admiring the view." Lily and I dragged chairs to the edge of the terrace overlooking the bay, and I took Edith's arm, practically forced her to sit. I said, "Did you enjoy your ride this afternoon? And did you manage to kill anything?"

Edith's eyes narrowed; she didn't answer. She took the chair I offered but pulled it around so that it faced sideways, and she watched Mele. I went to the railing of the terrace and looked at the little pier thirty feet below, where Denis' outboard bobbed alongside the big blue sampan. "I wonder what's going to happen to Eole's boat," I said.

"We're going to keep it," Edith announced. "To run tourists to Denis' valley. We're making a deal with him. We'll restore the old Hawaiian village there, and take ranch guests to see the natives pounding *poi*, making *tapa*, doing *hulas*. We'll have *luaus* at the village, the real thing—"

Mele called over her shoulder, "You can't run a sampan into that cove, Mrs. Farnham. It's not navigable."

"We'll make it navigable," Edith said.

Mele moved with her back to us and pulled Leslie to a half-upright position. "Lean against me," she said. "Now, drop your head forward, so I can get at those neck muscles."

She bent over Leslie and began to massage her shoulders; I saw her lips move but heard nothing except faint sibilance. Edith leaned forward, frowning. Just as she started to get out of the chair Mele slapped Leslie's bare back and said clearly, "Now. You must go upstairs and sleep for at least two hours." As Leslie rose, the Hawaiian woman looked into her eyes and added, "Rest, for you will need your strength."

She turned to Edith. "All right, Mrs. Farnham."

We were halfway up the steep path when we heard Howard slam out of the house. He rushed toward us with such livid fury on his face that we moved quickly out of his way. He paid no attention; he shouted, "Edith! I just got a call from Gilbert. Edith, listen to this!"

We watched Edith sit up on the bench with a silencing gesture; his voice dropped and we could hear no words, only agitated high notes of his voice. They turned then on Mele, who stood and faced them, moving her head in repeated denial.

Leslie had gone on ahead. I looked at Lily as we walked up the path together. "It looks as if Tropicana's man might be named Gilbert. And Mr. G. called Howard after his luncheon date with Steve."

Lily nodded. But she was not interested in the Farnhams at the moment; her concern was for Leslie. When we reached her again Lily asked, "What did Mele tell you?"

Leslie said slowly, "She is going to take me somewhere. Tonight."

I started to question her but Lily gave me a warning look. Leslie went on, "Mele said she was afraid to talk there, she said it wasn't safe with someone watching. I'm to meet her below the swimming pool, at the dock where the outboard is tied. She's going to put something in Karl's coffee to make him sleep, and she'll be there about ten o'clock."

She turned a puzzled face to us. "She said to be ready for a hard swim. What does that mean?"

"I have no idea," I told her. "But we'll find out."

She looked as if she were going to protest and I said decisively, "Leslie, there has already been one attempt on your life. You're aware of that, aren't you?"

"Yes." Her tone was indifferent.

"It's not wise to go out alone with anybody. We're going with you." To my relief, she nodded consent.

* * * *

The night was very still. The moon had not risen, so that the house lay surrounded by darkness. We came down the stairs in soft shoes, wearing slacks and long sleeves to conceal bare arms and legs. Under this Leslie and I wore bathing suits; Lily is not a strong swimmer, but she was going along as far as the boat would carry us. We left the house by the side door and walked along the front lanai. The radio was turned on in the living room; through a window we saw Howard and Edith sitting before the fireplace, Denis opposite them. They talked in low voices, their faces were serious. While Leslie and Lily waited in the driveway I went through the garden to the foreman's cottage, several hundred feet from the house. Karl was just finishing a cup of coffee. He rose from his chair and yawned, stretching powerful arms over his head.

"Can't keep my eyes open any longer. Guess I'll head for the bunk. Coming, Mele?"

Mele looked up from some sewing in her hands. "Not yet, Karl. I want to finish this."

He bent over her. "All right, *wahine*. Don't stay up too late." He murmured something, at which Mele rose. His arms went around her and I could see Mele's fists clench behind his shoulders. When he released her and left the room she sat down and picked up her sewing. I went back through the garden to the driveway where the others waited.

"She'll be along soon. Karl just went to bed."

We went down the sloping path, across the terrace to the wooden steps. We descended carefully, holding the railing. At the bottom step, in position to duck under the angle of the stairs quickly, we sat down to wait.

Water rushed in and retreated, waves foamed over jagged rocks near by. The air was chill and I shivered, I could hear Leslie's teeth chattering.

She whispered, "A long swim. There are no beaches near here; that doesn't make sense. Or did she say a hard swim? I can't remember."

Her cold hand touched mine. "You will need your strength. She said that. I don't know how much longer mine will last."

Lily said, "It will last."

I said, "I wish I had a cigarette."

Pale radiance crept over the horizon and silvered the ocean. The moon was rising, a pallid moon which gave faint intermittent light between dark scudding clouds. We waited in silence, sitting with elbows touching. Was that a footstep? I rose to look through the dark. Mele wouldn't make a sound, she would be barefoot. I peered up toward the terrace, where steeper stairs began. Someone moved there, someone who walked without sound, on feet that were bare.

The others heard it too. They stood up. Leslie called, "Mele?"

In moon-glint we saw Mele raise her arm. "I am coming." Then the wooden steps began to vibrate, and Mele's figure, like a dark blot in the night, moved down toward us. What was that larger, darker blot behind her? Black and monstrous, it rushed across the terrace toward the descending figure.

"Mele!" I warned.

Too late. The shadow pounced and drew back. With a terrible scream, Mele fell, she hurtled headfirst onto the rocks at the edge of the sea.

Then we were scrambling, slipping over seaweed, stumbling on lava rocks, toward that limp figure. I went to my knees in water, pulled myself up and struggled on, Lily beside me.

As we reached Mele she groaned. She said faintly, "*He nui loa kuu hewa.*"

My wickedness is too great.

She made no further sound or move.

CHAPTER FIFTEEN

HOURS LATER we went to Karl's bungalow to see whether there was anything we could do for him. The doctor had finally arrived; his services were not needed for Mele, whose body lay in the bedroom, surrounded by her people. They had found Karl heavily asleep; he was beginning to revive under stimulus of a hypodermic. He seemed unable to comprehend what had happened; he sat by his wife's bed holding her hand, saying, "Mele. Mele."

"This man has been drugged!" the doctor said. He turned to Leslie and demanded, "What's been going on here?"

Leslie knew nothing. She told her story again, simply, as we had rehearsed it. She had left her watch by the pool that afternoon, she took it off when Mele gave her the massage. Afraid of the dark, she had asked Lily and me to go with her to retrieve it. When we reached the place we sat at the foot of the wooden steps to watch the moon come up. We heard nothing until Mele's scream, until her body plunged past us to the rocks.

Howard and Edith listened. There was no expression on her painted face, but her husband was uneasy, closing his lips tight over whatever he wanted to say. Denis had arrived with them. He stood at the foot of Mele's bed clutching the brass post. He looked around him at Hawaiians who filled the room, at Hawaiian eyes which held knowledge that he had been Mele's lover. He shuddered violently, and rushed out of the house.

More Hawaiians came; some stood in the front room, others joined watchers who lined the walls of the bedroom. They waited for something. Presently Eole's mother entered. She wore a black *holoku* which made her grief-lined face more haggard; gray-streaked hair fell past her waist. She bent over Mele and chanted, low-voiced, a long Hawaiian prayer. Finally she stood upright, she uttered a terrible cry, raised both fists, and beat herself in the temples. Tears streamed down her cheeks and she wiped them away with her unbound hair, she sank to the floor and began to rock back and forth, wailing, beating her breast. Other voices joined her until there was a concerted outcry of grief.

Through it Karl sat unseeing, unhearing, holding Mele's hand.

Lily caught my eye and pantomimed that we should go. I signaled

Leslie and we left the cottage and started back to the ranch house. At the garden we stopped. Something was huddled on a bench there. Denis, sobbing. I felt a brief twinge of pity; not many hours ago he had held Mele in his arms, had kissed her warm mouth. Now he had just seen her mutilated and cold with death. I turned to my companions and found only one; Leslie had gone inside. Lily stood there.

No pity showed on Lily's face. In the moonlight her eyes glinted, her lips curled with contempt.

"Denis," she said.

When he did not move she touched him with her foot. He lifted his contorted face. "Why do you weep?" she asked. "You are surely not surprised. Mele told you this would happen."

He dropped his head onto his arms again.

Lily moved closer. "We saw you and Mele together today. We know that you killed her."

His head came up, he turned horrified eyes to her. "You're crazy! I could never have—oh, God!" He began to sob again.

Lily stood before him. She began, "You killed her, nevertheless. Mele begged you to stop what you are doing. She warned you that otherwise something dreadful would happen."

He sat rigid.

She continued: "You thought it might happen to someone else; Leslie, perhaps, or another unfortunate Hawaiian who tried to interfere. They did not matter. But it happened to Mele. She told us today that she was finished with protecting you, she was going to tell the truth. And so she died."

He made a smothered protest. Lily went on talking.

"You realize now, don't you, that you will never use that coffin? You will never be permitted to enjoy the money. It is not necessary for you to live longer; you have almost finished your time." *Like the most subtle of Oriental tortures, letting water fall a drop at a time, on a bound prisoner's forehead.* "Soon you will die, too, as the boy Eole died of a broken neck two nights ago. As the *paniolo* named Kolea died of poison last night. As Mele died with a crushed skull tonight." *Eventually, under those tiny drops of water, the victim goes insane.* "Perhaps tomorrow will bring the night for you." *Denis was bound only by his own guilt, Lily's voice dropped only cool syllables.* "You may be splattered on those black rocks. Or you'll break your neck in a fall. Or your little boat will explode—"

He groaned. He lurched to his feet. "Leave me alone!" He shoved her aside and started down the driveway.

Lily turned to me. "Go and get Don's wife."

I ran into the house. When I came out with Leslie they were on the path to the terrace; I dragged the dazed girl by the hand after them.

Denis reeled down the path, Lily at his elbow, still talking. At the terrace he halted, he jerked his head from side to side. He stared into space, then said in a loud voice, "I've got to get away from here!" He started down the steps to the water, but Lily was quicker—she darted ahead while I pulled Leslie at his heels.

On the dock Lily faced him. He shoved her aside. "Get out of my way! I'm getting out of here!"

Lily said, "You can't get anywhere. This is an island."

He stood still, breathing heavily.

"Mele came down here to meet us tonight," she told him. "She was going to take us somewhere. Where?"

He shrugged and started toward his boat. Again she moved in front of him. "Where was she taking us? To Don Farnham?"

"Yes!" he cried, like a man who answers on the rack.

At this Leslie screamed and sprang forward, clutching his arm. "Where is my husband? Where is he?"

Denis pulled free. "I don't know. I never touched the man. I swear it!"

Leslie began to claw at him. "Where is Don? You've got to tell me, or—"

Lily said, "Stand back, Leslie. He's going to help us."

Denis lunged past her and began to fumble with the mooring line of his boat. We three scrambled aboard. Lily motioned us to the bow, she took the center. Denis got into the stern and jerked the starter rope. The motor failed to catch.

Lily said, "Mele was going back to the valley tonight, wasn't she? Now, you can take us there."

He jerked the rope again. The motor coughed and then began to roar. He reached into a toolbox under his seat and found a flashlight which he handed to Lily. "Point it ahead," he said, "where the rocks are."

The boat bounced over dark water, salt spray stung our faces, and we clutched wood and hung on. It was impossible to talk until we rounded a point which jutted into the sea a couple of miles from the ranch. There Denis throttled the motor and we headed toward the valley which lay like a narrow cleft in the island. Moonlight glittered on the freshwater channel that flowed from the valley, and he steered into it. As soon as the boat touched land he jumped out and splashed toward shore.

"Where do you think you're going?" Lily called.

He said without stopping, "I'm going to pack my clothes and get the next plane away from here."

"Go, if you wish." At her significant tone he halted. "But you will be picked up in Honolulu. You will be arrested for murder."

He whirled. "But I'm innocent, I tell you! I never touched Don Farnham, I wasn't anywhere near his boat."

"But you pushed Mele. We saw you. Three of us. We will testify to it."

He came back. "You know that's not true. I've never hurt anybody."

"Three of us will testify to what we saw."

He turned to Leslie. "I never touched your husband, I swear it! Help me to get away, for God's sake!" he whined. "I've got a wife and children, they need me."

Lily said, "Take us to Don Farnham."

He threw up his hands and groaned. "I don't know where he is. I don't know, I tell you. I can't help you."

"Then who can?"

"The old witch. She lives up there—" He waved at the head of the valley, then started to run toward his house.

Lily watched until he disappeared inside. She bent over his boat, using something she took from the toolbox. She stood upright and put a small object in the pocket of her slacks. "Let us go now."

As we waded cautiously across the lagoon I asked, "What did you do to the motor?"

"I took out the spark plug. We may need the boat ourselves. The innocent Denis can walk."

We reached land again and went along the trail toward the interior of the valley. Leslie tried once to run, fell to her knees, and picked herself up, breathing heavily. As we went deeper into the island, valley walls seemed to move together; far above us indifferent stars shone in gunmetal sky. The moon disappeared, leaving us in darkness studded with blacker trees and bushes which menaced like phantoms. Finally we heard the rush of falling water; we slowed our pace and drew closer together. I stumbled and made a small outcry and Lily flashed on the torch. Light showed the cobbled old path but made towering wild growth seem more immense.

A voice spoke in Hawaiian. "Put out that light."

I gasped. I said, "Turn off the flash, Lily."

The next moment we were in smothering blackness, the roar of water surrounding us. We waited. The voice spoke again, directly ahead. "How many are you?"

I answered, "We are three women."

"Which women have come?"

"The wife of Don Farnham and two of her good friends."

"Mele?" When I did not reply immediately she said, "Mele is dead."

"Yes. We came because—"

"Follow me."

I took the lead, since our conversation had been entirely in Hawaiian. I followed a grayish blur along the trail into a clearing by the side of a large pool. The moon came out and shone on moving waters; a lunar rainbow tilted through mist of the waterfall. Away from the pool, its walls built against the face of the valley, stood the house of Mele's grandmother. Its roof slanted sharply; we followed the old woman into a small, bare room. She struck a match and held it to a kerosene lamp, setting the chimney back in place with a dry, wrinkled hand. Light reflected on her white hair—the blur we had followed along the path. She held the lamp before her and looked intently at each of us in turn from immense black eyes in a mummy-like face which might have been centuries old. She was shrunken; the ragged gray *holohu* she wore was big enough for three such withered bodies. Her feet were bare, with the look of feet which have never worn shoes.

"Sit down," she said.

I sat on the matting floor and signaled the others to do likewise. Leslie began breathlessly, "Denis said that you know where my husband is. Won't you—"

She stopped as she realized from the cold blank stare on the wrinkled face that her words were not understood.

"Talk to her, Janice." She sent me a look which begged me to hurry, and I smiled reassurance although I knew that hurry would not be possible here.

Kaula spoke to me. "I saw you give flowers to the *akua* today. Who are you? Tell me what you want."

I began to talk, choosing words with care. I told her of my father and his kinship with Hawaiian people. I pointed out that Eole's father had known him, had remembered me as a child when I visited this island.

She nodded. "I know of this. Go on."

Encouraged, I went on and told her of Eole's call for help, and of what had happened to him, of events which followed our arrival at the ranch. I finished the long story by explaining what Don's cousin wanted to do to the ranch, and how we were trying to forestall him, in order to protect the property not only for Leslie but for the Hawaiians whose welfare depended on it. I repeated our conversation with Mele, and her announced decision, and what had happened to her, how we had come here for help.

Leslie and Lily Wu waited; Leslie tried to be calm but could not stop wringing her hands. Lily sat straight as a carved ivory goddess, eyes very bright in her impassive face. When I finished the old woman was silent for a long while. Then she went and squatted before Leslie; she leaned forward and placed a brown hand on Leslie's brow, while her lids dropped. She was trying to sense Leslie's *mana,* her spirit, before she spoke in her presence. I was relieved to see that Don's wife did not shrink from the touch of those dry, skeletal fingers.

Kaula straightened. "You have married *alii,* you are *alii* now," she said in Hawaiian. "And fortunate that you are *pololei,* you can be trusted. Mele told me today. But I had to see for myself."

Leslie nodded as if she understood, and I didn't try to break the moment by translating. The old woman moved away from us and began to rock back and forth, chanting an interminable prayer to the gods, asking mercy for her dead grandchild.

When she had finished I reminded her, "Mele promised to help us. But now Mele is dead."

The white head nodded. "She will join the spirits of her ancestors. By death she paid for her betrayal."

I said, "Can you tell us where Don Farnham is?"

Kaula nodded vigorously and I heard Leslie draw in a quick breath. My own heart leaped, to plunge again as Kaula said, "I will take you to where he sleeps."

When I tried to speak she stopped me with an imperious hand. "No more talk. There is not time. Obey me and you will find him."

She started out of the house, leaving us to follow. As we went along the path, matching the amazingly rapid pace of the old woman, I explained to the others. At the point where the trail started up the face of the valley we heard someone climbing far above us. Denis had fled.

We reached the shore and Kaula said, "Give me your light."

I took it from Lily and handed it to her; she searched until she found the prow of a canoe hidden under some palm branches. She went to it, her bare feet treading lava rock as if it were feathers. We scrambled after her, and when the canoe was ready Kaula pointed to Leslie and me.

"Get in."

"But our friend—" I began.

"No. You two white girls have kinship with the land—it is not so bad if you break the *kapu* of the dead. But the Chinese woman cannot come with us."

I explained to Lily. "What shall we do?"

"Go with her. I'll run the outboard back and get Hong. She is taking you somewhere on water; as soon as daylight comes we'll cruise the shore looking for you."

I turned reluctantly. Lily said, "Are you afraid, Janice?"

"Yes."

"Be careful. And good luck."

She stood and watched as we began to float away from her.

Kaula had picked up a paddle. I started to help but she said, "You hold the light. Keep it pointed toward the land."

The tide was ebbing. Water lapped at the canoe's sides as Kaula began to paddle steadily, her eyes turned shoreward. We went toward Alohilani, around the point that concealed the valley's opening. Presently the old woman stopped paddling and turned her face to the east. Faint light shone there, paling scattered stars.

"That is Wanaao," she said. "The Ghost Dawn. For a while there will be low water. You both are strong swimmers?"

"Yes."

"Take off your clothes. You must swim under water for a long distance."

I explained to Leslie. She began immediately to take off slacks and shirt and I followed her example, shivering in the chill air. Kaula looked at Leslie, very thin in her one-piece suit. She turned to me and said, "You are a child of the islands, you can swim. Tell her that if she is not strong enough she will die."

I hesitated, then repeated the warning. Leslie said, "When can we start?"

The canoe had drifted close to the island's edge. Kaula gestured and we followed her pointing finger. Nothing was visible except black rock walls which plunged straight into the sea. She took the flashlight from me. "See that crack?" She moved light over it.

There was a break in the face of the cliff, where molten lava had split into two streams as it touched the ocean.

"You must dive," the old woman said. "Search the wall with your hands as you go down, until you find an opening. Go through it. Then swim straight ahead for nine long strokes before you come up. If you cannot swim under water long enough, you will drown. Can you do this?"

"Yes." I bit hard to keep my teeth from chattering.

Kaula grunted. "Good. Take this light. If it is waterproof it will be useful." I stuffed it down inside my suit until it lay cold and hard across my stomach.

She laid a bony hand on my arm. "I have been the guardian of this place for many years. Now I am helping you to break the kapu. When you come out—if you come out—do not expect to find me here. I shall be in my house praying to the gods for forgiveness."

She maneuvered the canoe in front of the fissured rock and steadied it with quick little sweeps of the paddle. "Now!"

I said to Leslie, "I'll go first. You follow as soon as I'm out of sight."

She nodded. I stood in the canoe and took one last look at the wan light of the Ghost. Dawn. I turned from it, filled my lungs to the last inch, and dived into the dark water.

CHAPTER SIXTEEN

DOWN—DOWN—DOWN. My outstretched hands followed a wall of rock. It ended in a submerged ledge. I kicked through it and swam on, counting strokes, swimming blind through inky water. Three—four—five. My lungs began to heave, my heart pounded. Seven—eight—the flashlight slipped across my middle and I redoubled my efforts. Nine—and I could hold out no longer. I put one hand over the flashlight and extended the other as I kicked toward the surface.

I emerged in total darkness. Treading water, chest heaving as I gulped air, I clung to a slippery ledge and fumbled for the light. Something touched my legs and I almost shrieked. It was Leslie; she came up slowly beside me, laid her hand on my arm. I recovered, fumbled for the light again. As I pulled it from my suit the bulb lit and I saw beneath us two pairs of frail white legs—our own legs—in what looked like a bottomless pit of ink. I laid the light on the ledge and pulled myself up while Leslie did likewise. We sat huddled with shoulders touching as I directed the narrow beam into darkness.

We were in a cave. Vast, seemingly without walls, it arched over an oval pool which moved with the ocean's ebb and flow. I pointed the beam behind us and saw a lantern on a rock shelf. When I got up to investigate I discovered a tin box of matches beside it.

I lit the lantern. Leslie clutched my ankle; we both gasped at what wider illumination disclosed.

A burial cave. Walls of lava rock carved into shelves on which lay skeletons. Some were wrapped in rotting tapa cloth, others sprawled on woven mats. Bundles of bones were tied together or heaped in hewn rock niches. I reached for Leslie and pulled her upright. Clinging together, she carrying the lantern while I held the flashlight, we moved toward the end of the pool, where the cave widened.

It was dry, and it smelled of mold and rot. I glanced frequently toward our bare feet, alert for centipedes. Set along the wall at regular intervals were old coconut calabashes which had contained whale oil. But as my light swung briefly to the opposite edge of the pool I saw an object which was not old—a thermos. I said nothing, for as yet there was no sign of a living person, and Leslie's hand in mine had begun to tremble uncontrollably.

A few feet farther we found a second lantern. When it was lighted the walls of the cave seemed to move closer; everywhere we looked we saw skeletons. Human bones lay surrounded by carved gourds and calabashes, *olona* fiber nets, baskets, adzes in various sizes and weights, drums covered with sharkskin, *poi* bowls, wooden daggers, arrows, shark-tooth swords—personal possessions of long-dead Hawaiians who once had lived in the valley called Auohe.

A few—the chiefs—had been laid in their war canoes. And one, whose canoe was set apart from the others, lay wrapped in his *mamo* cape, the cloak of golden feathers. I pulled Leslie closer.

"Look!" I whispered. "He was highest of them all. He is wearing a *mamo* cloak."

We stared at it in silence. No wonder there was such a dread *kapu* on this cave; it was the burial place of a very great chief. The cloak he wore, product of the labor of generations of skilled Hawaiians, was a thing beyond price. Coveted by museums, by collectors who panted over Hawaii's mountains and risked their lives scaling perpendicular rock walls in search for places such as this in which we stood, it was one of the rarest treasures in the world today. The golden feathers shimmered in the light, and I knew that if I touched them I'd feel softness like ermine.

His skeleton indicated that the chief had been a big man. Over the breast lay a *pahoa*, a necklace of whale teeth fastened to braided human hair, symbol of royalty. Finger bones were folded around a spear shaft of shell-inlaid *kauila* wood, with a blade of polished white bone.

"Look at his spear," I whispered. "It's exactly like the ones over your fire—"

Her fingernails dug into my hand. "What is that?"

Something rattled on the other side of the pool. We faced it, and I sent light in that direction. Nothing there but more bones, and a *tapa*-covered canoe with a fish net draped over its prow. I could hear my heartbeat. The sound came again, the faintest crepitation—could it be an air current? No. The atmosphere of the cave was utterly still.

I remembered then that this cave had been formed by lava, flowing centuries ago from Haleakala. As it made its slow way down the mountain, cold air congealed its surface while the molten heart of the stream continued to flow to the sea, leaving lava tubes which widened into caves.

There could be another entrance to this place; if such existed, if someone were making his way through it, Leslie and I were as good as trapped. I looked around for weapons. I had never attacked another human being, but if it meant defending ourselves—

I clamped the flashlight under one arm and reached into the chief's canoe, gingerly removing the spear with its barb of human bone. Finger bones rattled and fell apart; I bit my lip hard. At the side of the canoe was a long-handled adze with a stone edge. I kept this for myself and held the spear out to Leslie. She shrank away. I thrust it toward her again; she tried shudderingly to touch it and couldn't; the face she turned to me was pitiable with shame and fright.

"Leslie!" I hissed. "We may have to—"

There was a splash. We whirled, the spear clattered between our feet. We saw two hands thrust above the water, and then a head appeared.

It was Karl.

He swam to the edge of the pool, grasped the ledge as he waited for laboring lungs to bring oxygen to him. He pulled a cord and brought a plastic bag from the water and laid it on the ledge. He flexed powerful arms and lifted himself to the rim of the pool.

"Karl!" Leslie's voice shook with relief. "How did you know where to find us?"

Karl rose to his feet. We saw then that he was naked. Relief faded from Leslie's eyes; she stood transfixed with shock of realization.

Karl said, "Who brought you here? Kaula?"

Her face told him.

"I knew it couldn't be Denis, the fool never knew how to find this place." His shoulder was bleeding. He brushed a hand over it and said conversationally, "Came up too soon and cut myself."

Pretense was useless. I said, "You killed Mele, didn't you?"

He nodded as he wiped a bloody hand on his thigh. "Then I went back and drank some of the doped coffee she fixed for me. I should have got rid of that woman long ago. I couldn't, until Denis showed up and started mooning around. When he found out she wasn't going back to their love nest he was willing to make a deal. We planned to show this stuff to Barnet after we got it moved."

The waterproof coffin. Hawaiians used such means to bring bodies into the cave. Mele had told him that, when she confided the most safely guarded secret of her people.

Karl took a step, slipped, and regained his balance. "I was glad when you came home, Leslie, not only because you kept Howard in line, but because I liked you."

Leslie's voice trembled. "Karl! What are you going to do?"

In lantern light his shadow on the wall of the cave was monstrous. "It won't be so bad, girl." His tone was reassuring. "It took only a second for Eole; I did it while you went to the house, then I rode out and came back later."

I said, "Kolea saw you in the stable, didn't he?"

Karl gave me a look which said he'd take care of me later.

Leslie began to retreat, holding both hands before her. "Karl, you don't want to kill me."

"Of course I don't. Howard probably didn't want to, either. He would have preferred a miscarriage."

I said, "If Howard gets the land you'll be fired; you'll have to leave."

He said, "At least I'll get the feather cape." He moved toward Leslie.

She backed into a ledge. Bones rattled. A skull rolled past her feet and bobbed on the water.

She drew in a shuddering breath. Karl said, "Don't be so terrified. If you don't struggle it won't take a minute. And they'll find you tomorrow, when they find Don's body."

"Don's not dead!" she sobbed. "I won't believe it! Mele's grandmother told us—" Her lie died in her throat.

"Of course he's dead, you poor little fool!" Karl turned, strode to the canoe on the other side of the pool, and grasped the *tapa* which covered it. "I'll show you his body, where I dumped it a week ago."

I sidled after him, holding the stone adze behind me. Karl tugged at *tapa* and it broke in his hands. Leslie moaned and hid her eyes. But I looked; I saw a still profile, two white feet with bare toes turned upward—

Karl tossed *tapa* aside and started back to her.

And a voice spoke from the canoe.

"Why don't you make sure I'm dead, Karl?"

For an instant Karl froze. Then he pivoted, slipped and righted himself, and was at the canoe. He reached inside and lifted, lifted Don, alive. His shoulder was bandaged, his eyes were sunken, but he grinned as Karl held him by the hair. And then Karl was laughing.

"You can't move! Who tied you up—Mele?"

"Wouldn't you like to—" Don's body sprang upward and he threw both arms over Karl's head, holding him with bound wrists behind his back.

"Get out, Leslie!" he yelled. "Get out of here, quick!"

If I could get behind Karl, could hit him without hitting Don at the same time . . .

But Karl had stooped, he began to slide from Don's grasp. His feet slipped. The bound wrists tightened, the canoe tilted, they fell under it in a shower of bones and rotten *tapa,* calabashes, and fish net. They rolled and struggled, kicking and grunting, and I moved around to them, raising my weapon. Then Karl rose with Don clinging to him and heaved the canoe; it knocked me down and fell over me, fishnet tangled my arms and legs. As I floundered, I heard Don groan with despair when the big man pulled free. Karl towered over the gasping figure near the edge of the pool, he reached for a *koa* paddle which lay at his feet.

"This time, damn you, you'll stay dead!" He raised the paddle with both hands.

A hoarse cry tore from Leslie's throat. Karl halted, turned, and retreated. She was coming at him with the chief's spear. Karl swung at her with the paddle, missed, raised it again. She reached him and thrust; blood spurted as the smooth white blade went into his neck. He dropped the paddle and clawed air, he reeled with hands clutching the spear shaft, and fell into the pool. There was a splash, and when it subsided, bubbles began to rise to the surface.

Leslie saw none of this. She was kneeling, reaching for Don.

By the time I got myself disentangled from the fishnet they were able to notice me. I said as I sat near them and washed the rotten smell from arms and legs, "What's the matter with your shoulder, Don?"

He grinned at me from where he lay with his head on Leslie's bare thighs. "It's broken. That's why I couldn't handle Karl."

Leslie smoothed hair back from his brow. "You'll be all right now."

She wasn't interested in details, but I was. While we recuperated, Don filled in facts which I didn't know.

"It was Karl who came to the boat instead of Eole. He clubbed me. Next thing I knew I was in here, soaking wet, Mele was giving me artificial respiration. Karl had towed me in with a rope and dumped me into the canoe for dead. I would have been, of course, except for Mele. She and her grandmother had been watching Karl ever since they discovered what he and Denis planned to do."

"What was it?"

"They were going to move these old relics out of here, and plant them in another cave, an ordinary cave, on Denis' land. Then he would 'discover' it."

"Did Eole tell you this?"

"Just part of it. Eole used to spend a lot of time in the valley; it fascinated him. His mother brought him up on stories of their people before the *haoles* came here. He knew there was a burial cave somewhere, and he knew how the Hawaiians got the dead and their treasures through underwater tunnels. When he found the coffin that Denis was waterproofing, he guessed what it was for—he was too frightened to talk unless we could be certain of secrecy; that was why I told him to come out to the boat. But Karl reached me before Eole did; after he knocked me out he set a small charge of dynamite to explode the galley. He couldn't let my body be found, you see, because that would give Howard the ranch immediately. He wanted Leslie there, helpless and bewildered, while he pretended to search for me."

"How did you find all this out?" I asked.

"Mele told me. Gradually, for I was unconscious on and off for a long time. She put me back in the canoe and set my shoulder—" he moved and winced—"guess it's unset now. The old woman guarded the cave entrance, nothing could make her break the *kapu* by entering. But she brewed the stuff Mele gave me to drink, and it kept me pretty docile, I can tell you. I've been in a half stupor until today, when Mele didn't arrive for her regular visit."

"Why did you take it, Don?" Leslie asked. "Couldn't you refuse?"

"Sweetheart, I was dying of thirst. I raised a helluva row when I found myself here like a steer trussed for barbecue. After that Mele strengthened the dose. She kept telling me she'd let me out as soon as she could persuade Karl to leave Maui. I asked about you all the time and she said you were fine, I was not to worry. Worry! When I was lying here helpless—"

Leslie kissed his whiskered cheek. "Mele is dead, Don."

"I heard what Karl said. I heard you, too, when you came in, but didn't speak because I didn't know who it was. So Karl killed Mele. Well, the spear that got him was made with a bone from one of her ancestors."

Water rushed into the cave with a loud smack! which startled us. Don said, "That's the tide coming in. If you stay here much longer you'll have to wait hours for next low water. Better go now."

"And leave you here?" Her voice rang protest.

"With this shoulder I can't swim well enough to make it. You go and get help from the ranch—Mahoe can be trusted."

I got to my feet with a sigh. "I'll be back as soon as I can make it. We'll figure a way to get Don out of here intact."

I turned to say good-by but they had forgotten me. I took a deep breath and went into the water.

The first thing I saw when I emerged was Lily's face, turned anxiously toward my subterranean exit. She was in the outboard, Hong beside her, and Mahoe was with them. Several feet away the sampan grated against the rocky wall of the island; it had been their guide.

They helped me into the boat and while I caught my breath Lily said, "We were worried. We thought there must be a cave here somewhere, but couldn't find it. And when we saw the sampan, and knew that Karl was missing—"

"Karl will be missing for a long time," I said grimly. I told them what had happened.

Mahoe's eyes lighted with joy at news of Don's welfare. Hong bounced on the wooden seat. "Hot damn!" he squealed. "Don come home. No more bad time."

"But how will we get him home?" I asked. I slumped; I felt very tired.

"I know," Lily said. "We'll use the coffin. It is waterproof; when the lid is sealed it will hold enough air to last until we get him to the surface. We'll have to find weights to drag behind it and counteract the buoyancy of the wood—how about the sampan's anchor, Mahoe? We can use motor power to pull it through the tunnel."

She turned to me. "Do you think you can go into the cave again, Janice, and help Leslie?"

I groaned.

Mahoe said, "I'm stronger. I'll go. *Wikiwiki,* now. Let's get started."

I've never seen anything more expert than the way those two old men accomplished that project. By the time I was finishing a third cigarette they were back from the grass house, carrying the coffin between them; they floated it alongside the smaller boat while Lily and I waited in the sampan. The four of us managed to heave the anchor into the box and Hong tightened the lid while Mahoe attached a strong line to the handle at one end and dived with the line tied to his ankle, tools dangling from a cord around his waist.

We waited. The black box sank, the line grew taut, and we sat with eyes fixed to the rocky wall of the island.

At last Leslie emerged with the line. Hong tied it to the stern of the outboard, and she held it away from the motor while the little craft moved slowly out from shore, the line tightened, creaked, and began to slip through the water. Then the coffin was out, Mahoe swimming immediately after it. He unscrewed the lid and, we heard Don say, "Thanks. That air smells good!" Hong pulled him into the outboard, from which he was boosted to the deck of the larger boat, with Leslie scrambling up beside him..

We started to the ranch with the outboard in tow, Don supported on the sampan's leather cushions by Mahoe's brown arm while Leslie held his hands. The morning breeze brushed gently around us, the motor purred, and we moved over placid waters in silence.

Then Don said, "Look!" and we followed the direction of his gaze.

Galleons of clouds floated low in the east, while behind them the sky was irradiated with light which touched the sea with gold.

"Alohilani—light from heaven before the sunrise," Don said to Leslie. "Remember our first day here? I promised we'd see it together thousands of times."

Leslie nodded, and tightened her clasp of his hands. Hong was at the wheel. He swung the sampan, and we watched the rose flush of dawn spread over the horizon while we neared the shore of the island.

By the time that sun traveled over us to disappear behind Haleakala, a few changes had taken place at Alohilani.

Don was attended to first. The doctor who set his shoulder departed grumbling because the man wouldn't permit X-rays until the next day. Leslie had laughed and wept and laughed again, and finally permitted us to give her a sleeping tablet and put her into the twin bed beside Don's. They emerged several hours later, Leslie in a white dress, hair burnished, mouth pink, Don shaven and combed, freshly bandaged, eyes in his thin face already alert as he asked questions about the stock, the pastures, recent rains—everything which pertained to his land.

Lily and I agreed, discussing it later, that certain highlights of that day would long be vivid. The first was Mahoe. He had gone to Auohe to reassure Kaula that the burial place would never again be disturbed, and that someone from the ranch would visit her with food and other necessities as Mele had done.

Mahoe added, belatedly, that he had returned with Denis, whom he had met trudging toward the ranch house with a suitcase.

"My horse, he feel too spook today," Mahoe told Don with a straight face. "No carry man and suitcase at same time. So I *kokua*—help out. I take suitcase, give fella little help so he travel more quick."

Denis had arrived at the end of Mahoe's lasso.

Don's mouth twitched. "He's here now?"

"He rest little bit in stable. Got few scratches; we fix with horse medicine."

"What are you going to do to Denis?" I asked.

"Nothing. I've made out a check payable to his wife for the valley land. She's taking him back to North Dakota."

Lily smiled and murmured, " '. . . ice is also great and would suffice.' "

Don gave her a quick look. "Exactly."

Another memorable scene took place when Howard and Edith went, on command, to the room across the hall. I had to miss part of it because I went to get Lily. We tiptoed into my room and left the door ajar and heard:

"—so I will give you thirty days to settle your affairs and leave Hawaii. After that I shall expect to receive your forwarding address somewhere out of this Territory."

"But, Don!" Howard's voice was a bleat. "We've got friends here—our home—my office—"

"If you aren't gone in thirty days I give you my solemn promise that I'll come over with a snake whip and give you a beating as unmerciful as the treatment you gave my wife. If that isn't enough, I plan to give each of the ranch hands, say about a week apart, a free trip to Honolulu, with permission to do whatever they please when they find you. Now, start packing. One of the boys will drive you down. And as you go, pick up that character in the stables and take him with you."

After Howard and Edith had slunk past the door I looked at Lily. "Some fun, dis kin', eh, keed?"

Lily nodded. "Some fun."

Steve arrived that evening with Bessie Watson, whom I had invited, after discussion with Leslie, to visit the ranch for a while. I stilled her protests by telling her that Leslie had lost her housekeeper, she was really needed. While Mrs. Watson explored the place, getting acquainted with Hong and the maids, Lily and I settled on the lanai with Steve, drinking frosted rum punches.

Lily asked, "Did the Tropicana people make a decision?"

"They'll probably buy the Overholt ranch." Steve wiped froth from her mouth with the back of her hand. She said, "You know, I met that guy Barnet, the one Karl was planning to make a deal with. He's a shrewd cookie. Born in the islands, made a lot of dough playing Tarzan roles in the movies. He knows his film career is over, so now he's got this publicity agent building him up—revealed-for-the-first-time stuff—as a descendant of early Hawaiian royalty. He's opening a nightclub in Hollywood called the Grass Shack, and plans to display authentic Hawaiian relics. People will flock to see it, to thrill to the atmosphere of early Polynesia. So he gets his investment—fifty, a hundred thousand—back with interest."

I said, "How?"

Lily gave me a pitying look. "Janice, you're literate. Didn't you read recently about the New York hotel manager who replaced a bookshop in his building with a cocktail lounge? The bookshop was earning $450 per month."

"All right," I said, "I'll bite. How about the cocktail lounge?"

"Their first week netted $4000."

"Oh." I took a long drink.

Steve said, "I've got a call in now to Brownsville—the police there. Thanks to you two, we discovered who Karl really was."

At my puzzled look Lily explained. "The religious cards he had were printed in Spanish. And his hat had the initials C.R. and the name of a hatmaker in Brownsville."

"So," Steve added, "when Lily told me that, I called the place and he said he'd made the hat for one Carlos Reyes—Karl King, see?—who worked on the King Ranch near there. This Reyes was wanted for manslaughter; he beat another Mexican to death in a bar six years ago. That's why he was such a loyal employee, never left this ranch; he didn't want to run into anyone who knew him.

"When Don forced him to take a vacation he took Mele to Honolulu. There he met Barnet, the guy who wanted to buy a feather cloak. And there he also—remember the cattlemen's convention?—met a Texan who recognized him. Karl knew it was only a matter of time until he was found. He wanted to get out of the Territory as soon as possible—but with enough stake to take him somewhere. Barnet told me Karl had asked him about South America."

"Was he going to take Mele?"

"I doubt it. That marriage, so far as Karl was concerned, was strictly from hunger. He probably hated her, knowing she was still in love with Denis. It must have given him satisfaction to use both of them."

"Yes. As long as he could keep on searching for Don, with Leslie trusting him, he could continue preparations for emptying the cave. His wife did all she could to stop him, even to getting Howard and Edith to come here. Mele must have lived in hell this last week."

Leslie and Don came out to the lanai then, Bessie Watson fluttering behind them. They got Don settled in a reed chair with a hassock under his feet, and Mrs. Watson bustled to the kitchen and came back with a glass of some kind of revolting concoction for Don. There seemed to be slight competition as to which of the two women was going to wait on him. While they were getting settled the phone rang, and Steve said, setting her drink down, "That's my call. I'll tell the Brownsville police they can save the taxpayers' money."

She came back saying, "It's for you, Leslie. San Francisco calling."

When Leslie returned Don said, "That was your sister, wasn't it? I hope she's not sick again."

"Drink your medicine, Don." Leslie watched anxiously until he finished it. "Yes, it was Peggy. She's all right, just a little upset over something. She wants to pay us a visit."

"When is she coming?"

"I told her she could come next spring, perhaps, if you're perfectly well by then—and if we aren't too busy."

She turned to the plump woman who hovered in the background. "Mrs. Watson, don't you think he should go back to bed soon?"

"Oh, have a heart!" Don's face wore the expression—half harassed, half gratified—of a man overwhelmed by females determined to coddle him.

The older woman reached for Don's wrist and concentrated. "It's a bit fast," she said. "But—suppose we fix a place for him out here with us?"

Don was hoisted again and ensconced on a *punee* with pillows at his back. He had settled into a comfortable position when the first of the ranch hands came. Ikua, his sour old face stretched into a smile, a gardenia *lei* in his gnarled hands. He placed it around Don's neck.

"Aloha ino oe, Don. We are very happy today."

Others trooped after him: fat Hawaiian women with children clinging to their hands, cowboys with spurs jingling as they strode across the floor, kimonoed maids bowing and smiling, stable hands, yard boys, each with a touch, a phrase of affection—soon Don's bed was covered with flowers.

Hong came to the doorway and watched for a minute; when the last person filed away he clapped his hands. "Hot damn! I go fix dlinks. Numbah one headache tomollow, mebbe, but tonight—*welakahao!"*

As his shirt flapped out of sight the first chord of music sighed toward us from the group which had gathered in the driveway. Guitars, ukuleles, and an accordion gradually joined, and then the sound of many voices filled the night and rose toward quivering Hawaiian stars as the people of Alohilani began to sing.

THE END

About The Rue Morgue Press

The Rue Morgue vintage mystery line is designed to bring back into print those books that were favorites of readers between the turn of the century and the 1960s. The editors welcome suggests for reprints. To receive our catalog or make suggestions, write The Rue Morgue Press, P.O. Box 4119, Boulder, Colorado (1-800-669-6214). The Rue Morgue Press tries to keep all of its titles in print, though some books may go temporarily out of print for up to six months.

Catalog of Rue Morgue Press titles July 2002

Titles are listed by author. All books are quality trade paperbacks measuring 9 by 6 inches, usually with full-color covers and printed on paper designed not to yellow or deteriorate. These are permanent books.

Joanna Cannan. The books by this English writer are among our most popular titles. Modern reviewers favorably compared our two Cannan reprints with the best books of the Golden Age of detective fiction. "Worthy of being discussed in the same breath with an Agatha Christie or a Josephine Tey."—Sally Fellows, Mystery News. "First-rate Golden Age detection with a likeable detective, a complex and believable murderer, and a level of style and craft that bears comparison with Sayers, Allingham, and Marsh."—Jon L. Breen, *Ellery Queen's Mystery Magazine.* Set in the late 1930s in a village that was a fictionalized version of Oxfordshire, both titles feature young Scotland Yard inspector Guy Northeast. *They Rang Up the Police* (0-915230-27-5, 156 pages, $14.00) and *Death at The Dog* (0-915230-23-2, 156 pages, $14.00).

Glyn Carr. The author is really Showell Styles, one of the foremost English mountain climbers of his era as well as one of that sport's most celebrated historians. Carr turned to crime fiction when he realized that mountains provided a ideal setting for committing murders. The 15 books featuring Shakespearean actor Abercrombie "Filthy" Lewker are set on peaks scattered around the globe, although the author returned again and again to his favorite climbs in Wales, where his first mystery, published in 1951, *Death on Milestone Buttress* (0-915230-29-1, 187 pages, $14.00), is set. Lewker is a marvelous Falstaffian character whose exploits have been praised by such discerning critics as Jacques Barzun and Wendell Hertig Taylor in *A Catalogue of Crime.* Other critics have been just as kind: "You'll get a taste of the Welsh countryside, will encounter names replete with consonants, will be exposed to numerous snippets from Shakespeare and will find Carr's novel a worthy representative of the cozies of two generations ago."—*I Love a Mystery.*

Torrey Chanslor. *Our First Murder* (0-915230-50-X .$14.95) When a headless corpse is discovered in a Manhattan theatrical lodging house, who better to call in than the Beagle sisters? Sixty-five-year-old Amanda employs good old East Biddicutt common sense to run the agency, while her younger sister Lutie prowls the streets and nightclubs of 1940 Manhattan looking for clues. It's their first murder case since inheriting the Beagle Private Detective Agency from their older brother, but you'd never know the sisters had spent all of their lives knitting and tending to their garden in a small, sleepy upstate New York town. Even a hardened homicide cop like Inspector Moore is impressed with the tenacity displayed by the two women. Lutie is a real charmer, who learned her craft by reading scores of lurid detective novels borrowed from the East Biddicut Circulating Library. With her younger cousin Marthy in tow,

Lutie is totally at ease as she questions suspects and orders vintage champagne. Of course, if trouble pops up, there's always that pearl-handled revolver tucked away in her purse. It's no wonder a contemporary reviewer announced that Lutie was now at the top of her list of favorite fictional detectives. *Our First Murder* is a charming hybrid of the private eye, traditional, and cozy mystery, written in 1940 by a woman who earned two Caldecott nominations for her illustrations of children's books. "Quaint but funny."—Will Cuppy, *Books.* "Charming."—*Boston Transcript.* "Delightful ." —*New York Times.*

Clyde B. Clason. Clason has been praised not only for his elaborate plots and skillful use of the locked room gambit but also for his scholarship. He may be one of the few mystery authors—and no doubt the first—to provide a full bibliography of his sources. *The Man from Tibet* (0-915230-17-8, 220 pages, $14.00) is one of his best (selected in 2001 in *The History of Mystery* as one of the 25 great amateur detective novels of all time) and highly recommended by the dean of locked room mystery scholars, Robert Adey, as "highly original." It's also one of the first popular novels to make use of Tibetan culture. Locked inside the Tibetan room of his Chicago apartment, the rich antiquarian was overheard repeating a forbidden occult chant under the watchful eyes of Buddhist gods. When the doors were opened, it appeared that he had succumbed to a heart attack. But the elderly Roman historian and sometime amateur sleuth Theocritus Lucius Westborough is convinced that Adam Merriweather's death was anything but natural and that the weapon was an eight century Tibetan manuscript.

Joan Coggin. *Who Killed the Curate?* Meet Lady Lupin Lorrimer Hastings, the young, lovely, scatterbrained and kindhearted newlywed wife to the vicar of St. Marks Parish in Glanville, Sussex. When it comes to matters clerical, she literally doesn't know Jews from Jesuits and she's hopelessly at sea at the meetings of the Mothers' Union, Girl Guides, or Temperance Society but she's determined to make husband Andrew proud of her—or, at least, not to embarass him too badly. So when Andrew's curate is poisoned, Lady Lupin enlists the help of her old society pals, Duds and Tommy Lethbridge, as well as Andrew's nephew, a British secret service agent, to get at the truth. Lupin refuses to believe Diane Lloyd, the 38-year-old author of children's and detective stories could have done the deed, and casts her net out over the other parishioners. All the suspects seem so nice, much more so than the victim, and Lupin announces she'll help the killer escape if only he or she confesses. Imagine Billie Burke, Gracie Allen of Burns and Allen or Pauline Collins of *No, Honestly* as a sleuth and you might get a tiny idea of what Lupin is like. Set at Christmas 1937 and first published in England in 1944, this is the first American appearance of *Who Killed the Curate?* "Coggin writes in the spirit of Nancy Mitford and E.M. Delafield. But the books are mysteries, so that makes them perfect."—Katherine Hall Page. "Marvelous."—*Deadly Pleasures* (0-915230-44-5, $14.00).

Manning Coles. The two English writers who collaborated as Coles are best known for those witty spy novels featuring Tommy Hambledon, but they also wrote four delightful—and funny—ghost novels. *The Far Traveller* (0-915230-35-6, 154 pages, $14.00) is a stand-alone novel in which a film company unknowingly hires the ghost of a long-dead German graf to play himself in a movie. "I laughed until I hurt. I liked it so much, I went back to page 1 and read it a second time."—Peggy Itzen, *Cozies, Capers & Crimes*. The other three books feature two cousins, one English, one American, and their spectral pet monkey who got a little drunk and tried to stop—futilely and fatally—a German advance outside a small French village during the 1870 Franco-Prussian War. Flash forward to the 1950s where this comic trio of friendly ghosts rematerialize to aid relatives in danger in *Brief Candles* (0-915230-24-0, 156 pages, $14.00), *Happy Returns* (0-915230-31-3, 156 pages, $14.00) and *Come and Go* (0-915230-34-8, 155 pages, $14.00).

Norbert Davis. There have been a lot of dogs in mystery fiction, from Baynard Kendrick's guide dog to Virginia Lanier's bloodhounds, but there's never been one quite like Carstairs. Doan, a short, chubby Los Angeles private eye, won Carstairs in a crap game, but there never is any question as to who the boss is in this relationship. Carstairs isn't just any Great Dane. He is so big that Doan figures he really ought to be considered another species. He scorns baby talk and belly rubs—unless administered by a pretty girl—and growls whenever Doan has a drink. His full name is Dougal's Laird Carstairs and as a sleuth he rarely barks up the wrong tree. He's down in Mexico with Doan, ostensibly to convince a missing fugitive that he would do well to stay put, in *The Mouse in the Mountain* (0-915230-41-0, 151 pages, $14.00), first published in 1943 and followed by two other Doan and Carstairs novels. *Staff pick* at The Sleuth of Baker Street in Toronto, Murder by the Book in Houston and The Poisoned Pen in Scotsdale. Four star review in *Romantic Times*. "A laugh a minute romp…hilarious dialogue and descriptions…utterly engaging, downright fun read…fetch this one! Highly recommended."—Michele A. Reed, *I Love a Mystery*. "Deft, charming…unique…one of my top ten all time favorite novels."—Ed Gorman, *Mystery Scene*. The second book, *Sally's in the Alley* (0-915230-46-1, $14.00), was equally well-received. *Publishers Weekly*: "Norbert Davis committed suicide in 1949, but his incomparable crime-fighting duo, Doan, the tippling private eye, and Carstairs, the huge and preternaturally clever Great Dane, march on in a re-release of the 1943 Sally's in the Alley, the second book in the dog-detective trilogy. Doan's on a government-sponsored mission to find an ore deposit in the Mojave Desert, but he's got to manage an odd (and oddly named) bunch of characters—Dust-Mouth Haggerty knows where the mine is but isn't telling; Doc Gravelmeyer's learning how undertaking can be a 'growth industry;' and film star Susan Sally's days are numbered—in an old-fashioned romp that matches its bloody crimes with belly laughs." The editor of *Mystery Scene* chimed in: "If you write fiction, or are thinking of writing fiction, or know someone who is writing fiction or is at least thinking of writing fiction, Davis is worth studying. John D. MacDonald always put him up, even admitted to imitating him upon occasion. I love Craig Rice. Davis is her equal."

Elizabeth Dean. Dean wrote only three mysteries, but in Emma Marsh she created one of the first independent female sleuths in the genre. Written in the screwball style of the 1930s, *Murder is a Collector's Item* (0-915230-19-4, $14.00) is described in a review in *Deadly Pleasures* by award-winning mystery writer Sujata Massey as a story that "froths over with the same effervescent humor as the best Hepburn-Grant films." Like the second book in the trilogy, *Murder is a Serious Business* (0-915230-

28-3, 254 pages, $14.95), it's set in a Boston antique store just as the Great Depression is drawing to a close. *Murder a Mile High* (0-915230-39-9, 188 pages, $14.00), moves to the Central City Opera House in the Colorado mountains, where Emma has been summoned by am old chum, the opera's reigning diva. Emma not only has to find a murderer, she may also have to catch a Nazi spy. A reviewer for a Central City area newspaper warmly greeted this reprint: "An endearing glimpse of Central City and Denver during World War II. . . . the dialogue twists and turns. . . . reads like a Nick and Nora movie. . . . charming."—*The Mountain-Ear.* "Fascinating."—*Romantic Times.*

Constance & Gwenyth Little. These two Australian-born sisters from New Jersey have developed almost a cult following among mystery readers. Critic Diane Plumley, writing in *Dastardly Deeds*, called their 21 mysteries "celluloid comedy written on paper." Each book, published between 1938 and 1953, was a stand-alone, but there was no mistaking a Little heroine. She hated housework, wasn't averse to a little gold-digging (so long as she called the shots), and couldn't help antagonizing cops and potential beaux. The Rue Morgue Press intends to reprint all of their books. Currently available: *The Black Coat* (0-915230-40-2, 155 pages, $14.00), *Black Corridors* (0-915230-33-X, 155 pages, $14.00), *The Black Gloves* (0-915230-20-8, 185 pages, $14.00), *Black-Headed Pins* (0-915230-25-9, 155 pages, $14.00), *The Black Honeymoon* (0-915230-21-6, 187 pages, $14.00), *The Black Paw* (0-915230-37-2, 156 pages, $14.00), *The Black Stocking* (0-915230-30-5, 154 pages, $14.00), *Great Black Kanba* (0-915230-22-4, 156 pages, $14.00), and *The Grey Mist Murders* (0-915230-26-7, 153 pages, $14.00), and *The Black Eye* (0-915230-45-3, 154 pages, $14.00).

Marlys Millhiser. Our only non-vintage mystery, *The Mirror* (0-915230-15-1, 303 pages, $17.95) is our all-time bestselling book, now in a sixth printing. How could you not be intrigued by a novel in which "you find the main character marrying her own grandfather and giving birth to her own mother," as one reviewer put it of this supernatural, time-travel (sort-of) piece of wonderful make-believe set both in the mountains above Boulder, Colorado, at the turn of the century and in the city itself in 1978. Internet book services list scores of rave reviews from readers who often call it the "best book I've ever read."

James Norman. The marvelously titled *Murder, Chop Chop* (0-915230-16-X, 189 pages, $13.00) is a wonderful example of the eccentric detective novel. "The book has the butter-wouldn't-melt-in-his-mouth cool of Rick in *Casablanca*."—*The Rocky Mountain News*. "Amuses the reader no end."—*Mystery News*. "This long out-of-print masterpiece is intricately plotted, full of eccentric characters and very humorous indeed. Highly recommended."—*Mysteries by Mail*. Meet Gimiendo Hernandez Quinto, a gigantic Mexican who once rode with Pancho Villa and who now trains *guerrilleros* for the Nationalist Chinese government when he isn't solving murders. At his side is a beautiful Eurasian known as Mountain of Virtue, a woman as dangerous to men as she is irresistible. Together they look into the murder of Abe Harrow, an ambulance driver who appears to have died at three different times. First published in 1942.

Sheila Pim. *Ellery Queen's Mystery Magazine* said of these wonderful Irish village mysteries that Pim "depicts with style and humor everyday life." *Booklist* said they were in "the best tradition of Agatha Christie." *Common or Garden Crime* (0-915230-36-4, 157 pages, $14.00) is set in neutral Ireland during World War II when Lucy Bex must use her knowledge of gardening to keep the wrong person from going to the gallows. Beekeeper Edward Gildea uses his knowledge of bees and plants to do the same thing in *A Hive of Suspects* (0-915230-38-0, 155 pages, $14.00). *Creeping Venom* (0-915230-42-9, 155 pages, $14.00) mixes politics and religion into a deadly mixture. *A Brush with Death* (0-915230-49-6 grafts a clever art scam onto the stem of a gardening mystery.

Charlotte Murray Russell. Spinster sleuth Jane Amanda Edwards tangles with a murderer and Nazi spies in *The Message of the Mute Dog* (0-915230-43-7, 156 pages, $14.00), a culinary cozy set just before Pearl Harbor. Our earlier title, *Cook Up a Crime*, is currently out of print.

Juanita Sheridan. Sheridan was one of the most colorful figures in the history of detective fiction, as you can see from Tom and Enid Schantz's introduction to *The Chinese Chop* (0-915230-32-1, 155 pages, $14.00). Her books are equally colorful, as well as showing how mysteries with female protagonists began changing after World War II. The postwar housing crunch finds Janice Cameron, newly arrived in New York City from Hawaii, without a place to live until she answers an ad for a roommate. It turns out the advertiser is an acquaintance from Hawaii, Lily Wu, whom critic Anthony Boucher (for whom Bouchercon, the World Mystery Convention, is named) described as an "exquisitely blended product of Eastern and Western cultures" and the only female sleuth that he "was devotedly in love with," citing "that odd mixture of respect for her professional skills and delight in her personal charms." First published in 1949, this ground-breaking book was the first of four to feature Lily and be told by her Watson, Janice, a first-time novelist. No sooner do Lily and Janice move into a rooming house in Washington Square than a corpse is found in the basement. In Lily Wu, Sheridan created one of the most believable—and memorable—female sleuths of her day. "Highly recommended."—*I Love a Mystery*. "This well-written. . .enjoyable variant of the boarding house whodunit and a vivid portrait of the post WWII New York City housing shortage, puts to lie the common misconception that strong, self-reliant, non-spinster-or-comic sleuths didn't appear on the scene until the 1970s. Chinese-American Lily Wu and her novelist Watson, Janice Cameron, are young and feminine but not dependent on men."—*Ellery Queen's Mystery Magazine*. The first book in the series to be set in Hawaii is *The Kahuna Killer* (0-915230-47-X, 154 pages, $14.00). "Janice Cameron's return to Hawaii is 'the signal to set off a chain of events which [bring] discord and catastrophe,' as well as murder. Originally published five decades ago (thought it doesn't feel like it), this detective story featuring charming Chinese sleuth Lily Wu has the friends and foster sisters investigating mysterious events—blood on an ancient altar, pagan rights, and the appearance of a kahuna (a witch doctor)—and the death of a sultry hula girl in 1950s Oahu."—*Publishers Weekly*. Third in the series is *The Mamo Murders* (0915230-51-8, $14.00). Older Hawaiians believe that the sweltering heat of the Kona season is a harbinger of disaster. With the cooling trade winds stilled, the islands cease to be a paradise. In the past, the season has brought tidal waves, earthquakes or volcanic eruptions. This time it brings death. Young, recently married Leslie Farnham returns to her Maui ranch from the mainland only to discover that her older husband, a wealthy Maui cattle rancher, has disappeared at sea. Her in-laws have seized the ranch and Leslie finds herself an unwelcome guest in her own home. A stableboy tries to warn her about impending peril but is killed in a sudden, questionable accident. Leslie's only ally is novelist Janice Cameron, who has made the trip from Honolulu to Maui on behalf of a friend of the missing rancher. While Janice snoops about the island, her friend Lily Wu does a little sleuthing on her own, back on Oahu. The missing rancher was very popular among the native Hawaiians, who fear that the missing man's relatives intend to sell off the ranch to developers with no love for native traditions. After two more deaths, Janice begins to wonder if the deaths and the rancher's disappearance have anything to do with the violation of ancient taboos? This 1952 mystery is a vivid portrait of a changing society whose native people are battling to hold on to—and preserve—their traditions and history.

Coming in autumn 2002

Craig Rice. *Home Sweet Homicide* (0-915230-53-4, $14.95). This Haycraft-Queen Cornerstone comic mystery shows what happens when a mystery writer's three kids decide she needs to solve a real murder.

Constance & Gwenyth Little. *The Black Shrouds* (0-915230-52-6, $14.00). Comic mayhem erupts as the bodies fall while potential lovers bicker, fathers fret and cops scratch their heads.